If a dozen or so masters of crime get together, what do they plot? Sometimes mischief, sometimes murder, but sometimes they scheme to share their killer expertise and love of mystery.

Do you know: What career choice shaped the work of Joe Gores and Dashiell Hammett? How did Holmes feel about marriage? What blueprint did Raymond Chandler leave other writers? Was Agatha Christie treated shabbily by her first publisher? What past master of the Golden Age is now virtually forgotten? Which Poet Laureate wrote successful crime novels? How much is a first edition of the first Perry Mason case worth? Is Sara Paretsky really the heir to Hammett and Chandler? How did Eric Ambler revolutionize the spy novel? Why did Brother Cadfael sleuth in Shrewsbury? Who made "impossible crimes" possible? How does Treasure Island still cast a spell? Who dared to write a bestseller with a main character dead before the opening chapter? Is the Detective Story dead?

What makes a mystery a classic? Here are Justin Scott (Stevenson), Laurie King (Conan Doyle), Joe Gores (Hammett), Michael Connelly (Chandler), Val McDermid (Hard-Boiled Detectives), Edward Marston (Carr), H.R.F. Keating (Sayers), Miriam Grace Monfredo (Du Maurier), Steven Saylor (Palmer), Robin Smiley (Gardner), Peter Lewis (Ambler), Susan Moody (Crispin, Innes, and Blake), Margaret Lewis (Ellis Peters), Janet Laurence (Publishing in the Golden Age), and Catherine Aird playing devil's advocate to tell you.

Az Murder Goes...Classic

AZ Murder Goes

...

Classic

Edited by: Susan Malling and
Barbara Peters

Poisoned Pen Press
Scottsdale, AZ

Published by: Poisoned Pen Press
First Printing, January, 1997
First Revised Edition, printed July, 1998
10 9 8 7 6 5 4 3 2 1

All rights reserved. No part of this publication may be reproduced, stored in, or introduced into a retrieval system, or transmitted in any form, or by any means (electronic, mechanical, photocopying, recording, or otherwise) without the prior written permission of both the copyright owner and the above publisher of this book.

Any characters in this publication are fictitious and any resemblance to any real person, living or dead, is purely coincidental.

Publisher's Cataloging-in-Publication
(Provided by Quality Books, Inc.)

AZ murder goes— classic / edited by Susan Malling and Barbara Peters; [introduction by Duly Brainard; conference papers by Catherine Aird ... et al.] — 1st rev. ed.
   p. cm. —(AZ murder goes—)
   Includes bibliographical references.
   "A collection of papers presented in Scottsdale, AZ in February 1996 at a Crime Convention bearing the same name."
   ISBN: 1-890208-08-6

1. Detective and mystery stories, English—History and criticism. 2. Detective and mystery stories, American—History and criticism. 3. Authors, English. 4. Authors, American. I. Malling, Susan. II. Peters, Barbara G. III. Aird, Catherine, pseud. IV. Title: As murder goes—classic

PN3448.D4A9 1998   809.3'872
                              QBI98-812

Printed in the United States of America
Copyright © 1998
Poisoned Pen Press
6962 E. First Avenue, Suite 103
Scottsdale, AZ 85251
www.poisonedpenpress.com

Table of Contents

Introduction by Dulcy Brainard

Conference Papers

Nice Work—If You Can Get It! 15
    Catherine Aird
Robert Louis Stevenson 27
    Justin Scott
Sir Arthur Conan Doyle 43
    Laurie R. King
Dashiell Hammett 55
    Joe Gores
Raymond Chandler 79
    Michael Connelly
Hard-Boiled Detectives 99
    Val McDermid
John Dickson Carr 125
    Edward Marston
Dorothy L. Sayers 143
    H.R.F. Keating
Daphne du Maurier 155
    Miriam Grace Monfredo
Eric Ambler 167
    Peter Lewis
Collecting Erle Stanley Gardner 181
    Robin Smiley
Stuart Palmer 195
    Steven Saylor
Oxford Detectives 209
    Susan Moody
Ellis Peters 231
    Margaret Lewis
The Golden Age of Publishing 245
    Janet Laurence

Appendices

Agatha Christie Quiz 275
    Carolyn G. Hart
Final Examination 277
Agatha Quiz Answers 283
Final Examination Answers 285

Acknowledgments

AZ Murder Goes... was conceived as a companion to the fan convention, yet another way of building bridges between authors and readers, of fostering appreciation for the "Art of the Mystery," and of developing a wider audience for its past and present practitioners. Limited in size, focused in topic, light-heartedly academic, each symposium brings together authors with a particular interest or expertise to share with the serious reader and the more casual fan.

AZ Murder Goes...Classic, convened on February 23–25, 1996, in Scottsdale, Arizona, was a forum for a series of lectures of such quality and interest to students and readers of crime fiction that the organizers, supported by the author lecturers, determined to publish the papers of the conference both to preserve them and to reach a wider-spread audience. The book that follows is the first of a planned series of publications by *AZ Murder Goes....* The 1997 topic was *AZ Murder Goes...Artful*, focused on art, architecture, and antiquities. *AZ Murder Goes...* is owned and operated by The Poisoned Pen.

We wish to pay special thanks to the following: Justin Scott, for brainstorming—and suggesting the initial topic; Susan Malling for suggesting the *AZ Murder Goes...* title; Dulcy Brainard, Sara Ann Freed, Susanne Kirk, and Keith Miles for developmental advice; Jean and Martin Hanus, Joyce Watson, and Carole Jarchow, the conference organizing committee; playwright Catherine Kenney and the actress, Sheila Mitchell, for the production of *Dorothy L— A Dramatic Portrait of Dorothy L. Sayers*; Edward Marston for his role as Chancellor and Peter and Margaret Lewis for grading examinations; Marjorie and Les Westphal for taping the lectures; and the Poisoned Pen staff for going the last mile. Extra thanks, of course, go to the speakers who gave so generously of their time; to Catherine Aird, Janet Laurence, and Val McDermid who shared papers written for the 1995 St. Hilda's mystery conference, and to Alanna Knight and William Nolan who contributed comments from the floor.

Poisoned Pen Press expresses its grateful acknowledgment to the following for permission to quote from their copyrighted material: the works of Dashiell Hammett, by permission of Vintage Books,

Knopf Publishing Group; the works of Raymond Chandler in *Novels and Other Writings, 1943–1954* and *Stories and Novels, 1933–42* (NY: Library of America, 1995), by permission of The Library of America; the works of John Dickson Carr, the Estate of John Dickson Carr by permission of Harold Ober Associates, Inc.; the letters of Stuart Palmer by permission of the Estate of Stuart Palmer; papers from St. Hilda's, Oxford, by permission of the authors; *A Classic Mystery Quiz*, by permission of Carolyn G. Hart. The articles by Robin Smiley on *Collecting Erle Stanley Gardner* (November, 1992) and by Steven Saylor on *Stuart Palmer* (November, 1996) first appeared in *Firsts: The Book Collector's Magazine* in a slightly different form.

Barbara Peters, President,
The Poisoned Pen

Introduction

On a dark and clement Friday evening in February, 1996, an exceptionally literate group of experts in homicide, evasion, deception, forensic psychology and overall perception lined up row by row in a meeting room of a Scottsdale, Arizona, hotel. While these hundred or so masters of crime might well have set about plotting any number of nefarious schemes, their purpose was benign and even scholarly—to examine the roots of the crime novel and some of its finest examples in order to identify the characteristics of the mystery "classic." Or, as we noted that night, to look at whodunits to see if we could put a finger on what was done when it got done right.

Three reviewers of mysteries sat before the audience as a panel: Helen Francini of the *Drood Review*; myself, and the illustrious H.R.F. Keating, whose distinguished career as mystery writer and critic would be honored on May 1of 1997 by Britain's Crime Writers Association with the presentation of its Diamond Dagger Award for lifelong devotion to and excellence in his craft.

In keeping with a key genre convention, we began by eliminating suspects. A classic mystery is not necessarily a reader's favorite work. It does not occur exclusively in one or the other of the genre's two main subdivisions, the hard-boiled or the mysteries of manners, and is not tied inextricably to one or another narrative element, that is, plot, character, setting or tone. It is not determined by its writer's renown; it is the work itself.

We suggested—referring to 1957 Thunderbirds and Volkswagen Beetles and to the movies *Gone with the Wind* or *Pulp Fiction*— that a classic of any sort was a notable example of excellence of its kind. We talked about cultural, social and political contexts and how a story—or a genre—can capture and even explain the interaction of such issues in a given era, fitting its time as a glove can fit a hand. We talked about the ineffable quality called talent and agreed that we could examine any number of mystery titles that suggest themselves as classics but had always to remember that a writer's unique talent, like the alchemists' quest, will always make the whole something much more splendid than the sum of its parts.

Then we began to look at titles of possible classics to probe for common elements. The discussion, which had shown signs of heating up, moved from the front of the room to the audience and became free-wheeling, impassioned, sometimes a little argumentative (though never less than polite) and utterly exhilarating. Here these undisputed authorities on crime demonstrated a harder-earned and rarer expertise: their deep-rooted and always thoughtful knowledge of the field in which they work.

Excellence in its practice was cited from Poe and his seminal *The Murders in the Rue Morgue* to Conan Doyle, through Chesterton, Christie, Tey and Sayers to Cain (James M.), Hammett, Chandler and Queen; Simenon, Creasey, P.D. James and Tony Hillerman. Questions were tossed out and taken up: Must there be a corpse on page one? Must there be a murder? Can the identity of the villain be known early on? Does character always determine plot? How does setting define character? Does tone matter? What's the place of morality? Whose morality?

This discussion wouldn't quit, though we finally left the room, continuing in smaller groups in other venues. It remains in my memory a very special evening, distinguished by bracing intelligence, good humor, powerfully held opinions and, finally, the nearly palpable respect and affection of this much awarded and top-of-their-craft group of writers for their colleagues and forebears.

In a fitting way this sense of our meeting reflects the most certain of many less defined conclusions put forth: A mystery classic is a tale that, while rooted in its time, lasts beyond it. A classic possesses such rightness in the way all its elements come together that it will inspire and sustain exactly this evening's kind of spirited, rewarding revisiting, generation after generation.

In the pages that follow you'll catch some of this spirit. You will surely be inspired to reread some of the writings discussed and to dip into the work of the authors who share their scholarship and reflections. You may even end up with a surer sense of what makes a mystery classic. Regardless of your own conclusions, the greatest rewards, you will find, come *as always* in reading the works themselves.

Dulcy Brainard, Mystery Forecasts Editor,
Publishers Weekly,
New York, November, 1996

Catherine Aird

♦

*Nice Work—
If You Can Get It*

Nice Work—If You Can Get It

I understand that there is a procedure in the Roman Catholic Church which is invariably invoked whenever it is wished either to beatify or canonize a person.

The case in favour of this is sent to Rome where a cardinal or some other high official of the church is appointed simply and solely to pick holes in the case presented by the proponents of it. I think you will already know the title under which he operates in this situation. It is that of *advocatus diaboli* or Devil's Advocate.

Like all other advocates, the Devil's Advocate owes no duty to the opposite side of the case. And like other advocates he is not expected to—indeed, must not—reveal his own feelings and beliefs in the matter. (By the way, I used the word "he" in this connection advisedly and after some deep thought. I do quite understand that in law still the male is said to embrace the female but at the present time the words "Cardinal" and "Devil" would seem to be definitely male.)

It is my duty today to act as Devil's Advocate and destroy—if I can—the case for the study of crime fiction being considered an academic subject. I propose to do this in the true tradition of a Devil's Advocate—and indeed of a detective novelist—that is without letting my own view be known, let alone prevail.... I do though strongly advise your keeping an eye open for an occasional tongue in a cheek!

And to beware of any habit of mind which I might have caught from that character in Ben Jonson's *Volpone* with the very revealing name of Sir Politic Wouldbe....

This concealment of the crime writer's own personal viewpoint is in my view an important point to be made in the argument against the study of detective fiction being considered an academic subject. I would postulate that one of the good reasons why some detective story writers take to crime so to speak is precisely because they do not wish to reveal anything—let alone, too much—about themselves, something surely which ought to make them very much less susceptible to accurate analysis than other writers.

Now I think you would agree that in mainstream fiction it is almost impossible for a novel to be written without its giving the reader some clues to the author's background and the author's cast of mind—and hence leave some remains, working material, I understand it is called—for the academic jackal to get its teeth into.

I would like to think, too, on the other hand, that it is perfectly possible to write crime stories without showing one's hand on any subject at all; thus leaving no carrion to speak of—or, worse than that—leaving instead ambiguous and misleading pointers with which to lead an academic astray, than which there is no worse fate for the bluestocking. You see, academics, poor things, have always to be absolutely accurate in their work. Crime writers, I am happy to say, enjoy a greater freedom.

Should we wish the noise from a peal of church bells to prove fatal, then fatal it is—leaving the medical profession to argue the point among themselves. Should it be deemed possible for a poisonous snake to be lured through a grating in an otherwise inaccessible room, we are quite happy to leave the fieldwork to someone else.

In fact, I would actually prefer to go further still and suggest that the crime writer is self-selected and goes to quite some lengths not to be among those whom that much-tried fellow Job had in mind when he expressed the wish "that mine adversary had written a book" (*Book of Job*, Ch. XXX1 v. 35). Job knew that that delivered you into the hands of the critics, all right.

I must admit though that I cherish the thought that it is perfectly possible to write a crime story without giving the reader or researcher any handles at all; and that this is done by a great many of my confreres—and that's not by accident either. Those who are closet novelists *manqués* are few and far between and not too difficult to identify.

I am, of course, willing to concede, as evidenced by the previous speaker, that a determined academic could probably unearth factors relating to background and personality. If you believe that opinions are a by-product of these then I will allow that inferences may be drawn—oh, dear! I'd quite forgotten that advocates weren't supposed to make concessions to the other side.

This is all, however, merely *en passant*. My real text for this Sunday morning is taken from the obituary of Elizabeth Ferrars published in the *The Guardian* newspaper shortly after her death on 30th March this year. She was, you will remember, the author of some seventy works of detective fiction. She had first tried her 'prentice hand at three or four novels of contemporary fiction of no special distinction. I quote: "Then, recognizing with characteristic clear-sightedness that she had nothing of great interest to say, merely an uncontrollable urge to write, she turned to crime fiction."

Surely, therefore, there can be no proper stuff for study there among those of us who have nothing to say?

It would, I think, be fair to call this view the exact antithesis of John Keats' despairing:

> When I have fears that I may cease to be,
> Before my pen has glean'd my teeming brain.

I would even advance the view that this latter state of mind is one which does not trouble the average crime writer to any great extent. Perhaps there are the lucky few who cherish a new mode of death not yet committed to paper, a method of murder by internet not yet quite worked out, or even a way in which magnetic resonance can locate a blunt instrument.

(But not, mark you, a new motive. I understand on the authority of that good writer about crime, F. Tennyson Jesse, that there are no motives for murder that Job wouldn't have known about—gain, revenge, elimination, jealousy, conviction, and the lust for killing—but should you be kind enough to bend your teeming brains to the matter and come up with a fresh one a letter to my publishers will always find me.)

But I feel fairly confident that by and large crime writers are quite happy to go to their graves with their ideas unused—whilst leaving no notes, naturally.

It must also be admitted, because it is I think relevant (although it did not apply in the case of Elizabeth Ferrars), that making the crossing of that wide, wide sagacious sea between the manuscript and the published book is easier in the sturdy vessel known as "S.S. Detective Fiction" than in the frail cockleshell called "M.V. Wannabe a real novelist."

I do not for one moment, of course, intend to imply that there is no room in the sacred groves of Academe for what I, no scholar, would think of as mere taxonomy—the hundred and one uses of a dead cat.... I mean, a dead body; the "ten thousand several doors" that John Webster said death hath; the many, many ways in which it is theoretically possible to accomplish a murder in a totally sealed room, without windows or chimneys or trapdoors and with doors locked beyond question.

That this latter should be categorized as "impossible crime" when the detective has bended his every talent to prove that it was quite possible is, to me, one of the minor mysteries of the genre.

Similarly—"similarly" was, I seem to remember, a technical term much used in the proving of geometrical theorems in my schooldays—similarly "the perfect crime" (i.e. one that is not recognized as a murder at all) has come to mean a killing that is perfect from the point of view of the murderer (in the sense of a bad deed well done) rather than that of the victim or the investigator.

Now, there is a nice little topic which I think might well be explored by someone with time (if nothing else) to kill "as a sad reflection of present-day society or something...."

Nor do I wish to denigrate those who can find social history in what detective novelists write. This is valuable. The diver tram recorded by Dorothy L. Sayers throws a nice little sidelight on London Transport history between the wars now lost to all but the specialist; the measure of "double elephant" used by Ngaio Marsh to describe the size of a newspaper headline; and what the butler saw and done—did—in Agatha Christie's *oeuvre* are all quite properly meat and drink to social commentators provided they remember that all period fiction is of its period. Today's Dr. John Watson, R.A.M.C. (retired), would have something better to do than run errands for Sherlock Holmes, but this doesn't mean that he necessarily would have done in Conan Doyle's day.

I have no quarrel with these sociologists, save that sometimes they appear to think the mannered mores of the nineteen twenties and thirties a myth invented by particular detective novelists for their own amusement. The days when "bad form" was in some circles arguably worse than murder and "not done" the equivalent of permanent banishment to St. Helena did exist.

I must also make it quite clear that in suggesting that writers of crime fiction do not always have something to say; in asserting that they often write crime fiction because there is a readier market for it; and postulating even more importantly that they write in a noncommittal manner which makes analysis difficult, I am not saying that they lack expertise.

If you truly want to understand the real-life mysteries of the British railway timetable system, the subtle—not to say arcane—world of Vicarage tea-parties or the finer points of Toi and Tiny-Toi gang warfare in Glasgow, then you will have no more readable sources to compare with than those which the well-informed crime writer serves up somewhere between the blood and the thunder.

This may be because the crime-writer is an expert in the field in real life or perhaps it may merely be that he has mastered the subject for one book and then shed the knowledge in the way that the moment a Judge has pronounced sentence a barrister forgets the details of his brief—or should it be her briefs? No matter. You may study this aspect of the genre as much as you will.

There is something else which worries me about the academic study of crime writing. Do those who do it realize that the academic is on the outside, looking in: and the writer is on the inside, not looking out.

The expression "on the tin" is one more commonly heard in Her Majesty's Prison establishments but it is very true of those of us for whom that even more famous Bingo injunction "eyes down" should apply for the larger part of each working day.

As Dean Sydney Smith remarked in the most famous pun of all time when observing two women haranguing each other from the windows of their houses on opposite sides of the street, "They never would agree because they were arguing from different premises."

I think it should therefore be admitted that the very different stances of academic and crime writer constitute a real impediment to the marriage of true minds. Remember that the hunter and the hunted have quite different objects in their view; even when it is an academic *quae* crime-writing author holding the pen.

At best the academic's quarry is alive and well and living somewhere on that broad avenue between an ivory tower and a Tower of Babel. At worst their prey is dead, and their works either elusive or already much-worked over—worse still, seminal, flawed, trivial, significant, or what you will.

The automatic response to this on your part is probably "the onlookers sees most of the game." But onlookers can only truly see the game if they know its rules and how it is best played. I don't think any onlooker, however percipient, can truly know what the game is about if they have not tried to play it, albeit they may recognize excellence.

Mistakes may be made, too. One of the commonest misapprehensions of those on the outside, looking in, is that detective story writers use stereotypes for their subsidiary characters. That this is not so can be apparent when someone working in a different medium—stage, film, radio, or art—comes to try to delineate them. This was attested by a film director at a recent colloquium on Agatha Christie. They will very quickly tell you that these people are not the cardboard cutouts that commentators are fond of describing as such.

And should any learned academic happen to notice that all the place-names in my own work always begin with the letters of the alphabet from A to O and seek to wonder why, I had better enlighten them now. I must tell you that the first two volumes of a topographical dictionary were given me by a friend who had retrieved them from a skip, but there was no sign of the third volume P to Z.

Another source of misleading inference can sometimes occur when those practitioners who feel they should not be writing a *vade mecum* of murder cause deliberate minor inaccuracies in their methods to appear in their work—and thus run the risk of having a researcher dismiss them as merely careless rather than concerned.

I should also perhaps, point out that our readers can be irritated by detective writers trying to slip in their views on class, race, politics—even crime and punishment. That is not why they read us and that is usually why we don't put them in.

I advance one of my last thoughts with considerable trepidation in this distinguished home of scholarship. I feel that there is a seeming lack of awareness among some academics that the writing of crime fiction is essentially a conjuring trick, a distraction of the mind's eye of the reader, a sleight of hand, a written prestidigitatory skill and that, like a conjuring act, it can actually be harmed by being laid bare.

The phrase "the unexamined life" has religious overtones but this rough magic is meant to remain unexamined.... In other words for "deconstructionist" do be very careful, won't you, that you aren't in fact being a "destructionist"?

There can be harms, too, to the devoted reader. I think this is best summed up in a few lines from Siegfried Sassoon's poem *The Grandeur of Ghosts*:

> When I have heard small talk about great men,
> I climb to bed; light my two candles; then
> Consider what was said;....
> They have spoken lightly of my deathless friends,
> (Lamps for my gloom, hands guiding where I stumble.)

This seems to me to be particularly the case at present where all that many academics seem to want to do is reveal the sometimes well-hidden sex lives of writers great and small. This was before I realized that Hugh Grant had been featured in the current issue of *The Oxford Ammonite* as the son of an alumna of this College. Had you thought, though, that the crime writer might not like being regarded as a species under observation?

Now, ladies and gentlemen, I must go and make my report to the Curia. I leave you with the imperishable thought for your further consideration that the writing of detective fiction should surely be an exercise for academics rather than writing about it can be considered an academic exercise.

> St. Hilda's College, Oxford, August, 1995

Catherine Aird
Biography

Catherine Aird, a pseudonym for Kinn Hamilton McIntosh, was born in Yorkshire but eventually moved with her physician father and her mother to an Edwardian house near Canterbury where she still resides in a nest of wondrous antiques. She was educated at Waverley School and Greenhead High School in Huddersfield. For many years active in the Girl Guides, she is a past chairman of the CWA and recipient of their Golden Handcuffs Award. She published her first Ins. C.D. Sloan mystery in 1966 and has gone on to write fifteen more, the most recent of which is *Stiff News*. Her 1967 *A Most Contagious Game* is not a Sloan but sets an amateur detective to solve a 100-year-old mystery by using church records. Set in the fictional county of Calleshire, the Sloan series embraces the careers of several policemen and displays both the author's erudition and her exuberant sense of humour, both showcased in her paper written for St. Hilda's crime conference and kindly shared with *AZ Murder Goes... Classic*. Its full force was best felt when read aloud with wicked pace by the Author.

Bibliography

Novels:
  The C.D. Sloan Series:
   The Religious Body, 1966.
   Henrietta Who?, 1968.
   The Complete Steel, 1969; *The Stately Home Murder* US, 1970.
   A Late Phoenix, 1971.
   His Burial Too, 1973.
   Slight Mourning, 1975.
   Parting Breath, 1977.
   Some Died Eloquent, 1979.
   Passing Strange, 1981.
   Last Respects, 1982.
   Harm's Way, 1984.
   A Dead Liberty, 1987.
   The Body Politic, 1990.
   A Going Concern, 1993.
   Injury Time, 1994.
   After Effects, 1996.
   Stiff News, 1998.

  Other:
   A Most Contagious Game, 1967.
   Gervase Fen and the Teacake School and *Benefit of Clergy* in *Murder Ink*, edited by Dilys Winn, 1977.

Other:
  Uncollected short stories, several local histories, and a play.

Justin Scott

♦

Robert Louis Stevenson

Robert Louis Stevenson
(1850–1894)

Biography

Robert Louis Stevenson was born in Edinburgh on 13 November, 1850. Handicapped by delicate health, he struggled all his life against tuberculosis. He studied law and was admitted to the bar in 1875, but never practiced. Instead he began contributing essays and stories to *Cornhill Magazine* in 1876 and then to other periodicals. His first published book was *An Inland Voyage* (1878), an account of a canoe trip in Belgium. That same year he married Frances Osbourne; gained a stepson and a stepdaughter. His first popular novel was *Treasure Island* (1883). In search of healthier climes he went first with his family to Saranac Lake, NY, 1887; and eventually to the South Seas, 1889, where they settled on Samoa. There he died on 3 December, 1894, and is buried high atop Mt. Vaea.

Treasure Island: Clueless Narrator; Charming Villain; Bodies Galore—So What's New?

Everyone knows *Treasure Island*. Everyone loves it. *Treasure Island* is the bedrock of pop fiction. So, if, three or four years ago, Barbara Peters had extended her kind invitation to speak to you about Robert Louis Stevenson's *Treasure Island* I would have asked, "Why me?"

Like most Americans, I was vaguely and affectionately familiar with the tale of hunting buried treasure: A mysterious treasure map; peg-leg Long John Silver; yo ho ho and a bottle of rum; parrot shrieking "pieces of eight;" and little Jim Hawkins running around with adults well past his bed time. Knowing no more and no less I'd have respectfully declined, despite the opportunity to visit Scottsdale with its reputation for stunning weather and perfect women.

(And I certainly would have declined had I known that upon my arrival yesterday I would be accosted by Edward Marston and Susan Moody, who took great delight announcing that in my audience would be Alanna Knight, a great RLS authority and a citizen of Edinburgh, no less. I spent all day going through my talk removing generalities.)

But I did not decline. In fact I accepted with delight because a lot's happened in those three years and I now stand before you, transformed, as an expert on *Treasure Island* and the writing habits of its author. A genuine expert. *Not* that I have academic qualifications—that noise you hear is my former professors snickering in their nursing homes—but I'll guarantee no one's been more intimate with Robert Louis Stevenson—with the possible exception of his wife.

My transformation began one dark winter night, when I was holed up in the country with a friend. Our fire was burning low. A nor'easter was howling and the rain was beating the windows, much like the day Stevenson himself started writing the novel in a cottage in the Scottish highlands. We had an ancient copy of *Treasure Island* and we began to read aloud to each other alternating chapters.

It's a supremely modern thriller in many ways, but its nineteenth century roots and eighteenth century pretensions are suited to reading aloud. The words roll comfortably. Short chapters end with provocative cliff hangers and in the course of several dark nights we read the whole novel right down to the final piece of eight.

It's a crackerjack story. A mysterious old sailor beset by scary pirates dies, leaving a boy the treasure map his enemies had sought. The boy rescues it from the pirates and shares it with good adults who take him along on the treasure hunt. The hunt is infiltrated by the diabolically clever leader of the scary pirates who attack when they reach the remote Treasure Island and try to kill the boy and his friends. Merciless war is waged on the island. The treasure is lost. The treasure is found. Seventeen men are killed—most graphically. The good people get the gold. The villain escapes to vill another day. And the boy comes home a giant step closer to manhood. To quote the beer commercials, it doesn't get much better than this.

In fact, it did get better. It had become apparent early on that there was more to *Treasure Island* than we remembered. We had read it in grade school English. Or we had read it in summer vacations. We had read the Classic Comic. And we had seen movies. I know of four movie versions—1934 with Wallace Beery and Jackie Cooper; a Disney version of 1950—memorable for the apple barrel scene when Israel Hands thrusts his knife into the nearly empty barrel and Jim Hawkins snatches up an apple and sticks it on the point. A British *Treasure Island* with Orson Welles; and a 1990 cable television version with Charlton Heston as Long John. All sail fairly true to the plot—they'd have been crazy not to—but none were especially true to fiction's greatest villain, Long John Silver.

I lay the blame for this mostly at the feet of Wallace Beery, who had the excuse of a smarmy screenplay, and partly on the dark brush of illustrator N.C. Wyeth, both of whom I will slander a bit more later on.

What struck me upon our reading was the modernity of the story, the subtle motivation, the deftly drawn characters: the innocent narrator—that hero of the modern adventure thriller mystery; the innocent victim of Eric Ambler; the wide-eyed narrator of Dr. Watson; the moralist of Chandler and Hammett; and the sly charming villain who has inspired writers from Graham Greene to Ian Fleming. And there is Stevenson himself, a cheerful soul shining through the novel. Jorge Luis Borges:

> I like the roots of words, the taste of coffee, and the prose of Stevenson.... If you don't like Stevenson, there must be something wrong with you.

Above all, I was struck by the sheer narrative power of Stevenson's story. He hurtles his plot forward, while never ignoring his descriptive responsibilities. This is quite a trick and one worth learning if you write novels for a living.

I'd been earning my living writing novels for a long time—but at that moment things weren't going too well. I had a dozen books published, but the one in the typewriter was foundering and in general I had grown displeased with what I felt was a certain ponderousness to my writing. It was time for some sort of refresher course. I'd been doing this too long to enroll in school. My former mentors were busy advancing their own work. So I thought why not go to school with Robert Louis Stevenson? Why not parse and outline the first chapter of *Treasure Island* sentence by sentence just to see how the master did it. I had done this occasionally with other books—notably *The Firm*, trying to figure out why Grisham was such a hit. The idea is you get close to the author's decisions.

So I started parsing *Treasure Island*. But immediately I discovered that the language was getting in my way. You see this is a nineteenth century writer—late nineteenth century—writing a historical novel set in the eighteenth century. So what we've got is a nineteenth century novelist's version of eighteenth century language. Language is very important in *Treasure Island* because it's a novel of the sea, which represented the high technology of the day. Sailor talk was both arcane and highly evocative and Stevenson used it forcefully to transport young Jim, and us, into the exotic world of his pirates.

In fact, the dialogue read like a foreign language. So I thought rather than outline the thing, why not update the novel's setting and translate its language into modern English, the way we talk in the 1990s? Problem. Immediate enormous problem. Robert Louis Stevenson's plot for *Treasure Island* cannot work any later than about 1955. It depends on a degree of isolation he took for granted in the nineteenth century and we have lost since the invention of modern electronics: miniature radio, satellite phones, Emergency Beacons, dependable radar, etc. A second problem in the novel is peopled by characters just recently home from war, ordinary characters who can reasonably be expected to bear arms.

Both problems were solved by setting my translation in the time of my boyhood in the 1950s. When I was growing up, every kid's father had fought in World War II. Communications were not as ubiquitous as they are today. Radios were big and clunky and failed spectacularly in the presence of salt water.

So the early 1950s it was—a kid's story told when I was a kid. I started it where I knew best, not on the coast of England but on Long Island's Great South Bay, and miraculously I began to remember how I had heard adults talk then.

To compare my writing exercise to refitting a sailing vessel with a modern powerplant would ignore the obvious fact that Mr. Stevenson had no need of improved propulsion. It was a translation, pure and simple, as if I were translating it from the French or the Russian, and it offered an interesting insight into the art of translation: it takes a novelist to translate a novel.

My main job was to clear the decks of archaic talk. Stevenson's descriptive style was remarkably clear, almost modern, as I'll demonstrate later. But his dialogue was often impenetrable. For that I used *Webster's Unabridged Second Edition*—last published in 1955 and still the best single dictionary in the English speaking world. Chambers Dictionary helped too, with its emphasis on derivations. And, of course, *The Concise Scots Dictionary*, for Stevenson was Scottish through and through. It was so much fun that when I had finished chapter one, I tackled chapter two. By the end of the third chapter my literary agent, Henry Morrison was questioning my career goals—if not my sanity.

Then I got greedy. Why not publish it? Translate the whole book? Perform a public service by making the old novel more accessible. Maybe get a few kids to read the old classic. Whatever, have some fun. Learn something. Graft some literary cachet to my name. Get invited to Scottsdale.

My agent still thought I was nuts, but he's a book man and when I showed him eight chapters he was hooked, too. He, and my sister, the novelist Alison Scott Skelton, offered excellent advice to break loose from Stevenson's language and time, for he still held me in thrall. My friend Jim Frye, a New York piano player, solved the "Yo-ho-ho and a bottle of rum!" problem with a wonderful suggestion to replace it with the U.S. Philippine Army song: *Oh the monkeys have no tails in Zamboanga.*

That song, more than anything, finally freed me of Stevenson's time, if not his genius. (Horse-mounted Revenue officers became

State Police Motorcycle cops, convenient icestorms eliminated telephones.) But while I stuck to Stevenson's structure, sentence by sentence, paragraph by paragraph, I discovered that whenever my modern instincts provoked me to rearrange the order of events, Mr. Stevenson's instincts proved the more reliable.

I translated half the book, then put it down to write my first Ben Abbott novel—where I discovered the lessons were sticking and that I had indeed managed to clean up my style and ram my story ahead in ways I had forgotten. During the first draft of *HardScape*, I found myself rejecting slow material with the thought that Stevenson would have done the business of this chapter with a single paragraph.

HardScape completed, I returned to *Treasure Island* and finished my story for "modern" men and women who once were boys and girls.

What did I learn? I learned about pace, about description, and about character.

Pace is the great strength of *Treasure Island*. Stevenson was a restless man. Dogged by poor health—coughing blood, while smoking handrolled cigarettes—he traveled constantly searching for healthy climates. The restless man was a restless writer. And restlessness rarely hurts a novel. *Treasure Island* races from threat to rescue to threat. No one gets to sit down very long, much less revel in his last escape.

"The only art is to omit" he wrote early on about travel writing, and carried the principle into his fiction. He knows when to stop. And in that he's modern, compared to the big book giants of his day.

His descriptive powers are rooted in the surveyor's skill, learned no doubt while he traipsed after his father who was a lighthouse builder. He has a daunting ability to lay out his scene and taught me that the scene is like a stage set: get it clear up front and your readers will follow your characters anywhere: here, they drop anchor in the harbor between the mainland and Skeleton Island.

> The place was entirely land-locked, buried in woods, the trees coming right down to high-water mark, the shores mostly flat, the hill tops standing round at a distance in a sort of amphitheatre, one here, one there. Two little rivers, or rather two swamps, emptied out into this pond, as you might call it; and the foliage round that part of the shore had a kind of poisonous brightness....

I learned how to create a character with a well chosen action on first meeting—a device that Stevenson had mastered forty-five years before F. Scott Fitzgerald said, "Action is character and character is action." (Yes, I know, Ernest Hemingway should have said it, but Fitzgerald beat him to it.)

I learned how he made pictures that printed themselves indelibly in the reader's mind. Here is Jim Hawkins' first sight of Long John. He sees him in Silver's tavern, The Spyglass:

> His left leg was cut off close by the hip, and under the left shoulder he carried a crutch, which he managed with wonderful dexterity, hopping about upon it like a bird. He was very tall and strong, with a face as big as a ham—plain and pale, but intelligent and smiling. Indeed, he seemed in the most cheerful spirits, whistling as he moved about among the tables, with a merry word or a slap on the shoulder for the more favoured of his guests....

(At this point Jim and the reader are both aware that a certain one-legged man is big trouble). But Jim is taken in:

> I had seen the captain and Black Dog, and the blind man Pew, and I thought I knew what a buccaneer was like—a very different creature from this clean and pleasant tempered landlord....

Wallace Beery take note. Not so dark a figure at first, not so sly—not all growls and scowls, not smirks and quirks, but "plain and pale, intelligent and smiling."

N.C. Wyeth take note, too. His magnificent illustrations for the Scribner's editions, while arrestingly harsh, have also turned our heads from Stevenson's very special achievement. A novel we might call the first modern mystery thriller is fueled by the sort of villain we've all tried to copy ever since, the villain with the smiling face and the smiling heart: Robert Louis Stevenson knew exactly what he was doing. He said:

> I had an idea for John Silver...to take an admired friend of mine, to deprive him of all his finer qualities and higher graces of temperament, to leave him nothing but his strength, his courage, his quickness, and his magnificent geniality....

The longer *Treasure Island*'s success, the greater the demands it put on subsequent fiction: pace, quick characterization, the memorable scene. He was writing for the movies twenty years before movies started. He would have feasted on MTV—the dreamy montage, the quick freeze.

G.S. Fraser writes that in fact his narrative is slowed by memorable scenes: the arrival of Blind Pew, the confrontation between Doctor Livesey and Billy Bones, Israel Hand's stalking Jim up the rigging—"Moments not of quickening, but arrest." It's an interesting point, though Fraser might miss the point that arrest in a novel is not necessarily a bad thing. Certainly, when we discuss favorite books and movies we do it in terms of high points like this:

Here Jim cowers behind a bush and sees Silver in action. Silver throws his crutch:

> It stuck poor Tom, point foremost and with stunning violence, right between the shoulders in the middle of his back. His hands flew up, he gave a sort of gasp, and fell....
> ...to judge from the sound, his back was broken on the spot. But he had no time given him to recover. Silver, agile as a monkey, even without leg or crutch, was on top of him next moment, and had twice buried his knife up to the hilt in that defenseless body. From my place of ambush, I could hear him pant aloud as he struck the blows.

James Ellroy, where are you? Not to mention the blood and guts Florida mystery crowd.

He's a writer's writer. He did what most of us do—blew his money, followed good short novels with bad long ones, and sometimes rewrote incessantly when he knew damned well it was better the first time, building and gardening in a happy attempt to lose himself in the real word. He didn't suffer much as a writer, compared to most. The words usually flowed. Interestingly, one time they didn't was in the middle of *Treasure Island*.

Years after *Treasure Island* and *Dr. Jekyll and Mr. Hyde* had made Stevenson the richest, most famous writer in the world, he reminisced about a nasty case of writer's block. The book had started as a map. He water-colored an elaborate map of an island as part of a game with a little boy, his twelve-year-old stepson Lloyd Osburne. From the map he got his story. And it flowed. He had written *Treasure Island* a chapter a day for fifteen chapters—the sort of pure writing that occasionally overtakes you and propels you along—and then suddenly it stopped and he went dry. Couldn't write a word. He had already sent the first fifteen chapters to his publisher to be serialized and the proofs came in the mail and he was looking at a half-written book that had died under his pen.

What he says next could be many writer's despair—only the details are Stevenson's. He writes that he was,

> A good deal pleased with what I had done, and appalled at what remained for me to do. I was thirty-one; I was the head of a family; I had lost my health; I had never yet paid my way, never yet made £200 a year.

(For half a century writers from Sir Walter Scott to Dickens and Trollope were pulling down twenty to thirty thousand pounds a year, which put them in the earning bracket of landed aristocracy.)

> My father had quite recently bought and cancelled a book that was judged a failure: Was this to be another and last fiasco?

There isn't a writer in this room who hasn't felt that awful, be it for an hour or a year. He traveled to Switzerland where he was to spend the winter. He did some reading, thought about other things. Suddenly a breakthrough. "It flowed from me like small talk." A chapter a day and in nineteen days he had finished his first novel.

He didn't seem to think it was important enough to mention in the reminisce, but the really interesting thing is that the turning point came when he fell upon a wonderful and very modern sounding device. Right smack in the middle of this first person novel Stevenson switched narrators—from young Jim to Dr. Livesey. I don't know if anyone had ever done that before in a novel. Maybe somebody in the audience does. I'd love to hear it during the question period. Anyhow, Livesey gets two or three first person chapters—Jim reappears—and we're off to the races.

Sprints. It's a short novel. I read Trollope, whom I love, to a point, and I ask, "Did the Victorians skim?"

After the rather succinct writing of Jane Austen, cheap printing, and a rising middle class gave birth to the "Modern" commercial novel invented by Sir Walter Scott. Dickens and Trollope expanded the tradition aided and abetted by a publishing-printing industry that fed an insatiable library business. RLS inherited a fifty year tradition of writing big. And turned his back on it. "The only art is to omit."

If I haven't cleared the room yet, let me warn those in the doorway you may be trampled because I'm about to careen into academic proclamations. I'm going to talk about *plot* and *theme*.

This is not my way, as a rule, but it's worth some mention while trying to figure out why Stevenson was so loved for so long. *Treasure Island*'s plot seems basic at first, and hardly new—basic good against evil—but it's really about three or four other things. First, it's about order versus chaos. With odds of nineteen pirates against six men and a boy, Jim and his friends still hold a slim advantage: they are orderly. They obey their captain. They're frugal. And they do nothing to excess.

The pirates are disorderly. They drink themselves silly, eat too much, sleep in the malaria infested swamp, waste their supplies, burn up their firewood, and refuse to plan ahead. These are villains in a deeply Scottish Presbyterian sense. They are, in short, what our sterner forefathers called undisciplined rabble. What we might call low life, low-rent slobs.

What makes them dangerous—more dangerous than their bloodthirsty cruelty—is that Long John Silver knows that chaos is his enemy. When he was Captain Flint's quartermaster he ruled with an iron hand: "When I was quartermaster, lambs wasn't the word for Flint's old buccaneers." Long John knows and fears that disorder, chaos, is his greatest weakness in the contest for the gold. "If you would only lay your course and point to windward you would ride in carriages, you would." Silver's almost wistful, as if for a moment even before the battle begins he senses that he is doomed by his comrades' fecklessness.

All is not perfect within the camp of Goodness. Stevenson's too smart for that. If it were, it would be boring. So we have Squire Trelawney, who embodies some chaos himself. The king pin of the plan to lift the treasure, the money man, the project manager, he's a big mouth, blabs the secret of the treasure, and is easily taken in by conmen like the shipyard owner Blandly and Silver. Dr. Livesey is a steadying influence. But our young hero, the boy Jim, is somewhat disorderly, taking foolish chances and running off onto the island. (Basically, Jim acts like a kid—not a particularly bright kid—who's constantly forcing our hearts into our throats—"No, don't run onto the island—No, get on the ship!")

Fortunately for the forces of good, Captain Smollet is the essence of order—dull, stolid, brave, and strong, and demanding— Stevenson allows us his protection just long enough to count on it, then takes him out of action with deadly wounds. Stevenson knows that threat upon threat makes a story fly.

Second, the novel is also one of the last pre-Freudian Freudian novels. It is, essentially, the story of a boy searching for his father.

Jim's father dies early on and chapter after chapter Jim attaches himself to a father figure, is disappointed, and finds another: Old Billy Bones, the sailor who comes to the Admiral Benbow Inn; Squire Trelawney; Dr. Livesey—the one perfect man in the story; Captain Smollett; and ultimately Long John Silver himself. Whenever Long John Silver lets him down, Jim must grow.

Third, it's a novel of friendship—something which Stevenson the man took very seriously—the ease and comfort of mutual understanding and mutual admiration felt by good old friends Squire Trelawney and Dr. Livesey is beautifully handled. Friendship is fairly rare in fiction. Writers write about love. And I'm no exception, so I thought why not for the fun of it make Dr. Livesey a woman. Make them bachelor lovers—busy with their own lives, but bound by the pleasure of their company. It was the only substantive change I made in Stevenson's story. (Interestingly, I've been told that the reason the attempts to turn *Treasure Island* into a Broadway musical failed was because there was no love interest.)

Another theme of *Treasure Island* is rebellion. Stevenson tweaked the whiskers of Victorian certitude. Being a Scot he found the English, who dominated the culture, to be dull and overbearing.

Stevenson fancied himself a bohemian, a bohemian and of a younger generation that was getting bored with Victorian march of progress and the long, long Pax Britannica. Keep in mind that thirty years later WWI broke out largely from boredom.

Darwinism, Socialism, and Atheism were the new ideas of his day, the sorts of ideas perfect for driving your parents up a wall. And indeed, he drove his indulgent father nuts.

One of his biographers, Ian Bell, writes that "Stevenson was debauched on a part time basis only." That is, after a night of adventure in Edinburgh's Old Town, he slept in his bed in his father's substantial house in the New Town. To be blunt, he was a rebel with a rich father. But to be fair, he mingled beyond his class, sort of as Turner had on the London Docks, and he listened to their speech and observed their foibles, and seemed to have his eyes open wide enough to keep a sense of humor: "My circle," he said, "was being continuously changed by the action of the police magistrate."

But the one time he managed to get himself arrested, it was a riotous snowball fight.

Still, like any bohemian worth his salt, his rebellion sprang from serious roots. Religion dominated Scottish lives, even the lives of those who didn't partake of the sacrament daily. Right and wrong were important, but so was the usually unspoken Calvinists' belief that none of these really mattered a whole hell of a lot since God had already thrown the dice and their lives were predestined. Godly behavior was, ironically, a doomed attempt to rewrite what was already written. Thus the fascination with duality. Good and evil in the same man—right and wrong in the same heart.

Could this be the secret to *Treasure Island*'s extraordinary success? Could it have survived so long—despite archaic language—because it was so modern that it took three or four generations to catch up with it? Does its success stem from the central theme embodied in Long John Silver and Jim Hawkins—the theme that good and evil can and do reside in the same soul?

Jim Hawkins? Like Silver? You bet. That little bohemian Jim Hawkins: the outsider, the lone wolf, the non-team player. (If Jim hadn't run away to the island his friends could have retaken the ship from the skeleton crew that Long John Silver left behind to guard them. Of course if he hadn't, we'd have no novel.)

Captain Smollet wasn't fooled: "You're too much of the born favorite for me," Captain Smollet dismisses him in the end, and doubts they'll ever sail together again.

But the good captain misses the point that enthralls Stevenson's readers. *Treasure Island* resonates with the promise, the hope, the dream that—We can pull it off. We can be both good and bad and *not get caught.* Jekyll and Hyde live. Long John Silver gets away. Now there's a fairy tale. There's a fantasy. There's a novel.

So what did Stevenson leave us in this novel about a fatherless boy looking for a father? This sea story about friendship? This treasure hunt? This tale of good and evil? This mystery?

Well, he and Henry James had a big debate about art. (Years later he met Mark Twain and I'm willing to bet that the discussion centered on royalty statements and the newfangled typewriter. But with Henry James, you talked art.) James, in fact, admired Stevenson's work, and was a generous booster in the face of literary snobbishness. Anyhow, Henry James talked about the art of fiction. RLS said no, there was no such thing as the art of fiction; there is the art of narrative. Fiction was too general. The novel is not a transcript of life—but a simplification of some side or point of life. This is how Stevenson saw his job. Leave your life, he whispers to us. Run off with me awhile. Figure it out later—when you're too old to play.

Bibliography

Novels:
- *Treasure Island*, 1883.
- *Prince Otto*, 1885.
- *Kidnapped*, 1886.
- *The Strange Case of Dr. Jekyll and Mr. Hyde*, 1886.
- *The Merry Men*, 1887.
- *The Black Arrow*, 1888.
- *The Master of Ballantrae*, 1889.
- *The Wrong Box*, with Lloyd Osbourne, 1889.
- *The Wrecker*, with Lloyd Osbourne, 1892.
- *The Ebb Tide*, with Lloyd Osbourne, 1894.
- *The Weir of Hermiston*, incomplete, 1896.

Other:
- *An Inland Voyage*, 1878.
- *Travels with a Donkey in the Cevennes*, 1879.
- *Verginibus Puerisque*, essays, 1881.
- *Familiar Studies of Men and Books*, essays, 1882.
- *New Arabian Nights*, short stories, 1882.
- *A Child's Garden of Verses*, 1885.
- *A Footnote to History*, 1893.

Critical Studies:
- Graham Balfour, *The Life of Robert Louis Stevenson*, 1901.
- David Daiches, *Robert Louis Stevenson*, 1947.
- J. C. Furnas, *Voyage to Windward*, 1952.
- Ian Bell, *Dreams of Exile*, 1992; US, 1993.
- Several works by Scottish authority Alanna Knight that include *Stevenson in the South Seas* and *Bright Ring of Words*.

Justin Scott

Biography

Justin Blazer Scott resides in New York City and Connecticut where he set his Ben Abbott series. His first mystery, *Many Happy Returns*, was a 1974 Edgar Best First Mystery nominee. He has written numerous historical sea thrillers and in 1994 conceived a modern version of the Stevenson classic, *Treasure Island*. His short story *An Eye for an Eye* was a 1994 Edgar nominee.

Bibliography

Novels:
- The Ben Abbott Series:
    - *HardScape*, 1994.
    - *StoneDust*, 1995.
    - *FrostLine* (UK), 1997.

- Other:
    - *Deal Me Out* (as J.S. Blazer), 1973.
    - *Lend a Hand* (as J.S. Blazer), 1974.
    - *Many Happy Returns*, 1973.
    - *Treasure for Treasure*, 1974.
    - *The Shipkiller*, 1978.
    - *The Turning*, 1978.
    - *The Man Who Loved the Normandie*, 1981.
    - *A Pride of Royals*, 1983.
    - *The Auction* (UK), 1984.
    - *Rampage*, 1986.
    - *The Widow of Desire*, 1989.
    - *The Nine Dragons*, 1991.
    - *The Empty Eye of the Sea* (UK), 1992.
    - *Treasure Island*, 1994.

Short Stories:
- *The White Death* in *Beastly Tales*, 1989.
- *Katherine's Faces* in *A Body Is Found*, 1990.
- *The Commission's Moll* in *Missing Manhattan*, 1992.
- An *Eye for an Eye* in *Justice in Manhattan*, 1994.
- *A Shooting Over in Jersey* in *Murder On The Run*, 1998.

Laurie R. King

♦

Sir Arthur Conan Doyle

Sir Arthur Conan Doyle
(1859–1930)

Biography

A. Conan Doyle was born in Edinburgh on 22 May, 1859. He was educated in Lancashire at the Hodder School and at Stonyhurst College, 1870–75; the Jesuit School, Feldkirch, Austria, 1875–76; studied medicine at the University of Edinburgh: 1876–81, M.B. 1881, M.D. 1885. He practiced medicine in Southsea, Hampshire, 1882–90, then became a full-time writer. From 1899–1902 he served as senior physician at a South African field hospital during the Boer War. He twice stood for Parliament. He was a member of the Society for Psychical Research, 1893–1930 (resigned). His honours include the L.L.D., University of Edinburgh, 1905; Knight of Grace of the Order of St. John of Jerusalem. Widowed, he married Jean Leckie in 1907; two sons and one daughter. He died on 7 July, 1930.

Sir Arthur Conan Doyle

Let it be said straight off: I am not a Sherlockian. I am no Holmesian, I have not memorized the canon backwards and forwards, I belong to no scion such as the Baker Street Irregulars (although I agree that the idea of being an Adventuress of Sherlock Holmes does have a certain appeal). I will even admit that until I began actually writing a book in which Conan Doyle's detective plays a major part, I had not read the stories since *The Speckled Band* and *The Hound of the Baskervilles* back—way back—in high school.

By now, of course, I am well aware of the multitudinous works of higher criticism on the Conan Doyle canon, critical volumes filled with essays concerning such pressing questions as how many times Dr. Watson married and the original color of Mrs. Hudson's hair before being the landlady of Sherlock Holmes turned it white. Most of these, although one suspects not all, agree firmly with the judgement of Dorothy L. Sayers when she wrote that the whole business of Holmesian commentaries "must be played as solemnly as a county cricket match at Lord's: the slightest touch of extravagance or burlesque ruins the atmosphere."

However, be they tongue in cheek or deadly serious, there is no getting around the fact that there are a lot of these essays and volumes, and that when relative neophytes such as myself are asked to give a talk on the subject, we are either left scratching around for some immensely arcane issue that has not been worked to death, or else dependent on those who have gone before.

I was trained as a theologian; I am not too proud to use the work of earlier scholars. Therefore, my talk largely consists of a series of quotations from minds better than mine. This may appear either as shameful laziness or as a rather obvious attempt to lend a spurious air of academic respectability to a worn garment, and I admit that when I first realized I had nothing but a string of quotes, I did come near to panic. However, I decided that really, as there is nothing new under the sun to be said about Conan Doyle or Sherlock Holmes anyway, I might as well present a few nuggets mined by others for the contemplation of my listeners.

In his introduction to John Gardner's brilliant *On Moral Fiction*, (not, by the way, the John Gardner who writes crime fiction),

Charles Johnson writes that very occasionally a writer "creates something that becomes emblematic for some sector of our experience. This happens when a writer stumbles, by genius or dumb luck, on an archetypal character. In some cases this naming, this dramatizing, crystallizes an experience we all know but until this creation occurs, have not found a way to utter."

Until the character of Sherlock Holmes crystallized under the pen of an out-of-work medical doctor in the end of the last century, Victorian England, and in its footsteps the rest of the world, did not have its defining modern hero, a man (I fear, inevitably a man) who could confront the truly awful problems of the age with the best weapons and values of that age: the power of science and knowledge arrayed against the immorality and chaos that threatened on all sides, a hero who depended not so much on swordplay (fisticuffs occasionally) as his mind. Problems, Sherlock Holmes says, are solvable, when the right person tackles them. That Holmes is as much adored in the late twentieth century as in the year of his birth says a great deal for the power of the image that Conan Doyle tapped into—or, if you insist, created.

Conan Doyle himself conceived of Holmes primarily as a thinking machine. In the first short story (not the first novel) he refers to Holmes'

> ...cold, precise, but admirably balanced mind. He was...the most perfect reasoning and observing machine that the world has seen.... He never spoke of the softer passions, save with a gibe and a sneer.... For the trained reasoner to admit such intrusions into his own delicate and finely adjusted temperament was to introduce a distracting factor which might throw a doubt upon all his mental results. Grit in a sensitive instrument, or a crack in one of his own high power lenses, would not be more disturbing than a strong emotion in a nature such as his. [*A Scandal in Bohemia*]

For those of us who had not read the Holmes stories since before we could vote, it sometimes comes as a surprise to find things going on in the stories other than this Thinking Machine *persona*. Indeed, it is a great joy not only as a literary discovery but as a bearer of psychological insight to stumble across this Holmes Who Laughs, a Holmes who shakes with passion.

The first we hear of Holmes is in the novel *A Study in Scarlet*. The narrator Dr. Watson is newly in London, having been invalided out of the army following an encounter with a Jezail bullet in Afghanistan. He runs into a friend, and over a drink tells the man

Stamford of his search for affordable rooms. Stamford recommends a young researcher he knows from the medical school, with the caveat, however, that "Holmes is a little too scientific for my tastes—it approaches to cold-bloodedness." He even suggests that Holmes might readily give a touch of poison to a friend (or, one wonders, to a roommate?) to see how it worked—although he admits that Holmes would be just as likely to take it himself.

And yet, the first we see of Holmes, working over a test tube in the hospital laboratory, he is springing to his feet with a cry of pleasure. He chuckles to himself, he seizes Watson's sleeve (this perfect stranger) in eagerness to show him the results of this thrilling experiment, and claps his hands, looking as delighted as a child with a new toy, his eyes glittering.

Not perhaps the image of cold-bloodedness Stamford's words had brought to mind. Fixation, perhaps, but not cold-bloodedness. About his work, at any rate, Sherlock Holmes is certainly passionate—but remember, the root meaning of passion is suffering. Webster's gives several meanings for the word passion. The first three refer to the Easter passion, the suffering on the cross. The fourth meaning mentions "emotion and an intense, driving, or overmastering feeling or conviction," and the sense of an outbreak of anger (to fly in passion at something.) Only in the fifth position do we get down to the idea of passion as "ardent affection."

In speaking of the person of Sherlock Holmes, not just as a scientist but as a human being, Conan Doyle uses a spare, almost mythic language rather than the more descriptive style of the novelist. The descriptions we are granted are few and specific, and make it necessary to look for the indicators of personality in something other than the straightforward story line. These often come in little bursts, as if the man Holmes occasionally thrusts his way into Conan Doyle's slow and deliberate account by the very force of his personality. Violent emotion appears, rapidly suppressed, and unexpected sparkles of humour pop to the surface.

Now Victorian humour is a very special thing. A classic of the type is Jerome K. Jerome's *Three Men in a Boat*, filled with dry, self-deprecating, and occasionally very heavy-handed humour. In the Holmes stories, it is poor Watson who generally bears the brunt of these humorous asides.

In *The Valley of Fear*, Holmes declares sarcastically, "Your native shrewdness, my dear Watson, that innate cunning which is the delight of your friends, would surely prevent you from enclosing cipher and message in the same envelope," and later on adds,

"Perhaps there are points which have escaped your Machiavellian intellect." In the *Three Students* Holmes berates Watson,

> By jove! My dear Watson, it is nearly nine, and the landlady babbled of green peas at seven-thirty. What with your eternal tobacco, Watson, and your irregularity at meals, I expect that you will get notice to quit, and that I shall share your downfall.

A rather different sort of jest is made in *The Hound of the Baskervilles* when Holmes admits to Watson that, although he has travelled to Devonshire by means of the Ordnance Survey maps, actually "My body has remained in this armchair and has, I regret to observe, consumed in my absence two large pots of coffee and an incredible amount of tobacco." He then explains his preference for the smoky fog he has generated in their rooms: "It is a singular thing, but I find that a concentrated atmosphere helps a concentration of thought. I have not pushed it to the length of getting into a box to think, but that is the logical outcome of my convictions."

Later in the Baskerville case, he says drily, "In a modest way I have combatted evil, but to take on the Father of Evil himself would, perhaps, be too ambitious a task."

Holmes may be a thinking machine with a sense of humour, but he is also capable of friendship and love. "Quick, man, if you love me!" he says to Watson…. After nearly killing Watson by burning a hallucinogenic powder in their closed rooms in the *Devil's Foot* adventure, he apologises, and Watson answers him "with some emotion, for I had never seen so much of Holmes's heart before." In the case of the *Three Garridebs*, when Watson is shot, Holmes cries, "You're not hurt, Watson? For God's sake, say that you are not hurt!" It was worth a wound (says Watson)—it was worth many wounds—to know the depth of loyalty and love which lay behind that cold mask. The clear, hard eyes were dimmed for a moment, and the firm lips were shaking. For the one and only time he caught a glimpse of a great heart as well as of a great brain. All his years of humble but single-minded service culminated in that moment of revelation.

"It's nothing, Holmes. It's a mere scratch." Holmes rips up Watson's trousers with his pocket-knife to examine the wound. "You are right," he cries, with an immense sigh of relief. "It is quite superficial." His face set like flint as he glared at their prisoner…. "By the Lord, it is as well for you. If you had killed Watson, you would not have got out of this room alive."

Admittedly, Holmes' friendship and companionship with a loyal partner such as Watson is a different thing from his feelings towards women. Holmes is described as having a good but slightly paternalistic attitude towards women, to whom he can demonstrate sympathy, but nothing much stronger. He does become extremely devoted to one woman, in the very first short story, whom he refers to henceforth as The Woman, but only because she outsmarts him at his own game. (Actually, this may not be a bad recommendation for a man, that he be devoted to a woman who has beaten him soundly....) In the *Copper Beeches*, troubled by a case without data involving a young woman, he mutters that he would not wish a sister of his to accept the situation that this woman is about to assume as governess to a very shady set of people in a remote area.

Interestingly enough, it seems clear in Conan Doyle's mind that, although Holmes will not marry, he could consider it. Again in the *Copper Beeches* story, Watson ends his narrative by noting sadly that, in spite of his hopes (and surely by this time in their partnership he would have known Holmes well enough to know if hopes were utterly impossible), Holmes manifested no further interest in the young lady of the case once it was solved. When in the *Devil's Foot*, Holmes speaks of Dr. Sterndale's dastardly act, he says, "I have never loved, Watson, but if I did, and if the woman I loved had met such an end, I might act even as he has done."

Similarly, in the *Charles Augustus Milverton* case, when Holmes wishes to insinuate himself into the blackmailer's household, one day he walks into Baker Street and announces to Watson that he is engaged. Watson, although surprised, is far from dissolving into hoots of laughter or otherwise expressing polite disbelief; indeed, he begins enthusiastically to congratulate him until Holmes cuts him off with the information that it is only a part of his role in the household.

And finally, in *The Valley of Fear*, Holmes reflects speculatively, "Should I ever marry, Watson, I should hope to inspire my wife with some feeling which would prevent her from being walked off by a housekeeper when my corpse was lying within a few yards of her." Holmes, ever the romantic....

There is a poem by Robert Browning, where he says,

> Our interest's on the dangerous edge of things. The honest thief, the tender murderer,
> The superstitious atheist...

The cold passion of Sherlock Holmes is another of these appealing dichotomies, this character who epitomizes both the rational mind and the bursts of escaping passion. Were he simply a cold theoretician, he would not still be so alive more than a century after he first appeared.

In an essay in the 1976 edition of the *Mystery Writer's Handbook*, John D. MacDonald addresses this question of the complexity of a character:

> Too often in mystery fiction, the attempt to devise a real and believable detective has degenerated into a complication of props rather than expanded into a complication of character, a subtlety and complexity of the spirit. The original fault is perhaps due to that misinterpretation of Sherlock Holmes which places too much weight on the needle, the violin, the pipe. We remember Holmes as a man who, primarily, was troubled in spirit, was obsessed with the sense of evil, whose arrogance was defensive. Yet we see around us today a score of fictional detectives who have been given merely the props without the spirit.

In the *Dying Detective*, his enemy calls Holmes an amateur of crime. I would remind you that the Latin root of the word means love. To borrow again from John Gardner (in reference to a book whose flaw he sees as its facile openness of sentiment):

> That is one great technical problem which modern fiction has as yet found no way to break through. Feeling, the heart of the novelist's business, sits waiting for the right incantation, nervous and bored.

I would like to suggest that Arthur Conan Doyle was doing just that. By using spare language (mythic in its form rather than novelistic), spare description, spare emotion, he forms a backdrop in which the slightest passion and fury resounds, where a whisper of love is as a shout, where a twitch of anger is more eloquent than another man's furious bellow.

To borrow a final time from Gardner:

> In the fictional dream, as in our dreams as we sleep, there is some urgent concern—something that needs to be achieved and cannot be achieved easily, something worth achieving in the first place, though possibly crazy.

For more than a century now, readers have been grateful that an underemployed medical doctor in Victorian England persisted in his craziness, and brought Sherlock Holmes to life.

Bibliography

The Sherlock Holmes Canon:
   Novels:
      A Study in Scarlet, 1888.
      The Sign of the Four, 1890.
      The Hound of the Baskervilles, 1902.
      The Valley of Fear, 1914.

   Short Stories (56 in all):
      The Adventures of Sherlock Holmes, 1892.
      The Memoirs of Sherlock Holmes, 1893.
      The Return of Sherlock Holmes, 1905.
      His Last Bow: Some Reminiscences of Sherlock Holmes, 1917.

   And later:
      The Case-Book of Sherlock Holmes, 1927.

Other:
   2 Crime Novels, 16 Novels, a vast collection of short stories including Professor Challenger, Brigadier Gerard, Horror, Supernatural, Science Fiction, Adventure, Plays, Poetry, History, Politics, Spiritualism, Memoirs, Essays, Letters.

Critical Studies:
   Extensive biographies of Doyle and Holmes, bibliographies, studies, chronologies, guides, and pastiches too numerous to list.

Laurie R. King

Biography

Laurie R. King of Watsonville, California, burst upon the mystery scene with her first Kate Martinelli novel, *A Grave Talent*, winner of the 1994 Edgar Allan Poe Best First Mystery Award and the 1995 John Creasey Award from the British Crime Writers Association as well as a nominee for other prizes. Her first Mary Russell novel, *The Beekeeper's Apprentice*, is an example of a hyper-modern or highly collectible first-in-series book. She has published two more Kate Martinellis and three Mary Russells and is currently working on a non-series novel. The mother of two, King—holder of a B.A. with honors in religious studies; an M.A. in theology; and was awarded an honorary doctoral degree (Doctor of Humane Letters) from The Church Divinity School of the Pacific in 1997— is deeply interested in religion, philosophy, and feminism. She's also a talented punter, practicing on the rivers of England.

Bibliography

Novels:
    The Kate Martinelli Series:
        A Grave Talent, 1993.
        To Play the Fool, 1995.
        With Child, 1996.

    The Mary Russell Novels:
        The Beekeeper's Apprentice, 1994.
        A Monstrous Regiment of Women, 1995.
        Letter of Mary, 1997.
        The Moor, 1998.

Joe Gores

◆

Dashiell Hammett

Samuel Dashiell Hammett (1894–1961)

Biography

Dashiell Hammett was born in St. Mary's County, Maryland, on 17 May, 1894. He was educated at the Baltimore Polytechnic Institute, but left at an early age. He worked variously as a clerk, stevedore, and advertising manager, and during World War I joined the Motor Ambulance Corps of the U.S. Army, 1918–19, during which time he contracted tuberculosis. In 1908 he had become a private operative with the Pinkerton Agency, where he returned until 1922, after which he became a full-time writer. He was a book reviewer for *Saturday Review of Literature*, 1927–29, and for the *New York Evening Post*, 1930, and wrote screenplays and collaborated with his long-time lover, Lillian Hellman, variously. From 1946–56 he taught creative writing at the Jefferson School of Social Science, NY. In 1951 he was convicted of contempt of Congress and served a six month prison term. He served as president of the League of American Writers, 1942, and of the Civil Rights Congress of New York, 1946–47. Married to Josephine Dolan, 1920; two daughters. He died on 10 January, 1961.

Dashiell Hammett

In 1925, a short, dumpy, fortyish man told a self-styled Russian countess who was trying seduce him:

> You think I'm a man and you're a woman. That's wrong. I'm a manhunter and you're something that has been running in front of me. There's nothing human about it.

In 1956, a tall, solid, fortyish man said to himself, after interviewing a teen-age hooker who was mainlining heroin:

> The problem was to love people, try to serve them, without wanting anything from them. I was a long way from solving that one.

Both are fictional private investigators. The first, never named, is known only as The Continental Op. He is Dashiell Hammett's essential detective. The second is Lew Archer, Ross Macdonald's durable detective hero.

That Hammett is Macdonald's literary grandfather—by way of Raymond Chandler's Philip Marlowe—there can be no doubt. Macdonald said that, "As a novelist of realistic intrigue, Hammett was unsurpassed in his own or any time." He even named Lew Archer after Miles Archer, whose murder in the opening stanzas of *The Maltese Falcon* sends his partner Sam Spade out into the San Francisco streets in the quest for the jewel-encrusted black bird.

So why is this picture out of focus? Where did Hammett's singular detective hero come from, and what happened to him in the three decades between those two quotes?

Samuel Dashiell (Dashiell was his mother's maiden name) Hammett was born in St. Mary's County, Maryland, in 1894. His father (a Democrat) ran for political office from the wrong party (Republican) and was virtually run out of the county, so Hammett grew up in Philadelphia and Baltimore. He left school at the age of 14; during the next few years he held several kinds of jobs—messenger boy, newsboy, office clerk, timekeeper, yardman, machine operator, and finally stevedore.

Probably at about 18, he became an operative for the Pinkerton Detective Agency. Based on my own experiences as a private detective, I have a hunch he perhaps started out as office boy rather than field man, but there are no records from those years, and in any event he soon became an operative.

WW I interrupted his sleuthing and injured his health. He was an ambulance driver (not in the war zone), and in a one-vehicle accident rolled an ambulance full of sick and injured soldiers. No one was damaged further, but Hammett was so shaken by the incident that he never drove a motor vehicle again.

He also contracted TB in the service and was in and out of veterans' hospitals for several years until he grew tired of it, discharged himself, moved to San Francisco in 1920, married Josephine Dolan—a nurse whom he'd met in a VA hospital in Seattle—and returned to sleuthing for Pinkerton's.

He and Josie had two daughters, but his tuberculosis eventually made it necessary for him to live apart from his family. They never really got together again as man and wife, although Hammett bought Josie a house, supported her all his life and provided for the education of his daughters. They were never divorced, contrary to the impression left by Lillian Hellman in her autobiographical writings, and Hammett never stopped spending several weeks each year with his family.

He finally quit detective work and started writing ad copy for Al Samuel's Jewelry store on Market Street. A co-worker there, Peggy O'Toole, served as his major inspiration for Brigid O'Shaugnessy in *The Maltese Falcon*. In 1975, while researching my novel *Hammett*, I tracked down Peggy O'Toole; she would only talk to me on the porch of their Sonoma home, because her husband was still suspicious about her and Hammett from those long-ago days in the 1920s. She didn't know she had served as a major literary inspiration—and had never read *The Maltese Falcon*!

During these early years he was trying to write—fiction, poetry, fact pieces, criticism—and had his first crime story published in 1922; in 1923 his first Continental Op story was published in *Black Mask*. During this brief eight-year creative burst in San Francisco (1923–1930), he turned out four novels (*Red Harvest*, *The Dain Curse*, *The Maltese Falcon*, and *The Glass Key*), and an even sixty short stories and novelettes.

His fiction made him the unquestioned master of detective-story fiction and made a lasting impression on American letters. But the 1934 publication by Knopf of his fifth novel, *The Thin Man*, virtually marked the end of his creative career: during his last 27 years he wrote a few book reviews, a few radio scripts, and motion picture rewrites, and for a few months the continuity of the Alex Raymond-drawn comic strip, *Secret Agent X-9*.

During WW II, Hammett again served in the Army, this time in the Aleutian Islands where he edited a post newspaper that has since become famous in its own right. After the war, he was hounded by HUAC—House Unamerican Activites Committee—commie-hunters in Congress and jailed for contempt by refusing to state whether he was a member of the Communist Party and because he said he "didn't know" the names of any card-carrying Communists. This jail-time gave him emphysema, which completed the destruction of his health begun during his Army service in WW I.

During subsequent testimony before the Senate came the famous exchange between Hammett and "Tail-Gunner" Joe McCarthy, the red-baiting Senator who almost destroyed the American system of government. McCarthy asked, "If you were me, Mr. Hammett, would you allow your books to be on the shelves of American libraries?" To which Hammett replied, "If I were you, Senator, I wouldn't allow there to be any American libraries."

He died in 1961 in the home of his long-time consort, Lillian Hellman.

Many theories have been advanced for Hammett's long creative silence. Some say his chronic alcoholism destroyed his ability to work; others that his ill-health did the same thing.

More pragmatic observers like San Francisco private detective David Fechheimer, one of the country's great Hammett experts—he even has X-rays of Hammett's teeth—disagree. Fechheimer feels that Hammett was earning huge amounts of money ($60,000–$75,000 a year) from rights, royalties, and residuals during the 1930s and 1940s when federal income taxes were idiosyncratic at best and a very good income was $2,000 a year. So why should he write?

Writers know very well why he should write even though he didn't need the money: for a writer, it is impossible not at least to try. The best argument against the "why write?" theory is that during many of those years, he was trying desperately to complete a non-mystery novel called *Tulip* of which a sizeable fragment exists. I know Bill Nolan disagrees with me on this, but I find the fragment, about a writer trying to write, anything but compelling.

My own theory about the long silence is what I call the "*Mr. Roberts* Syndrome." *Mr. Roberts* was a Pulitzer-Prize winning play and subsequent high-grossing movie by Thomas Heggen about Heggen's adventures on a non-combat naval vessel during World War II. The trouble for the very-successful Heggen was that the only thing he had to write about were his wartime experiences. He hadn't had any other experiences, but the imperative to write was still there. So he drowned himself, if I remember correctly, in his bathtub.

I think a variant of this is what happened to Hammett's career as a novelist. When he left San Francisco in 1930 for the big bucks and bigtime of Hollywood and then New York, he was riding the crest: he had created a new kind of American fiction. In Hollywood he met Hellman and her circle of friends who all considered detective fiction low-class and definitely not "literature"—in quotes, of course.

The irony is that Hammett was already being recognized as a major American novelist, but because he was a Pinkerton op moving in a smart set with radically different concerns, he came to have contempt for what he had been writing about and for himself. The *Tulip* fragment bears poignant testimony to the fact that he couldn't write about anything that wasn't rooted in his Pinkerton experiences.

His solution was to write nothing at all. Instead of drowning himself, he drowned his talent.

The urge to write remained, of course, so he poured his creativity into Lillian Hellman's plays. There are many critics who claim they can isolate huge hunks of Hellman's work which actually were written by Hammett; there is no doubt that his fingerprints are all over her plays.

I find it significant in the extreme that while Hellman wrote extensively after Hammett's death—memoirs, screenplays, adaptations, and translations of European dramatists—she never wrote another original play of her own after his death in 1961. So far as I know, not even a single scene of her own.

Could the disapproval of the literati really carry such weight with someone struggling to be a writer? Well, in 1955, when I wanted to do my Master's Thesis at Stanford on the stories of Hammett, Chandler, and Macdonald, I was informed by the University that since these stories were not literature, obviously graduate papers could not be written about them. I took comfort from the fact that back about 300 years, the Bodleian Library of Oxford University refused shelf room to the manuscripts of William Shakespeare's plays on the same grounds.

The term most often applied to the hard-boiled detective novel, even today, is "realistic." The writer is primarily a creator, not a commentator. He is less concerned with realism in a literary sense than with reality in a literal sense. Realism is a word that critics and reviewers love—John Mason Brown rhetorically asks, "If realism isn't real, then isn't it trash?"

Mike Avallone has always called critics "one-legged runners" and there are many of us who would say he is not in every instance wrong. Anyway, let's look at the critics' "realism" for a moment. Realism of character is very far from Lillian Hellman's sort of hothouse creations—I think Hammett's help to her was more in the way of construction of scene and movement of story than in *whom* she chose to write about.

Realism in its best sense equals truth; and ironically it was perhaps that element in Hammett's work that Hellman's friends—and many critics—scorned. But it is that truth which makes his work so seminal and successful. Fiction's truth takes what is there and refines it until the very essence of truth—more true than fact itself—is there on the page.

Of course in some ways, realism is subjective—as any judge learns from listening to eyewitnesses of the same event. On the other hand, real people look, dress, and act in certain ways; when they talk, they talk in certain ways. It is the writer's job, whatever his subjective feelings, to take these true elements of real people and heighten and shape them without losing the underlying reality.

Never easy to do. It is a commonly held maxim that artistic realism is the miner's canary of a civilization: extreme realism in sculpture and drama marked the beginning of the decline for both the Greek and Roman empires. Could it be that a coarsened realism that anticipates artistic decline is emotional? That the writers begin to believe that the emotion surrounding the reality is the reality itself?

Anyway, such extreme realism (as is often seen in today's novels, film, and television) gives a certain hard reality to Hemingway's off-hand comment about New York when he was hand-delivering a manuscript to Knopf. In his hotel room he found that the row of books on the shelf were only fake backs of books, and said, "I think we are an outfit on the way out."

Let's stick with Hemingway for a moment. He once wrote of Mark Twain:

> All modern American literature comes from one book by Mark Twain called *Huckleberry Finn*...it's the best book we've had.

> All American writing comes from that. There was nothing before. There has been nothing as good since.

My wife Dori and I think several others in this room would give *Moby Dick* the honor of the Great American Novel; I'd split the honor between the two. I think the Great American has to appear every fifty years or so anyway because society keeps changing.

There is a whole school of literary thought, by the way, that believes Ernest Hemingway was a major literary influence on Hammett. However, the late Lee Wright, mystery editor for many years at Random House, always held that Hemingway learned his clipped, precise style from Hammett. Indeed, in *Death in the Afternoon*, Hemingway remarks that his wife is reading *The Dain Curse* ("Hammett's bloodiest yet") aloud to him. Of course in one of the Op short stories a woman the Op interviews is reading *The Sun Also Rises*. Tit for tat.

But I still agree with Lee Wright. Hammett, flat broke in San Francisco, would have had no access to Hemingway's earlier stuff published only in Europe. Furthermore, he had been appearing in *Black Mask* for two years before Hemingway's first collection of short stories, *In Our Time*, was published by Scribner's in 1925.

It is the writer's job *as writer* to chronicle life as he sees it, as Twain chronicled life on the Mississippi, as Melville chronicled life on a New Beford whaler, rather than directly comment on it. His subjective appraisal of that reality he is interpreting will seep through—as Twain's and Melville's did—because the writer is always concerned with the *real*—as opposed to the *realistic*. English novelist John Braine says, in a discussion of Charles Dickens' work:

> An intense concern for the real—that's what the novel is all about. It starts with a passionate and devouring interest in things as they are.

So are Hammett's detective stories "real"? Is any hard-boiled detective novel "real"? When I started writing, Hammett, Chandler, and Macdonald were the gods of the hard-boiled field. If you wanted to write in this genre, you had to read these men; and if you read them, you found in their works—despite the necessities of genre—all the hallmarks of fine literature: economy of expression, creation of character with a few bold strokes, realistic depiction of milieu, and sentiment without sentimentality. Raymond Chandler wrote of Hammett:

Hammett was spare, hard-boiled, but he did over and over what only the best writers can ever do at all. He wrote scenes that seemed never to have been written before.

The private eye tale, as created in the 1920s and developed in the 1930s, faced a special challenge because of the English countryside murder mysteries so epitomised by the wonderful novels of Dame Agatha. The American private eye tale had to put fictional murder back where it realistically belongs, in a dark alley at three in the morning. It had to do this while being coarse, gutty, tough, and gritty—or it wouldn't sell to its primary market, the pulps.

Again, it is Raymond Chandler, writing of himself and his fellow writers at *Black Mask*, who put it best:

> We were trying to get murder away from the upper classes, the week-end house party and the vicar's rose garden, and back to the people who are really good at it.

Detective novels present the writer with very specialized problems. First, the mystery or detective novel demands a *plot*. And I don't mean the loosely-knit tapestry a mainstream novelist can get away with—500 pages of navel-gazing doesn't cut it. The mystery demands a tightly-knit series of causes and effects. There is a stern logic involved here that, if ignored, will destroy the effectiveness of the novel.

Second, while demanding this tightly-knit series of causes and effects, the mystery also demands a compression of many of the essential dimensions of the story. Something—in the hard-boiled tale a lot of somethings—has to be happening all the time. Often at the *same* time.

Raymond Chandler put it this way: "The detective story deliberately outrages probability by telescoping time and space."

So what does a writer do if he wishes to be at once mysterious and realistic? How to give a "flat response," as they sometimes like to say in the music field, while at the same time being evocative and compelling? Why is *The Maltese Falcon* so much more real—and to my mind readable—than *The Unpleasantness at the Bellona Club*? What did Hammett do that Dorothy L. Sayers did not?

Very simply, in Hammett's work the people are real even when his plot is full of twists and turns, even if the time and space in which these events take place is outrageously telescoped. Hammett's characters and the backgrounds against which they move are meticulously true to life.

The reader feels that these things *could* happen to these people, maybe even are *likely* to happen to them. The author cheats not in what happens, but in making it happen in a few days, rather than months or years, and in making it happen here and now in a single case rather than on a dozen different investigations in a dozen different places.

This balancing act, this uneasy alliance between plot and incessant action on the one hand, and character, setting, and atmosphere on the other, is the true art and accomplishment of the hard-boiled detective story. Understanding this is the key to understanding the literary form Hammett created. As Fred Dannay (under the Ellery Queen pseudonym he shared with his cousin, Manny Lee) writes:

> We would not label Hammett a "realist" and merely let it go at that.... We would call him a "romantic realist".... The secret is in Hammett's method. Hammett tells his modern fables in *terms* of realism.... His *stories* are the stuff of dreams; his *characters* are the flesh-and-blood of reality....

Okay. We've got it. Romantic realist. But wait a minute. There were other private eye writers before and after Hammett just as realistic in character and setting, just as masterful of time and story, just as fanciful in plot and purpose. What made Hammett somehow stand out? What made his, apart from Hemingway's and Chandler's very different prose styles, the most emulated style of story-telling in American letters? How did he turn the crude stuff bequeathed him by Carroll John Daly into lasting literature?

Howard Haycraft, writing about Hammett, almost gets it—but doesn't understand the point he himself is making. He says:

> Because of their startling originality, the Hammett novels virtually defy exegesis even today.... As straightaway detective stories they can hold their own with the best. They are also character studies of close to top rank in their own right, and are penetrating if shocking novels of manners as well....

Then, merely in passing, Haycraft also notes that Hammett was for eight years a field operative with the Pinkerton Detective Agency. He adds off-handedly:

> It was this last experience...which principally gave him the backgrounds and many of the characters for his stories....

What Haycraft fails to realize, or at least fails to state, is that Hammett was writing about a different set of manners: those of the hunter and the hunted. The mores he was examining were those of the criminals he knew—and hunted. *Hunted.* No other writer before Hammett had been a manhunter. His detective experience gave Hammett a *mind-set* that no other writer of his day, and damned few of ours, has had.

His novels stand or fall by the quality of their detectives *as detectives.* This is what sets Sam Spade and The Op apart from other detective heroes. Hammett was to stress this in his introduction to the Modern Library edition of *The Maltese Falcon*:

> Spade...is what most private detectives I worked with would like to have been and what quite a few of them in their cockier moments thought they approached. A hard, shifty fellow, able to take care of himself in any situation, able to get the best of anybody...whether criminal, innocent bystander or client.

David Fechheimer, my nominee for today's most creative, offbeat, and successful real-life private detective, remarks, in the Preface to the gorgeous North Point Press edition of *The Maltese Falcon*, that:

> The San Francisco I live and work in as a detective is still Spade's city.... Just as Joyce created Dublin, Hammett created San Francisco. The City is not just a setting for the novel; it is a character, flowing through the dialogue like fog.... Looking again at *The Maltese Falcon*, a story about a detective written by a former detective, from my perspective as a detective, I see the authenticity of Spade's character and the plausibility of the details.

This stubborn hewing to the reality of the private detective, based on his own Pinkerton experiences, is what set Hammett's central character apart from all who went before and all who were to come after. No matter how exotic and fanciful his plots, he never abandoned that reality. Not because he was worried about Literature with a capital *L*. He was worried about the rent.

He was not a writer learning about private detection in order to create a detective hero; he was a detective learning about writing in order to make a living. This meant that as he wrote, he retained the detective's subconscious attitudes toward life. It is this subconscious state of mind, I believe, that separated his work from that of Chandler or Macdonald and their followers. The stories he told were about *real* private eyes, because real private eyes were what he knew about most intimately, and the reading public recognized it instantly.

But not necessarily the critics. According to Leo Gurko, the fictional private eye is:

> A variant of the tough guy...(a) sensual and utterly amoral man who, like the males in Hemingway, lives by the quickness of his reflexes rather than by the keenness of his intelligence.... He makes love to three or four sexually magnetic women, consumes four or five quarts of hard liquor, smokes cartons of cigarettes, is knocked on the head, shot, bruised in fist fights from seven to ten times—while groping through a dense fog as far as breaking the case....

Well, all right, okay so far. We certainly all have met this chap Gurko describes. But then he goes on:

> This unstained biological egotism, in its literary context, is best seen in...Dashiell Hammett's *The Maltese Falcon*. Its central figure, Sam Spade, is a characteristic specimen.

Sutherland Scott expands upon the theme with the same carelessness of observation and analysis:

> Sam Spade...is father to all the tough private investigators.... He loves and leaves his women with catholic abandon; he must be held responsible for the bottle in the desk drawer.... *The Maltese Falcon* introduces the inevitable fat, sinister man.... There is also the usual collection of seductive blondes and brunettes....

Let's measure the foregoing criticisms against the novel ourselves and see where it takes us. Gurko's stupid, punchdrunk, alcoholic, chain-smoking letcher bears no resemblance to Sam Spade at all. Or to *The Maltese Falcon*, a subtle novel of intrigue and innuendo, things half-understood, half-seen through San Francisco's pervasive fog.

True, Spade takes guns away from Joel Cairo and the murderous youth, Wilmer Cook—but he gives them back again. He is punched in the face by a cop once, is drugged by Casper Gutman and kicked in the head by Wilmer. He shoots nobody; he does not even carry a gun. Four men are murdered in *The Maltese Falcon*, none of them on-camera, none of them by Spade. He is smarter than anyone else in the novel, and he outwits everybody—cops and bad guys alike.

Spade's office is small, but it is not shabby. It is a suite of rooms and is not, when the book opens, a one-man office. The appearance of Spade's office bottle of booze is of such startling brevity that it deserves quotation in full here:

> Spade...took a bottle of Manhattan cocktail and paper drinking cup from a desk-drawer. He filled the cup two-thirds full, drank, returned the bottle to the drawer, tossed the cup into the wastebasket....

Spade is not celibate, but he is hardly a satyr. He has had an affair in the past with Iva Archer, his partner's wife, but that is finished as far as Spade is concerned. We catch a glimpse of Brigid O'Shaugnessy asleep in Spade's bed, but nothing more than that. Many assume that Spade has been sleeping with his secretary, Effie Perrine, but there is no evidence of this at all. The only other attractive woman in the book is Rhea Gutman, daughter of Spade's fat antagonist. Spade does no more than impatiently walk her around a hotel room to get knock-out drops out of her system so he can question her.

Are the antagonists in detective stories as crude and rude as the critics would have them? Is Casper Gutman so sinister? By any objective appraisal, he is a bumbler. So much so, in fact, that Spade at one point scowls at him and bursts out irritably:

> Jesus God! is this the first thing you guys ever stole? You're a fine lot of lollipops! What are you going to do next—get down and pray?

Those Gutman hires betray him; Spade outwits him; when he finally possesses the black bird he has spent seventeen years of his life pursuing, it is a worthless lead substitute; and in the end, worst bumble of all, he is shot dead by Wilmer. Is Gutman a master criminal, or is he Everyman—Gutman, after all, literally means Good Man—with his impossibly, hopelessly romantic quest? If so, isn't his portrayal a throw-away bit of virtuosity that scorns the capital *L* in favor of a compelling story and an unforgettable character?

As for the charge of unstained biological egotism, Spade solves the crimes by using his intellect and his knowledge of human nature, not his fists or his guns, and turns both of the murderers over to the police. And they are the actual murderers. No one is framed. Justice is done—deliberately—by Samuel Spade, Esq.

When Hammett published the first Continental Op story in the October 1, 1923, *Black Mask*—a rural tale called *Arson Plus*—he did not, as is so often thought, create the American tough private eye in fiction. That distinction, if such it can be called, must go to Carroll John Daly, who fathered Race Williams and Terry Mack. But it is instructive to glance at Daly's work for a moment. Here we meet Race Williams in *Knights of the Open Palm*:

> "Race Williams, Private Investigator," that's what the gilt letters spell across the door on my office. As for my business; I'm what you might call a middleman—just a halfway house between the dicks and the crooks. It don't mean nothing, but the police have been looking me over so much lately that I really need a place to receive them.

Daly was never one to abandon a good thing. When we meet his other private eye, Terry Mack, we might notice a certain similarity of phrasing and content:

> So for my line, I have a little office which says "Terry Mack, Private Investigator," on the door; which means whatever you wish to think it. I'm in the center of a triangle; between the crook and the police and the victim. The police have had an eye on me for some time, but only an eye, never a hand; they don't get my lay at all.

Both pieces were written in 1923, and Terry Mack and Race Williams are, perhaps, distant uncles to Sam Spade and the Continental Op. But anyone who has read Hammett's work—or even seen John Huston's superb adaptation of *The Maltese Falcon*—can see how unique and far from these precedents Hammett's hero was.

In analysing this hero, it is well to remember that Sam Spade appeared in only one novel and three indifferent short stories from the closing years of Hammett's creative surge. The Continental Op, on the other hand, appeared in two novels and 29 short stories. The Op is the fictional distillation of the genuine article. He is, above all, a superb detective. He is a better detective than Spade, because he does not get emotionally involved. Ellery Queen points out:

> The Continental Op might easily be Sam Spade's older brother. He's just as hard, just as hardbitten, just as hard-boiled. A less

spectacular workman at times (but only at times), he is equally efficient as a manhunter.

More efficient, in fact. The Op stories are a condensed course in the techniques of detection. He is more physical than Spade, and his San Francisco is filled with more underworld types than Spade's. Of course Spade has a one-man office, while The Op is a fieldman in the Continental Detective Agency's San Francisco office. No affairs with Iva Archers for the Op; he barely exists outside his work.

In this he is distressingly like a real agency detective. When I was a young field agent with the L.A. Walker Company, I might, in a single month, be sent to work in Eureka, Vallejo, San Francisco, Oakland, San Jose, Fresno, Bakersfield, and Palm Springs. If working out of DKA's head office in San Francisco, I would average 5,000 miles a month in my car without ever leaving the city. Everything except work, including eating, sleeping, and socializing, was on a catch-as-catch-can basis.

It is the Op who makes Hammett's art so seminal to the literary tradition that he founded. And it is to the Op, tough, pragmatic, not imaginative but with a detective's highly-developed intuition concerning his cases, that we must turn if we are to understand the very real detective that Hammett himself must have become during his Pinkerton years.

What are the characteristics of the Hammett detective? First, he's a man both mentally and physically competent in his job. Spade is more cerebral than the Op: he tends to think or talk himself out of sticky situations. The Op tends to find a more physical solution to his problems. Here he is at work in *The Whosis Kid*:

> I twisted around, kicking the Frenchman's face. Loosened one arm. Caught one of his. His other hand gouged at my face.... Clawing fingers tore at my mouth. I put my teeth in them and kept them there. One of my knees was on his face. I put my weight on it. My teeth were still in his hand. Both of my hands were free to get his other hand. Not nice, this work, but effective.

As I have said, Sam Spade doesn't even carry a gun. He tends more to take them away from other people. The Op, doing his work on the pulp pages of *Black Mask*, also tries to avoid gunplay; but if he has to use his gun, he makes sure he has whatever edge he can get so his gun will be effective. In a totally black apartment with a man who wants him dead, the Op crawls silently into the bedroom. Why? Only one door. The other man has to come through that door to get him. So...

> I...felt for my watch, propped it on the sill, in the angle between door and frame. I wriggled back from it until I was six or eight feet away, looking diagonally across the doorway at the watch's luminous dial. The phosphorescent numbers could not be seen from the other side of the door.... On my belly, my gun cocked, its butt steady on the floor, I waited for the faint light to be blotted out.

Unlike the stereotyped private eye of fiction, Hammett's detective lone-wolfs it only when he has to. Spade uses Effie Perrine for legwork whenever possible; consults his lawyer on legal angles; pumps Tom Polhaus of the local police for information; and shamelessly talks hotel dicks into rousting people he doesn't like and searching hotel rooms for him.

The Op is even less inclined to work alone. He brings in other operatives, he brings in the police, he uses any routine which promises to grind out the answers he needs. Above all else, the Hammett detective—especially the Op—is dogged.

In *The Scorched Face* there is more real investigative procedure in one page than will be found in most complete private eye novels. The Op sets out to make a list that he hopes will establish a pattern of linked suicides among the upper stratus of wealthy San Francisco women. Let him describe the process:

> We spent all the afternoon and most of the night getting the list...it looked like a hunk of the telephone book.... We could check off most of the names against what the police department had already learned of them.... The remainder we split into two classes...the second list was longer than I had expected, or hoped. There were six suicides in it, three murders, and 21 disappearances.... For four days I ground at this list. I hunted, found, questioned, and investigated friends and relatives. Three times I drew yesses....
>
> I had the names and addresses of 62 friends of the Banbrock girls. I set about getting the same sort of catalogue on the three women.... Fortunately, there were two or three operatives in the office with nothing else to do just then.
>
> We got something.

Can you imagine Mike Hammer doing that? Or even Philip Marlowe? But it is what real detectives do all the time. I spent my first week at L.A. Walker Company running down forty-two people at 122 different addresses in San Francisco. The last address was in Colma. In the cemetery. The absconder had died six months before he was assigned to me.

Dave Kikkert, my boss and later my partner in DKA, had known the man was dead when he assigned me the case. It takes a certain mentality and blind determination to pursue a maze of conflicting leads with the relish and certainty of a beagle after a rabbit when in reality nothing is certain. That would be a drawback in most professions, but Dave knew it is a plus to a detective. And Hammett, instead of growing softer and more fanciful as he matured as a writer, dug deeper into the reality of detection.

Although Hammett's detectives are on the side of the law, like contemporary detectives they are not scrupulously law-abiding. They have been hired to do a certain thing, discover a certain fact or object. There are municipal, county, state, federal agencies, and legislative bodies constantly churning out laws and regulations—many directly contradictory to the others. So if a detective must bend the law, well—so be it. Any detective who observed them all would get very little done.

At DKA our motto—unspoken by the field men except among themselves—was "a felony a week whether we need it or not."

Hammett's detectives, in an age when weaker law-enforcement agencies were all jealous of their own turf, have a much wider latitude of action than do private eyes of today. They break the law constantly, sometimes with deadly results. Almost everything the Op does to bring Poisonville to the boil in *Red Harvest* is illegal. He lies, cheats, suborns, even kills. It is not unreasonable to assume his actions are based on those of real operatives.

In *$106,000 Blood Money*, the Op learns that another operative has sold out to the baddies and that only one of the baddies who knows about the sell-out is still alive. He arranges that both operative and baddie are shot down and killed.

In *Zigzags of Treachery* he sends a blackmailer out to face the police with a gun the Op knows has a broken firing pin.

These stories all combine Hammett's superb imagination with the countless cases he worked as a Pinkerton Op; it is impossible to tell where fact ends and creative invention begins, and it matters little. What emerges rings with truth.

Hammett's detective goes by his gut feelings. Spade tells the fat man of Wilmer Cook:

> Keep that gunsel away from me.... I'll kill him. I don't like him. He makes me nervous. I'll kill him the first time he gets in my

way. I won't give him an even break. I won't give him a chance. I'll kill him.

In the end, of course, it is Wilmer who does the killing. Of the fat man. So Spade was right about him. Hammett's detective does not believe in chivalry, does not give the other fellow (or woman) an even break. Spade turns the killer of Miles Archer over to the police no matter what it costs him personally. The Op does the same thing with Princess Zhukovski in *The Gutting of Couffignal*.

The Op is ruthless—or merely realistic?—in *Fly Paper* when he must stop a huge criminal named Babe McCloor. The Babe is not at all intimidated by the Op's gun.

> "I can still get to you with slugs in me."
> "Not where I'll put them.... If you think smashed kneecaps are a lot of fun, give it a whirl."
> "Hell with that," he said, and charged.
> I shot his right knee.
> He lurched toward me.
> I shot his left knee.
> He tumbled down.
> "You would have it," I complained.
> He twisted around, and with his arms pushed himself into a sitting position facing me.
> "I didn't think you had sense enough to do it," he said through his teeth.

This passage may no longer represent a private detective's life, but even today it has a symbolic truth. And it was real for the tough-guy street culture of Hammett's day. As an *amateur* student of peleoanthropology, I must make a case for the accuracy of Hammett's perception of the nature of man.

Spade and the Op not only put the job first, they like the job. I've read and enjoyed many contemporary detective writers who make their detective heroes somber men or women who dislike themselves and their work, but these are not Hammett's detectives, nor are they real detectives. Both of them derive much of their enjoyment from their job, and take a lot of pride in it. As the Op says in one of the stories:

> I'm a detective because I happen to like the work.... And liking work makes you want to do it as well as you can.

Otherwise there'd be no sense to it.... In the past 18 years I've been getting my fun out of chasing crooks and solving riddles...and I can't imagine a pleasanter future than 20-some years more of it.

It seems to me that human nature hasn't changed too much in the genus Homo's 2.7 million year history. We are here today because a great many of us enjoyed the hunt and were very good at it; and a great many of us still enjoy the hunt. I have read and enjoyed many mysteries in which the detectives are strongly motivated by empathy and a desire to better society, but I think Spade and the Op know all too well that the fellow to whom you give the even break will often be the one who gets you.

One of our field agents was run off by a Lutheran minister with a loaded double-barreled shotgun, and the next day the same man of God tried to run me down with his car.

I think that in our deepest nature we all know the game, because we are all descended from survivors. But we don't want to think about this dark side of ourselves, and if we're lucky we won't have to. The detective, on the other hand, lives it every day, and he knows he is not always going to be popular with those around him.

When a character in *The Dain Curse* looks at the Op "as if I were something there ought to be a law against," and says sarcastically, "I hope you're satisfied with the way your work got done," the Op replies, "It got done."

The manhunter—real-life, or Hammett's—is, frankly, not concerned with truth in the abstract, only with enough truth to do the job he has been hired to do. Nora Charles complains of this at the end of *The Thin Man*, when Nick says to her:

> "Now, are you satisfied with what we've got on him?"
> "Yes, in a way. There seems to be enough of it, but it's not very neat."
> "It's neat enough to send him to the chair," I said, "And that's all that counts."

Again, it is Hammett himself who most neatly sums up his detective when he writes of the Op:

> I see him...a little man going forward day after day through mud and blood and death and deceit—as callous and brutal and cynical as necessary—toward a dim goal, with nothing to push or pull him to it except he's been hired to reach it.

When you're a manhunter, that goal is seeking out other human beings and taking from them something they treasure—their illusions, their gold, their freedom, perhaps only their chattels, perhaps their greatest treasure, life itself—and doing it dispassionately. It's all part of the job. In *The Maltese Falcon* is a passage I have often seen quoted, but which none of the commentators has really understood. Spade is talking with Brigid in the famous closing moments of the book:

> Don't be too sure I'm as crooked as I'm supposed to be. That kind of reputation might be good business—bringing in high-priced jobs and making it easier to deal with the enemy.

The Enemy. Right there is the core of Hammett's detective hero. The man he is tracking is *The Enemy.* The detective's pride, indeed his own estimation of his worth as a man, derives in part from his assessment of himself as a manhunter. Hunting *The Enemy.* Hammett's detective has the pitiless knowledge that when he faces *The Enemy*, it is going to come down to *him* or *me*.

Only one of them will walk away from it a whole person.

This is the detective Hammett has bequeathed us. A proud, independent, crafty, intelligent, tough, hard-minded protagonist who closely mirrors the ideal real-life investigator. Whether he is a scoundrel or a hero depends upon who hires him and the context within which history places his work.

For myself, I am grateful that Hammett, the detective who yearned to write, took the lumpy, unformed clay he was handed, and molded it into a new ideal, found in it the hard, clear fossil of our essential nature, without embellishment. It is not that the writers who follow him can't embellish and improve on his model; we can, and we must. But I'm glad that Samuel Dashiell Hammett went straight to the complicated heart of our most ancient nature to mold a new reality for American letters.

Bibliography

Novels:
  The Red Harvest (Continental Op), 1929.
  The Dain Curse (Continental Op), 1929.
  The Maltese Falcon (Sam Spade), 1930.
  The Glass Key (Ned Beaumont), 1931.
  The Thin Man (Nick and Nora Charles), 1934.
  $106,000 Blood Money (Continental Op), 1943; reissued as *The Big Knockover*, 1948.

Short Stories:
  The Adventures of Sam Spade and Other Stories, ed. by Ellery Queen, 1944.
  The Continental Op, ed. by Ellery Queen, 1945.
  The Return of the Continental Op, ed. by Ellery Queen, 1945.
  Hammett Homicides, ed. by Ellery Queen, 1946.
  Dead Yellow Women, ed. by Ellery Queen, 1947.
  Nightmare Town, ed. by Ellery Queen, 1948.
  The Creeping Siamese, ed. by Ellery Queen, 1950.
  Woman in the Dark, ed. by Ellery Queen, 1951.
  A Man Named Thin and Other Stories, ed. by Ellery Queen, 1962.
  Collections by other editors.

Other:
  Play, Screenplays, *Secret Agent X-9* (cartoon strip), Articles.

Critical Studies:
  Joe Gores, *Hammett: A Novel*, 1975.
  Richard Laymon, *Shadow Man: The Life of Dashiell Hammett*, 1981.
  William Nolan, *Hammett: A Life at the Edge*, 1983.

Photo Credit: Peter Papadopolus

Joe Gores

Biography

Joe Gores of San Anselmo, California, was educated at the University of Notre Dame and earned an M.A. at Stanford University. Like Hammett, Gores worked as a private eye before he became a mystery writer. The list of his other jobs is varied and fascinating, forming great experience for a writer. A past president of the Mystery Writers of America, Gores is the winner of three Edgar Allan Poe Awards—best novel, short story, and television series—and was an Edgar nominee for *Come Morning* and *32 Cadillacs*. The versatile Gores has written numerous screen and television plays and continues to write both DKA and stand-alone mysteries, his most recent DKA novel, *Contract Null and Void*, appearing to rave reviews in June, 1996. His novel, *Hammett*, combines fact and fiction.

Bibliography

Novels:
> The DKA Series:
>> *Dead Skip*, 1972.
>> *Final Notice*, 1973.
>> *Gone, No Forwarding*, 1978.
>> *32 Cadillacs*, 1992.
>> *Contract Null and Void*, 1996.

> Other:
>> *A Time of Predators*, 1969.
>> *Interface*, 1974.
>> *Hammett: A Novel*, 1975.
>> *Come Morning*, 1986.
>> *Wolf Time*, 1989.
>> *Dead Man*, 1993.
>> *Menaced Assassin*, 1994.
>> *Cases*, 1998.

Other:
> Numerous Short Stories, Screen and Television Plays, Non-fiction.

Michael Connelly

♦

Raymond Chandler

Raymond Chandler
(1888–1959)

Biography

Raymond Thornton Chandler was born in Chicago on 23 July, 1888. He moved to England with his mother and became a naturalized British subject; he again became an American citizen in 1956. He was educated in London at local school and at Dulwich College, 1900–05, then studied in France and Germany, 1905–07. In a varied career he worked in supply and accounting for the Admiralty; as a reporter for the *Daily Express* and the *Western Gazette*; upon returning to the US in 1912, on a ranch and in sporting goods; and also as accountant and bookkeeper for the Los Angeles Creamery. During World War I he served in the Gordon Highlanders of the Canadian Army and in the Royal Air Force. Returning to civilian life in 1919, he went into a San Francisco bank; to the Los Angeles *Daily Express*; and eventually to the Dabney Oil Syndicate as auditor, becoming a full-time writer in 1933. Chandler won two Mystery Writers of America Edgar Allan Poe Awards—screenplay, 1946; novel, 1954—and was MWA President, 1959. He was married to Pearl Cecily Hurlburt [Pascal] from 1924 until her death in 1954; no children. He died 26 March, 1959.

Raymond Chandler

I am going to turn the Chandler program into a double feature. I'll begin by talking about Chandler's work, his writing, and how it's influenced me and many other writers. I'm going to read a little bit of his work and some of what others have said about him. But then I'd like to bring up Bill Nolan, author of the recently published *The Marble Orchard*. In that book, Raymond Chandler is actually a character—he's the narrator of the book—and to have pulled that off, Bill's obviously had to delve deeply into Chandler's work as well as do a fair amount of research into the personal aspects of the author. He's in a much better position to talk to you about the man behind the words. My own research on Raymond Chandler probably amounts to going a couple of times down to his old watering hole, The Whaling Bar in La Jolla, and drinking too much. Maybe I was hoping that the ghost of Chandler's genius would possess me, or rub off on me, but I only got a hangover.

I jumped on the chance to come here when Barbara Peters invited me because no other writer has influenced me as much as Raymond Chandler and I feel a duty to sing his praise whenever I get the chance. Once having accepted the invitation, I realized that it was hard to put into words just how this man's writing has affected and influenced me. But I did know this, that I constantly reread his books in between writing my own. When I sit down at the computer to map out my story or build the character of the protagonist, I religiously use the blueprint that Chandler left behind in his essay *The Simple Art of Murder*.

Basically, Chandler was a writer in the hard-boiled genre and he is considered the most influential stylist in that genre. But I think most critics and authors would have to acknowledge that he's a very influential stylist in all writing in this century.

He started in the *Black Mask* pulp magazines writing short stories and then produced seven novels between 1939 and 1958. In these novels he had as protagonist Philip Marlowe, the private investigator.

I live in Los Angeles now, but I grew up in Florida and I did not meet Chandler until I was in college. I was about half way through school when I first came upon him. At the school I attended, the student union ran three or four year old movies for a dollar. It was the hot ticket event in those days—not because we liked the films or knew what was playing, but because they were a dollar. And on one Friday night in 1976 or 1977 what I saw was *The Long Goodbye*, which was a 1973 Robert Altman movie set in contemporary Los Angeles. It was my first exposure to Chandler. Not knowing how much the movie differed from the book, I really liked it...to the point where I spent another $1.00 and saw it again. Then I went and bought the book the movie was based on; this was the movie tie-in edition with Elliot Gould on the cover. That's where I really discovered Chandler.

To my surprise, I found the movie I'd so liked was based on a book written 20 years before, that the ending was quite different, and the character was quite different. As is often the case—at least being a writer I hope it's often the case—I found the book to be much better than the film, a better character study of this private eye, Philip Marlowe, a more cynical yet sympathetic and romantic view of Los Angeles. Last night, Steven Saylor said that when he read *The Name of the Rose* it was somewhat of an epiphany for him. Well, that's what happened to me when I read *The Long Goodbye*. Like most kids in college, I really didn't have a major yet, I wasn't sure what I wanted to do—in my case it was probably in my fourth year—but I was thinking about becoming a writer and this book inspired me. I could not buy Chandler's books in the student bookstore so I had to go off campus for them. Some I borrowed from a guy down the hall who had already discovered Chandler. I cut classes and read through them all in about a week, and then I read *The Long Goodbye* again, and I knew: this was it, this was what I wanted to do. What's strange is that even though I can clearly remember the revelation, I cannot say why this sparked it. I can only tell you that there is a style in the books that touched me, that hopefully touched my creativity, and that made me say to myself "I want to do this."

It was not the plots that were responsible, it was more the style and the way the story was used to make a point about the place called Los Angeles and about our society as a whole—the way each book was used as a character study of this man called Marlowe. I found that I immediately subscribed to Chandler's/Marlowe's suspicion of the rich, his disgust with phony people, his cynicism about law and justice. These are powerful themes for a twenty-year-old looking for a direction to his life. These were things I wanted to write about.

I'd never even been to Los Angeles, but through his books I found it to be greatly intriguing, a place that drew me. Chandler had an original way of showing the city for its good and its evil, its tainted beauty. He was talking about what was wrong with it while lamenting what it could have been, and what it once was. He saw the dark and the light at the same time, and he had this way that is hard to copy or imitate, a perfect way of describing it all at once.

This is the second paragraph of the opening of *The Little Sister*, which is one of my two favorite Chandlers.

> It was one of those clear, bright summer mornings we get in the early spring in California before the high fog sets in. The rains are over. The hills are still green and in the valley across the Hollywood hills you can see snow on the high mountains. The fur stores are advertising their annual sales. The call houses that specialize in sixteen-year-old virgins are doing a land-office business. And in Beverly Hills the jacaranda trees are beginning to bloom. [*Library of America* editions, vol. 2, p. 203]

There it is, right there, the light and dark together. He's got the call houses and the jacaranda trees blooming. It's in one paragraph. It's perfect. It might make you smile or chuckle now, but that's because that paragraph, written in 1948, has probably been imitated a million times by writers since then, and imitated badly. The thing you have to remember is that Chandler was the originator. He wasn't imitating anyone.

This is not to say that Chandler was not influenced by other writers. Dashiell Hammett in particular made a strong impression, as you heard from Joe Gores during this symposium. I think that Chandler once said that anyone who uses the word "yeah" in a novel is influenced by Hammett. But I think Chandler did what great writers always do and good writers try to do. He took what he learned from Hammett and went a step further. It's said that Hammett took the crime novel out of the drawing room and put it out on the street where it belonged. Chandler attempted and succeeded in many respects in carrying it to the next step, to the place where the crime novel could be seen as a metaphor for a time and a place and to where it might be considered an art form. I think with the unique, romantic cynicism that Chandler brought to his books, he also was lucky in that he had good timing. He was writing his stories during a time when the bloom was coming off the rose in America. We were coming out of the Depression, there was a war on the horizon, the cities were getting big, there were lots of poor people and crimes, gangsters were making headlines all the time and in some places even ruling cities.... This was the period when he started writing and when he formulated Philip Marlowe.

Robert Parker, the mystery writer, is an expert on Chandler and this is what he wrote about Chandler in an essay for the *New York Times* last year when Chandler's works were published in two volumes by The Library of America:

> Chandler had the right hero in the right place and engaged him in the consideration of good and evil at precisely the time when our central certainty of good no longer held.

I agree with that assessment and I think Chandler would have as well. His consideration of good and evil and his conclusion of the reality that good did not always reasonably triumph informed almost all of his work. When you think about that conclusion, it creates a fear in us. That fear is the engine that drove his stories. In trying to explain the power of his stories, this is what Chandler wrote in the introduction of *Trouble Is My Business,* a collection of his early detective stories:

> It was the smell of fear which the stories managed to generate. Their characters lived in a world gone wrong, a world in which, long before the atom bomb, civilization had created the machinery for its own destruction, and was learning to use it with all the moronic delight of a gangster trying out his first machine gun. The law was something to be manipulated for profit and power. The streets were dark with something more than night.

The scenes outlined in that paragraph still have their grip on reality four and five decades later and I think that is one of the keys to why we are here and why Chandler is considered a classic. He has longevity. He wrote about things in his time that he might as well have been writing about right now.

Another key to this success and longevity is the fact that those themes he wrote about have no better foothold than in Los Angeles. I was recently at a conference in New York where the subject was a celebration: Raymond Chandler's inclusion in The Library of America—incidentally, the first and only hard-boiled mystery writer to be included. Somebody at the conference said that Chandler was such a great writer that if he had not written about Los Angeles and had chosen to write about Buffalo instead, that he'd still be celebrated by readers and revered by writers today. I don't think so. I think that Chandler and Los Angeles were a perfect match of time, talent and place.

In that essay I just mentioned by Parker, he also said that "Chandler did not capture Los Angeles, he invented it," and I don't think I wholly agree with that either. I live there now and I can drive around LA today and still see places he wrote about, see similarities to stories he wrote, see the tainted beauty he described so well. It's all still there. I don't think he invented Los Angeles. I think he put a romantic spin on it and lamented its faults, but he was deadly accurate about it and that's also a key to his longevity. He showed LA for what it was. It was a place that had high hopes and was proud, but somehow or somewhere, stumbled. It was a place that people came when they ran out of other places to go, and it was a place where nothing was as it seems. That's the way it was in his books, and that's the way it is still.

I want to read from *The Little Sister* again. I guess you could call this a Cook's Tour of LA through the eyes of Raymond Chandler and Philip Marlowe. It's one of my favorites because it's full of attention to detail and description, it has a lot of visual imagery in the development of the character through Marlowe's interior musings about the place he lived. This is three or four pages—with some editing by me to keep it as brief as possible—and yet this section has nothing to do with mystery, nothing to do with the plot of the story. It's only about life in Los Angeles. It's about despair and loneliness.

> I drove east on Sunset but I didn't go home. At La Brea I turned north and swung over to Highland, out over the Cahuenga Pass and down on to Ventura Boulevard, past Studio City and Sherman Oaks and Encino. There is nothing lonely about the trip. There never is on that road. Fast boys in stripped down Fords shot in and out of the traffic streams, missing fenders by a sixteenth of an inch, but somehow always missing them. Tired men in dusty coupes and sedans winced and tightened their grip on the wheel and ploughed on north and west towards home and dinner, an evening with the sports page, the blatting of the radio, the whining of their spoiled children and the gabble of their silly wives. I drove on past the gaudy neons and the false fronts behind them, the sleazy hamburger joints that look like palaces under the colors, the circular drive-ins as gay as circuses with chipper hard-eyed carhops, the brilliant counters, and the sweaty greasy kitchens that would have poisoned a toad. Great double trucks rumbled down over

Sepulveda from Wilmington and San Pedro and crossed towards the Ridge Route, starting up in low-low from the traffic lights with a growl of lions in the zoo.

Behind Encino an occasional light winked from the hills through thick trees. The homes of screen stars. Screen stars, phooey. The veterans of a thousand beds. Hold it, Marlowe, you're not human tonight.

The air got cooler. The highway narrowed. The cars were so few now that the headlights hurt. The grade rose against chalk walls and at the top a breeze, unbroken from the ocean, danced casually across the night.

I ate dinner in Thousand Oaks. Bad but quick. Feed 'em and throw 'em out. Lots of business. We can't bother with you sitting over your second cup of coffee, mister. You're using money space. See those people over there behind the rope? They want to eat. Anyway they think they have to. God knows why they want to eat here. They could do better home out of a can. They're just restless. Like you. They have to get the car out and go somewhere. Sucker-bait for the racketeers that have taken over the restaurants. Here we go again. You're not human tonight, Marlowe.

.... I stepped out into the night air that nobody had yet found out how to option. But a lot of people were probably trying. They'd get around to it.

I drove on to the Oxnard cut-off and turned back along the ocean. The big eight-wheelers and sixteen-wheelers were streaming north, all hung over with orange lights. On the right the great fat solid Pacific trudging into shore like a scrubwoman going home. No moon, no fuss, hardly a sound of the surf. No smell. None of the harsh wild smell of the sea. A California ocean. California, the department-store state. The most of everything and the best of nothing. Here we go again. You're not human tonight, Marlowe.

All right. Why should I be? I'm sitting in that office, playing with a dead fly and in pops this dowdy little item from Manhattan, Kansas, and chisels me down to a shopworn twenty to find her brother. He sounds like a creep but she wants to find him. So with this fortune clasped to my chest, I trundle down to Bay City and the routine I go through is so tired I'm half asleep on my feet. I meet nice people, with and without ice picks in their necks. I leave, and I leave myself wide open, too... Why? Who am I cutting my throat for this time? A blonde with sexy eyes and too many door keys? A girl from Manhattan, Kansas? I don't know. All I know is that something isn't what it seems and the old tired but always reliable hunch tells me that if the hand is played the way it is dealt the wrong person is going to lose the pot. Is that my business? Well, what is my business? Do I know? Did I ever know? Let's not go into

> that. You're not human tonight, Marlowe. Maybe I never was or ever will be. Maybe I'm an ectoplasm with a private license. Maybe we all get like this in the cold half-lit world where always the wrong thing happens and never the right.
> Malibu. More movie stars. More pink and blue bathtubs. More tufted beds. More Chanel No. 5. More Lincoln Continentals and Cadillacs. More wind-blown hair and sunglasses and attitudes and pseudo-refined voices and waterfront morals. Now wait a minute. Lots of nice people work in pictures. You've got the wrong attitude, Marlowe. You're not human tonight.
> I smelled Los Angeles before I got to it. It smelled stale and old like a living room that had been closed too long. But the colored lights fooled you. The lights were wonderful. There ought to be a monument to the man who invented neon lights. Fifteen stories high, solid marble. There's a boy who really made something out of nothing. [*Library of America* editions, vol. 2, pp. 267–269]

I can read a description like that today and find it's still valid forty or fifty years after it was written. I happen to live in the hills that look out over Hollywood, just as Philip Marlowe did in the pages of Chandler's books. I can look out my window and see what Marlowe saw so long ago. Believe me, a lot of it hasn't changed. He is as accurate now as he was then, and that's the key to timelessness, to being a classic.

This is my all-time favorite Chandler passage. It's short, and it's from *The Long Goodbye*.

> When I got home I mixed a stiff one and stood by the open window in the living room and sipped it and listened to the groundswell of the traffic on Laurel Canyon Boulevard and looked at the glare of the big angry city hanging over the shoulder of the hills through which the boulevard had been cut. Far off the banshee wail of police or fire sirens rose and fell, never for very long completely silent. Twenty-four hours a day somebody is running, somebody else is trying to catch him. Out there in the night of a thousand crimes people were dying, being maimed, cut by flying glass, crushed against steering wheels or under heavy tires. People were being beaten, robbed, strangled, raped, and murdered. People were hungry, sick, bored, desperate with loneliness or remorse or fear, angry, cruel, feverish, shaken by sobs. A city no worse than others, a city rich and vigorous and full of pride, a city lost and beaten and full of emptiness. [*Library of America* editions, vol. 2, p. 645]

Chandler's work stands the test of time and that's what clearly separates him from the myriad imitators and it is why I'm standing here not talking about somebody else.

Last night in the discussion of what makes a classic, Dulcy Brainard brought up the ratio of how much of it is story and how much of it is character and plot and so forth. I think when you read Chandler's books you find that his devotion was to character and style and building the sense of place. Last came the plot. I sometimes think when I reread his books now that he might have in a sense been making it up as he went. What I mean by that is he started with A and B. In other words, this is what my case is going to be and this is who did it. But in between A and B he may have winged it. I do it myself when I'm writing and I find it's actually the best way to create. It gives you the most freedom and you enjoy it the most. About Chandler, that's just my guess. But I think it goes with his devotion to character over plot.

I think you can only do it that way—get away with it—if you are heavy on character and place and other things besides plot. You can win the day with character if your plots are going to be—not necessarily bad—but only serviceable. I think Chandler probably viewed it this way and I think to underline that there's a story that when the movie director Howard Hawkes was preparing *The Big Sleep* to become a movie with Humphrey Bogart, he was analyzing the book and preparing to do the screenplay and he realized that of the seven murders in the book, one of them is not solved. It's not clear in the book who would have killed the guy. I think it's the butler who is killed and it's never explained who did it. So Hawkes fired off a telegram to Chandler saying "Who killed the butler, Ray?" and Chandler sent one back and it just said "I have no idea." I think maybe if they hadn't charged by the word for telegrams he would have said, "I have no idea, and I don't care." What he clearly cared about was Marlowe as a character and it was that character he used to move the story along. You have to subscribe to Marlowe, you've got to get into him, then you can put up with any kind of shortcoming in plot and elsewhere.

I don't think his plots are very intricately designed. In them the protagonist moves in linear fashion gathering clues toward a hidden truth. Often violent acts like murders are used to propel the action forward. That's not an original thing. I think his plots are almost like great scenes or set pieces that were cobbled together and that's how he wrote, which also gives rise to the thought that maybe he was winging it through the books. Basically, the plots were quests. He built Marlowe as a weary knight on a quest through a perilous city and the allusions to this are pretty clear through the books. In *The Little Sister*, he's hired by a woman named Orfamay Quest to find a guy named Orrin Quest. In his very first book, *The Big Sleep,* the allusion is clear on the first page. This is the second paragraph:

> The main hallway of the Sternwood place was two stories high. Over the entrance doors, which would have let in a troop of Indian elephants, there was a broad stained-glass panel showing a knight in dark armor rescuing a lady who was tied to a tree and didn't have any clothes on but some very long and convenient hair. The knight had pushed the vizor of his helmet back to be sociable, and he was fiddling with the knots on the ropes that tied the lady to the tree and not getting anywhere. I stood there and thought if I lived in the house, I would sooner or later have to climb up there and help him. He didn't seem to be really trying. [*Library of America* editions, vol. 1, p. 589]

Chandler is pretty clearly saying this is my knight, so begins the quest. And so the real muscle behind these stories is the knight, the tarnished knight—it's Marlowe. In Marlowe, he succeeded in creating a classic American hero. He's sentimental and lonesome, wise and cynical, a hardened romantic. Marlowe is a vector Chandler uses to cut through all social strata, and he takes you, the reader, along for the ride. Marlowe is at home whether he's in a crumbling rooming house in Bay City—which is actually Santa Monica—or in the rich mansions of Beverly Hills. By virtue of his position as private detective, it seems that he has the right—or it's not unusual for him—to step into both these places, yet the guy who lives in the crumbling rooming house would never step into the mansion, and the guy who lives in the mansion wouldn't be caught dead in the crumbling rooming house. So it's left to Marlowe to go back and forth between these things. Marlowe is the instrument used to move safely, comfortably, and believably through these different arenas. As such, Marlowe is a character who must be ready for all possibilities, and of course, usually is.

It's probably been read too many times at conferences like these, but I personally can't hear it enough, so I'm going to read a couple of edited pages from *The Simple Art of Murder*. It's the best description of Marlowe that I know, and as I've said before, it's the blueprint for a thousand other detectives who came after him from Kinsey Millhone to my guy, Harry Bosch. This was written, I think, in 1950, so it's very male-oriented, but Chandler could be talking about men or women and as we know, there are probably more women PIs out in fiction right now than men.

> The realist in murder writes of a world in which gangsters can rule nations and almost rule cities, in which hotels and apartment houses and celebrated restaurants are owned by men who made their money out of brothels, in which a screen star can be the finger man for a mob, and the nice man down the hall is a boss of the numbers racket; a world where a judge with a cellar full of bootleg liquor can send a man to jail for having a pint in his pocket, where the mayor of your town may have condoned murder as an instrument of money-making, where no man can walk down a dark street in safety because law and order are things we talk about but refrain from practicing; a world where you may witness a holdup in broad daylight and see who did it, but you will fade quickly back into the crowd rather than tell anyone because the holdup men may have friends with long guns, or the police may not like your testimony, and in any case the shyster for the defense will be allowed to abuse and vilify you in open court, before a jury of selected morons, without any but the most perfunctory interference from a political judge.

It's not a fragrant world but it is the world you live in....

> But down these mean streets a man must go who is not himself mean, who is neither tarnished or afraid. The detective in this kind of story must be such a man. He is the hero; he is everything. He must be a complete man and a common man and yet an unusual man. He must be, to use a rather weathered phrase, a man of honor—by instinct, by inevitability, without thought of it, and certainly without saying it. He must be the best man in his world and a good enough man for any world.... The story is his adventure in search of a hidden truth, and it would be no adventure if it did not happen to a man fit for adventure. He has a range of awareness that startles you, but it belongs to him by right, because it belongs to the world he lives in. If there were enough like him, the world would be a very safe place to live in...[without becoming] too dull to be worth living in. [*Library of America* editions, vol. 2, pp. 991–992]

Each time I sit down to write a new book, I read that before I type the first page. For me, it's like a refresher course of what I'm writing about, all in two pages.

Now I'm standing here saying what a genius he is, but clearly Chandler is not without his critics. He has been criticized by some for being morally pretentious in Marlowe. After all, what gives a lowly private eye the right to look down his nose at the rich, at the police, at all of society? In his work, Chandler is politically incorrect by today's standards—and maybe by all days' standards. Minorities are often if not always treated with suspicion, women are generally cast as bimbos or pathological liars or psychotic killers, or sometimes as all three. It's in these segments where I think Chandler fails the test of time. You read about these characters and it does feel dated, the one place where he stumbles. In the extreme, there are even those who believe that Chandler's style may ultimately have harmed the crime novel, helping to set it on a repetitive path from which it rarely breaks away. My friend James Ellroy, a writer who grew up in Chandler's LA, often rails against Chandler and his legion of followers. In a recent issue of *New Yorker* magazine Ellroy is quoted as saying:

> I see hardboiled crime fiction as heavily ritualized horseshit, and largely spun off of Raymond Chandler. Chandler's a very easy writer to imitate, which is why so many people have been able to adapt his formula with such success. But I hate that formula, and I hate his sensibility.

I agree that a large part of today's crime fiction is formulaic and spun off of Chandler, but I don't agree with all of the rest. It may be easy to imitate Chandler; it's not easy to imitate him well. The point that I think Ellroy is making, and that I would also make, is that Chandler was such an original that it was inevitable that his style would be imitated—whether well, or badly. Today it's the crime novelist's duty to expand or grow from Chandler and to take it to the next step, just as I think Chandler took Hammett to the next step.

Recently there's been a renaissance of talk about Chandler, a celebration of him, and largely this is because his work was published last year in two volumes by the prestigious Library of America. His inclusion as the first crime writer in this pantheon of great American writers secures his spot as not only the master of the crime novel but as the master of the novel. Still, his very publication by The Library of America spawned debate. It's the old question of whether a mystery novel can ever be more than entertainment: can it actually be art? Well, for my money, it can be art, and Raymond Chandler was an artist.

Let me read one last thing. In that same issue of the *New Yorker* from which I just quoted Ellroy, James Walcott said this about Chandler's inclusion in the Library of America:

> Chandler was an inside outsider as a writer, jimmying loose the iron jawed formulas of the pulp magazines like *Black Mask* and using the detective genre for his own artistic ends. Like Hemingway, he put a high premium on style, believing it the best investment a writer could make for posterity. Some styles endure. Some dry to a thick, cracked coat. In the best pages of the Marlowe novels, you can feel Chandler's creative pleasure. The lawns wet with rain seem minted in heaven. In the worst pages, the mean streets that Marlowe walked echo with the hollow footsteps of a movie studio backlot. The bad pages may outnumber the good, but it's the good pages that stick if you're lucky. Raymond Chandler was lucky.

I think this shows a grudging acceptance by the literary establishment of Chandler the crime writer. I don't know if he would even care, or if he would react to it, if he even gave a whit about how he would be viewed by posterity. In his first book he wrote that nothing mattered to you anymore once you were sleeping the big sleep. But he also once said: "The average critic never recognizes an achievement when it happens. He explains it after it's become respectable."

* * *

Author William R. Nolan is a two-time winner of the Edgar Allan Poe Special Award Scroll. His science fiction novel *Logan's Run* was an international bestseller made into a film and a CBS television series. In 1994 he published *The Black Mask Murders*, the first book in a series featuring classic crime writers Hammett, Chandler, and Gardner as sleuths. *The Black Mask* was written in the style of Dashiell Hammett. *The Marble Orchard* belongs to Chandler. Nolan's knowledge of all three writers was of great benefit to members of the symposium. Here, at Michael Connelly's invitation, he says a few words about the man behind the words.

* * *

No writer in history was ever less likely to be hard-boiled than Raymond Thornton Chandler. He would have been as surprised as anyone else if someone had pointed out in the early years the

Chandler of later years. "That isn't me, I don't know who the fellow is but he certainly doesn't have anything to do with me."

Chandler was born in 1888 in Chicago. His father was an alcoholic bastard—Chandler called him a swine—who left the family when Raymond was very young. Suddenly this six or seven year old boy was without a father. His mother, who had relatives in London, immediately took her son there to live with them. He grew up with British characteristics. He reported that when he later got to Los Angeles, he had "an accent thick enough to cut with a breadknife," one tweed suit, and 12 cents in his pocket. The point is, he grew up in England, attended Dulwich Preparatory School, learned rugby and soccer, Greek and the classics, and was exposed to a very high level education. He reported he considered himself to be a pretentious young intellectual who would have made a fairly good second-rate essayist if anyone had encouraged him, but thankfully no one did. He wrote for *The Spectator* and *Westminster Gazette* and several high quality magazines, delivering terrible verse, romantic nonsense, near gibberish, and book reviews—high flown, critical, cynical, pretentious—which luckily we've all forgotten. They were collected in the early writings of Raymond Chandler which I do not recommend to anyone. He would certainly be upset to think you were reading these things now. I'm sure he could shoot Matthew Bradley [former publicist at Viking Penguin] for bringing them together after his death.

At any rate, here he was, a British intellectual with a background in the classics and suddenly he read about America and thought, my mother was an American, my father, the swine, was an American, I should go to America and see what it's like. In his mid-twenties, he borrowed some money from friends and booked passage. On the boat, he met a man from the Dabney Oil Syndicate who invited him to Los Angeles with a possible job offer. Chandler had quit the British Civil Service because he couldn't stand it, he was at loose ends, and he knew—he was convinced—he wasn't going to be a writer. After all, he'd published awful stuff and he was intelligent enough to recognize how truly awful it was. He was very caustic about his early work always, reporting he'd managed to fool people with a lot of drivel. He was right to be so dismissive.

He arrived in LA in 1913, penniless, and began to string tennis rackets for 12 cents an hour. He eventually landed a job with Dabney as a bookkeeper, and he rose in the oil business to the point where in the late 1920s to the early 1930s he was managing thirteen or fourteen small oil companies, kind of running the show. He was drinking a lot, having affairs with secretaries, driving around in his big car, not showing up for work...and so they fired him. There he was, without work in the midst of the Depression. Not knowing what to do, he drove up and down the coast in his big car, and read pulp fiction. In *Black Mask* he read a man named Dashiell Hammett. Now that, as Michael just said, that did it. Chandler thought he could do as well as Hammett, and he knew he could do better than many other less talented contributors.

Being a British intellectual, he felt like an alien in America. He had to learn slang, to learn tough-guy vernacular like a foreign language. Here was Hammett, ex-Pinkerton detective, hard-boiled, left school at fourteen, factory worker, a real authentic tough guy writing about mean streets. Here was Chandler, classicist with tweed coat, deciding to go down those same streets. So he spent six months of 1933 on a novelette called *Blackmailers Don't Shoot*, 18,000 words, and he sent it off to Joe Shaw at *Black Mask* who bought it for $180. $180 for six months work—maybe he shouldn't be a writer. But what else could he do? Joe Shaw when he got the manuscript thought Chandler must be a great natural writer, or a complete phony who was trying to copy all the other writers in *Black Mask*. Of course, Chandler wasn't trying to copy anyone, he was simply trying to pick up the mantle that Hammett had dropped when he quit the magazine in 1930.

Chandler was a direct descendant of Hammett, but he wrote an entirely different kind of novel in an entirely different vein. The difference between them is vast and fascinating. Chandler was the romantic, the knight, and Philip Marlowe was that knight. The last thing Hammett ever thought about was his detective as a knight. The Continental Op, Sam Spade, these were hardboiled characters who didn't give a damn about knighthood and would laugh at the suggestion. They were job-holders, out to get a job done, that's the way Hammett thought of them. Marlowe, on the other hand started out as "Mallory"; it was Cissy who changed his name.

Cissy is a fascinating story. When Chandler got to LA, he used to attend concerts. There was a musician named Julian Pascal who used to play the piano in these social evenings who had a wife named Cissy Pascal. Chandler was erotically titillated to discover she had once in her early youth posed nude for a painter. Chandler was a man who found sex very difficult but he was always titillated by it and he found Cissy extraordinary. He began to write her love letters when he served in the Canadian Army during the war, and she began to love Raymond more than Julian. Being a gentleman, Julian decided to step aside and get a divorce. He did. Cissy was eighteen years older than Chandler; he waited until his mother died before he married Cissy, not wanting to upset his mother by marrying someone the same age. The truth is, they had a wonderful marriage. When I wrote *The Marble Orchard*, I dealt in depth with this relationship which has rarely been explored in fictional form. She was a hothouse flower, rarely left home, drifted in and out in pink chiffon almost like an ethereal fairy figure...the heart of *The Marble Orchard* is thus not a murder mystery but an exploration of the mystery of the marriage. I hope I have brought some intuitive truth into it.

A few final comments about Chandler's work. The looseness of Chandler's plotting accounts for one of his oft-quoted maxims: whenever you're stuck, just have a man come through the door with a gun and a hat...generally followed by a blonde. Chandler had a great sense of humor but at the same time he was an old curmudgeon, not liking writers, critics, even himself much. Hell would break loose if someone corrected him; when confronted with a copyeditor who fixed a split infinitive, he struck back by saying if he split an infinitive, it was to stay split. He hated screenwriting and he wrote *The Blue Dahlia* under the condition that he would remain drunk the whole time he wrote it and there would be an ambulance parked outside his house to take the script pages to the studio where they could film...or to take him to the hospital. When he was working on *Strangers on a Train* with Alfred Hitchcock, they did not get along, each being a supreme egoist convinced his own creative world was supreme. They clashed like two bulls. Chandler made Hitchcock come all the way out to La Jolla each time for the script conferences. Finally one day, Chandler looked out through the screened window, and in a clearly audible voice as he watched Alfred's struggles to extricate himself from the limousine, called out "There's the fat bastard now." That was their last meeting in La Jolla. Another writer was hired to finish the film.

Hammett and Chandler left a remarkable legacy that has shaped the course of American literature. As to what each would have thought of posterity's view...well, that remains a mystery.

Bibliography

Novels:
   (Philip Marlowe in all titles):
     The Big Sleep, 1939.
     Farewell My Lovely, 1940.
     The High Window, 1942.
     The Lady in the Lake, 1943.
     The Little Sister, 1949.
     The Long Goodbye, 1953.
     Playback, 1958.
     Poodle Springs (unfinished); completed by Robert B. Parker, 1989.

Short Stories:
   Five Murders, 1944.
   Five Sinister Characters, 1945.
   Finger Man and Other Stories, 1946.
   Red Wind, 1946.
   Spanish Blood, 1946.
   The Simple Art of Murder, 1950 (as *Trouble Is My Business, Pick-Up on Noon Street, The Simple Art of Murder*, 3 vols, 1951–53).
   Smart Aleck Kill, 1953.
   Pearls Are a Nuisance, 1953.
   Killer in the Rain, ed. by Philip Durham, 1964.
   The Smell of Fear, 1965.
   The Midnight Raymond Chandler, omnibus ed. by Joan Kahn, 1971.

Other:
   Library of America editions, 1995:
     vol. 1, *Novels and Other Writings, 1943–1954* (includes essays and letters).
     vol. 2, *Stories and Novels, 1933–42* (includes short stories).
   Plays, Screenplays, Notebooks, Letters.

Critical Studies (Among the vast number available):
   Philip Durham, *Down These Mean Streets a Man Must Go*, 1963.
   Frank McShane, *The Life of Raymond Chandler*, 1976.
   William Marling, *The American Roman Noir: Hammett, Cain, and Chandler*, 1994.

And for insights, see William Nolan, *The Marble Orchard*, 1995.

Michael Connelly

Biography

Michael Connelly was born on 21 July, 1956, in Philadelphia. He attended St. Thomas Acquinas High School in Fort Lauderdale, Florida, and he earned a B.S. in journalism at the University of Florida, Gainesville. Today a resident of Los Angeles, Michael Connelly is a Pulitzer Prize winning journalist and a former police reporter for the *LA Times*. Now a full time writer, he launched his mystery career with *The Black Echo*, winner of the 1993 Edgar Allen Poe Best First Mystery Award. He has been an Anthony Award and Hammett Prize nominee for subsequent books. *The Last Coyote* and *The Poet* won the 1996 and 1997 Dilys Award as the books independent mystery bookstores most enjoyed selling. In 1997, Connelly and wife Linda collaborated on a new work, their first child. Always generous with his time and supportive of new or established authors, Connelly has appeared at numerous conferences and workshops.

Bibliography

Novels:
    The Harry Bosch Series:
        The Black Echo, 1992.
        The Black Ice, 1993.
        The Concrete Blonde, 1994.
        The Last Coyote, 1995.
        Trunk Music, 1997.

    The Jack McEvoy Series:
        The Poet, 1996.

    Other:
        Blood Work, 1998.

Val McDermid

◆

Hard-Boiled Detectives

Hard-Boiled Detectives

The year is 1929, right in the middle of what literary historians tell us is the Golden Age of detective fiction. In England, in that place of which we in Oxford do not speak, that other, pale blue university city, the clock still stands at ten to three and there is, of course, honey still for tea. Queen of Crime Agatha Christie is celebrating the publication of her latest popular detective novel, *The Seven Dials Mystery*. It begins;

> That amiable youth, Jimmy Thesiger, came racing down the big staircase at Chimneys two steps at a time. So precipitate was his descent that he collided with Tredwell, the stately butler, just as the latter was crossing the hall bearing a fresh supply of hot coffee. Owing to the marvellous presence of mind and masterly agility of Tredwell, no casualty occurred. "Sorry," apologised Jimmy. "I say, Tredwell, am I the last down?"

Across the Atlantic, something very different is stirring.

> I first heard Personville called Poisonville by a red-haired mucker named Hickey Dewey in the Big Ship in Butte. He also called his shirt a shoit. I didn't think anything of what he had done to the city's name. Later I heard men who could manage their r's give it the same pronunciation. I still didn't see anything in it but the meaningless sort of humour that used to make richardsnary the thieves' word for dictionary. A few years later I went to Personville and learned better.

So opens *Red Harvest*, Samuel Dashiell Hammett's first novel. It's an arresting opening that announces with a fanfare of raspberry-blowing trombones that things definitely ain't what they used to be in the sedate world of murder. I can still remember the shock of reading that first paragraph. Strangely enough, it was within the precincts of this very college, twenty one summers ago when I was an undergraduate. I was supposed to be reading English literature, but I'd decided early on that as far as I was concerned, that included crime fiction. I can still recall the afternoon I discovered Hammett. I was lying in the shade of the copper beech in front of Garden building with a secondhand green Penguin bought from Jeremy's 10p Bookshop in the Cowley Road, aware that my reading life was never going to be quite the same again.

Like, I suspect, a large number of my fellow crime readers, I'd cut my teeth on Sherlock Holmes, followed by the Big Four—good title for a novel, that!—The big four of the Golden Age—Allingham, Christie, Marsh and Sayers. I enjoyed their complexity, their relentless drive towards a solution and the sense of visiting an alien society. Being working class and Scottish, I didn't have the same sense of unreality that another reader might have had, confronted with that world. I simply assumed for years that they were telling the truth. I arrived at Oxford convinced that England was crammed with villages like St. Mary Mead, populated by elderly women with private incomes and an unhealthy obsession with herbaceous borders. I think I was quite disappointed that none of the dons at St. Hilda's had been poisoned at High Table by the end of my first Michaelmas term. Of course, by then I had realised that the world of the Golden Age bore the same approximate relationship to English middle-class life as Monty Python's Flying Circus. I could still enjoy the plots, but I yearned for characters and ambience that struck some chord in me.

I had discovered Chandler two or three years before Hammett, thanks to an English teacher who was enough of a romantic to be a fan of Chandler as well as Keats and Shelley. I recognised that Chandler was profoundly different from the other mystery novelists I'd read, but his style was literary enough to disguise the enormity of the gulf that separated him from what for want of a better word I'm going to have to call the Cosy tradition.

It took Hammett's economical and muscular prose to make me feel that what I was reading was rooted in reality. When he wrote about a gambling den, I was convinced he'd been in gambling dens. When he wrote about speakeasies, I believed he knew these places and the people who hung out in them. I don't have that sense of conviction when Dorothy Sayers writes about the Duke of Denver, or Margery Allingham about the charmingly comic criminal classes. As Chandler himself says in his essay, *The Simple Art of Murder*:

> Hammett took murder out of the Venetian vase and dropped it into the alley.... Hammett gave murder back to the kind of people that commit it for reasons, not just to provide a corpse, and with the means at hand, not hand-wrought duelling pistols, curare and tropical fish. He put these people down on paper as they were, and he made them talk and think in the language they customarily used for these purposes. He had style, but his audience didn't know it, because it was in a language not supposed to be capable of such refinements.

It's a style that relies above all on deception. Although Hammett's dialogue sounds as if he's simply taken dictation and replicated it on the page, the most superficial analysis soon reveals how tightly constructed it is. Although his stories seem to flow naturally and naturalistically from one scene to the next, it doesn't take the deconstructive skills of Derrida to reveal that the novels are structured carefully and precisely so that the protagonist is never, as they say, disempowered. By which I mean that he remains at the centre of the action, and he alone controls the strands that must be woven together in the correct pattern to give us a satisfactory conclusion. As André Gide so perceptively remarked, "Dashiell Hammett's dialogues, in which every character is trying to deceive all the others and in which the truth slowly becomes visible through the haze of deception can be compared only with the best of Hemingway."

It's not easy, with hindsight, to recapture the sense of shock I felt that day under the beech tree. But for the purposes of this talk, I wanted to try. So I went back to one of my favourite critical works, Colin Watson's *Snobbery with Violence*, to see how he characterises the traditional murder mystery and how that compares with the novels of Chandler and Hammett. Watson reminds us that, according to Chandler, the English are, "incomparably the best dull writers [in the world]." Watson goes on: "Chandler was not seriously exaggerating when he declared that 'the only reality the English detection writers knew was the conversational accent of Surbiton and Bognor Regis." In book after book they appear:

> ...the diffident, decent young pipe-smokers; the plucky girls with flowerlike complexions; the wooden policemen, slow but reliable; the assorted house-party guests, forever dressing for dinner or hunting missing daggers; the aristocrats concealing their enormous intellects beneath a veneer of asininity; the ubiquitous chauffeurs, butlers and housemaids and the rest of the lower orders, all comic, surly or sinister, but none of them quite human.

No pipe-smoker, here's Sam Spade reacting to the news of his partner's murder.

> He scowled at the telephone on the table while his hands took from beside it a packet of brown papers and a sack of Bull Durham tobacco.... Spade's thick fingers made a cigarette with deliberate care, sifting a measured quantity of tan flakes down

> into curved paper, spreading the flakes so that they lay equal at the ends with a slight depression in the middle, thumbs rolling the paper's inner edge down and up under the outer edge as forefingers pressed it over, thumbs and fingers sliding to the paper cylinder's ends to hold it even while tongue licked the flap, left forefinger and thumb pinching their end while right forefinger and thumb smoothed the damp seam, right forefinger and thumb twisting their end and lifting the other to Spade's mouth.

I can't imagine any other Golden Age novelist knowing enough about roll-ups to write that, never mind allowing their heroes anything so infra dig.

No plucky girls with flowerlike complexions either. Here's Chandler in *The Big Sleep*:

> Miss Carmen Sternwood was sitting on a fringed orange shawl. She was sitting very straight, with her hands on the arms of the chair, her knees close together, her body stiffly erect in the pose of an Egyptian goddess, her chin level, her small bright teeth shining between her parted lips. Her eyes were wide open. The dark slate colour of the iris had devoured the pupil. They were mad eyes. She seemed to be unconscious, but she didn't have the pose of unconsciousness. She looked as if, in her mind, she was doing something very important and making a fine job of it. Out of her mouth came a tinny chuckling noise which didn't change her expression or even move her lips. She was wearing a pair of long jade earrings. They were nice earrings and had probably cost a couple of hundred dollars. She wasn't wearing anything else.

And forget the wooden policemen, slow but reliable. Here's Hammett:

> The first policeman I saw needed a shave. The second had a couple of buttons off his shabby uniform. The third stood in the centre of the city's main intersection...directing traffic, with a cigar in one corner of his mouth. After that I stopped checking them up.

And back to Chandler in *The Long Goodbye*.

> The homicide skipper that year was a Captain Gregorius, a type of copper that is getting rarer but by no means extinct, the kind that solves crimes with the bright light, the soft sap, the knee to the groin, the fist to the solar plexus, the night stick to the base of the spine. Six months later, he was indicted for

perjury before a grand jury, booted without trial and later stamped to death by a big stallion on his ranch in Wyoming.

There are no house party guests in the *noir* novel, no aristocrats either, unless you count General Guy Sternwood.

> In the wheelchair, an old and obviously dying old man watched us come with black eyes from which all fire had died long ago.... The rest of his face was a leaden mask, with the bloodless lips and the sharp nose and the sunken temples and the outward-turning earlobes of approaching dissolution.

Not a bit like Lord Peter, is he?

Oh, and the servants, of course. Remember the chauffeur in *The Big Sleep*? The slim dark young man who managed to keep his job in spite of running off with the daughter of the house and having a record for attempted robbery? Imagine him in St. Mary Mead....

Of course, Hammett and Chandler didn't just emerge as fully fledged revolutionary novelists like Minerva springing fully-armed from the brow of Jove. They too had their tradition. But where the cosy novels sprang from conservatism and a desire to recapture a safe world where everyone knew their place, the hard-boiled, *noir* school came from dissatisfaction and a sense of frustration and failure.

The detective fiction of both Hammett and Chandler first saw the light of day thanks to the pulp detective magazine *Black Mask*. The pulps—so-called because they were printed on cheap wood pulp which gave the contents an appropriately coarse, grainy and cheap appearance—were seven by ten inches in size, with gaudy covers invariably showing scenes of improbably violent action, often involving improbably endowed and invariably young women. Each issue contained around 120 pages of short stories, with occasional extracts from novels.

The pulps began to appear during the First World War but didn't reach the height of their popularity until the early twenties. They were born of disillusionment with the increasing corruption of American life. The great American Dream seemed to have died somewhere along the line for millions of Americans. Prohibition had brought in its wake racketeering and corruption on such a scale that almost nobody's lives were untouched by it. Gangsters seemed to run big cities, with elected politicians apparently powerless to end their reigns of terror. As if that wasn't enough, the Depression followed, devastating the lives of people who had never imagined that poverty on such a scale would attack them. In fact, if it hadn't been for the Depression, chances are Chandler would never have become a crime writer. It was only because he lost his job as an oil company executive and took to the road, driving up and down the California coast in a fruitless search for another one, that he actually decided to try his hand at writing the kind of detective stories he was reading in bed at night in lonely motels.

Out of the despair felt by Chandler and his fellow countrymen came a fiction that was driven by the anger of its protagonists, men who were strong and who took power for themselves, unlike their impotent readers. This violent and primitive kind of American crime story made a complete break with the European tradition that more conventional writers like Ellery Queen and S.S. Van Dine had followed. Philip Marlowe has nothing in common with Philo Vance or Hercule Poirot except his gender. They don't even share a sexuality because, of course, Golden Age cosy heroes never had sex. The English audience were deemed to be so sensitive to sexual references that the English edition of *The Thin Man* was censored by its publishers. Nora asks Nick, after a violent tussle with a woman, "Tell me the truth: when you were wrestling with Mimi, didn't you have an erection?"

By the end of the 1920s, there were over two hundred separate pulp magazines on the bookstands, each dedicated to crude violent adventure, mostly written in embarrassingly bad prose. S.J. Perelman memorably satirised them in a piece about "Spicy Detective" magazine:

> And then from an open window beyond the bed, a roscoe coughed "Ka-chow!" I said, "What the hell—" and hit the floor with my smeller. A brunette jane was lying there, half out of the mussed covers. She was as dead as vaudeville.

Not surprisingly, perhaps, many of the pulp magazines had a short life, but some, like *Black Mask*, achieved legendary fame. The magazine survived into the 1950s, but reached its zenith in the decade between 1926 and 1936, when it was edited by Captain Joseph T. Shaw. Shaw was determined to make pulp fiction less crude, although he had no qualms about its violent content. He encouraged the better writers he had available by using their work consistently and upped their pay from a cent a word. He ruthlessly blue-pencilled any discursive writing that didn't drive the plot relentlessly forward and demanded the highest standards of any of the pulp editors. "We wanted simplicity for the sake of clarity, plausibility and belief. We wanted action, but we held that action is meaningless unless it involves recognisable human character in three dimensional form," Shaw himself said. It was a discipline that helped both Chandler and Hammett to refine their styles. Although both wrote many short stories for *Black Mask* and other dime magazines, reading them now it's hard to escape the conviction that they were practice runs for the novels. It's a view that's backed up by the habit both writers had of taking material from short stories and developing them in novels. Hammett did this with the Continental Op, a detective who works for a private eye agency. The Op started life in a series of short stories, but he is never as vividly realised as he is in *Red Harvest*, Hammett's first novel.

Chandler went further and recycled whole chunks of his plots from earlier pulp fictions. A substantial part of *The Big Sleep* was drawn from two *Black Mask* stories—*Killer In The Rain* and *The Curtain*. His second novel, *Farewell My Lovely*, owed various strands of its plot to three other short stories—*The Man Who Liked Dogs*, *Try The Girl* and *Mandarin's Jade*; and the fourth novel, *The Lady In The Lake*, cannibalized yet another three—*Bay City Blues*, *The Lady In The Lake* and *No Crime in the Mountains*. Cannibalized was Chandler's own word, and he was never comfortable with this writing technique. There was no reason why he should have been embarrassed about it—most of us writers scavenge our early work for fragments we can salvage to garnish our later stories. But Chandler was eager that his readers shouldn't know about his habit, so he consistently refused to allow the cannibalised stories to be reprinted during his lifetime. It's only since he died that we have been able to examine the original stories from which the novels grew. And it's fascinating to see how he worked on his material to improve it. Some scenes are lifted virtually verbatim, with just a little polishing here and there. Others are expanded. For example, this passage in *The Curtain*:

> The air steamed. The walls and ceiling of the glass house dripped. In the half-light enormous tropical plants spread their blooms and branches all over the place, and the smell of them was almost as overpowering as the smell of boiling alcohol.

In the opening chapter of *The Big Sleep*, this becomes:

> The air was thick, wet, steamy and larded with the cloying smell of tropical orchids in bloom. The glass walls and roof were

heavily misted and big drops of moisture splashed down on the plants. The light had an unreal greenish colour, like light filtered through an aquarium tank. The plants filled the place, a forest of them, with nasty meaty leaves and stalks like the newly washed fingers of dead men. They smelled as overpowering as boiling alcohol under a blanket.

Twice as many words, it's true, but at least five times the atmosphere!

So both men served their apprenticeship as writers in the same boiler-room. It's hard to imagine another career move that would have brought two such different personalities from such different backgrounds together.

Chandler was the elder. Born in Chicago in 1888, he was brought to England by his Irish Quaker mother at the age of eight and given an English public school education at Dulwich College where he excelled in the classics. He completed his education in France and Germany, becoming a free-lance writer of reviews and essays. He returned to America in 1912, but came back to Europe in the First World War, first with the Canadian Gordon Highlanders and later with the Royal Flying Corps. After the war, he moved to California where he became a writer of oil reports and a company director until the Depression forced him out of work. Once he'd discovered he could make a living out of writing detective fiction, he devoted himself to it as thoroughly as he had done to everything else in his life. He was a taker of pains, a committed worker at his craft. In spite of a deep-seated conviction that what he was doing was ultimately pretty frivolous, he took seriously the doing of it.

Hammett's background was considerably less privileged. Born in St. Mary's County, Maryland in 1894, he grew up in Philadelphia and Baltimore, leaving school at fourteen with no qualifications. He had an assortment of unskilled and semiskilled jobs, including newsboy, labourer, timekeeper, machine-operator and stevedore. Then he made the move that would shape the rest of his life. He joined the Pinkerton Detective Agency, the biggest private eye bureau in America. It was the start of a bizarre career. The highlights included the Fatty Arbuckle case, committing perjury to avoid arrest, and being promoted for his part in catching a man who stole a Ferris wheel. I have to say that last one sounds like a case for my own detective, Kate Brannigan. One of her cases started off with a series of missing conservatories. After that, a missing fairground ride seems like a natural progression. But it wasn't all fun and games, in spite of Hammett's own amusing anecdotes about life as a Pinkerton's op. His work was often dangerous, his opponents men to whom life really was cheap. By the end of his career, his legs and body carried the scars from his violent encounters, while his head bore a permanent indentation after one vicious attack.

Like Chandler, he volunteered in the First World War, serving as a sergeant with the Motor Ambulance Corps. That's where he caught the TB that permanently weakened his chest, leading to years of emphysema and, finally, lung cancer. He tried to go back to Pinkerton's after the war, but it was soon clear to everyone including Hammett that he just wasn't up to it any longer. Soon he was hemorrhaging so badly from his lungs that he and everybody else was convinced he didn't have long to live. The one thing he wanted to do before he died was to write in fictional terms about the life of a detective. So with remarkable single-mindedness, in 1922, he left his wife and child and started to write short stories.

I doubt the medical profession would prescribe living on soup and bashing a typewriter as a cure for chest problems. But it seemed to do the trick for Hammett. The more stories he sold, the better his health became. By the time *Red Harvest* was published in 1929, he was well enough to be drinking, gambling and smoking heavily and staying up all night working. Only the marriage never recovered, and in 1930 he met Lillian Hellman, with whom he was to have a tempestuous roller-coaster love affair until he died in 1961. His serious writing was over by 1934, however. After that, all he ever produced was Hollywood hack work. That may have had something to do with the phenomenal amount of alcohol he consumed before the DTs drove him on to the wagon in 1948. And after that, his involvement with radical politics occupied those of his energies not taken up with helping other writers, in particular Lillian Hellman, to realise their own abilities.

In spite of their widely differing backgrounds, Chandler and Hammett created heroes who had a remarkably similar idea of how a man should be. Their protagonists are always honourable but not always honest. That was a serious break with tradition. What must Hammett's original readers, raised on the high moral tone of the Cosies, have made of Sam Spade? He lies to the police, he's been sleeping with his business partner's wife not out of love but out of desire and convenience, he has sex with the book's heroine at a point where we cannot be sure whether she is on the side of the angels or the devils. Sam and Brigid

O'Shaughnessy broke the mould of upright, truthful investigator and virtuous heroine for good.

Chandler and Hammett brought moral ambiguity, ethical complexity and enigmatic endings to crime fiction for the first time. These were elements that had no real place in the certainties of Golden Age writers like Sayers and Christie. W.H. Auden argued, as has P.D. James, that detective fiction is more interesting as an exploration of moral choice if the murder takes place in an ordered, pre-lapsarian sort of world, where the crime can almost be seen as the serpent in the garden. In a newspaper interview, Agatha Christie once said, "I don't like messy deaths. Anyway, I'm more interested in peaceful people who die in their beds and no-one knows why. I don't like violence. I once collected the papers for three weeks and every day there was somebody murdered, some girl killed, some child missing and strangled. I think it's a sign of the times." But Hammett and Chandler demonstrated powerfully that in a world of violence and confusion, the impact of moral choices can be as devastating as in an ordered world.

As the German sociologist Max Weber, in his essay *Politics as a Vocation*, says:

> The world is governed by demons and he who lets himself in for...power and force as means, contracts with diabolic powers, and for his action it is not true that good can follow only from good and evil only from evil, but that often the opposite is true. Anyone who fails to see this is, indeed, a political infant.

That Hammett in particular sees this is evident in the way that his detectives typically work so hard to maintain control over all the various factions, using lies, evasions, blackmail and even truth to maintain the balance between them until the hero is ready to collapse all the houses of cards.

Hammett's first hard-boiled hero, the Continental Op, gets his full-length outing in *Red Harvest*. He doesn't sound like a traditional hero. He's shortish, fattish, not even the owner of his own business, but nevertheless, he's his own man. It's part of his heroic nature that he's an employee; no matter how well or how badly he performs, he will not enrich himself nor pay any financial price for his actions. Within hours of arriving in the obnoxious and corrupt Personville, the never-named Op is up to his ears in violence. Charting the deaths in this book is a job in itself, so much so that one chapter is headed "The Seventeenth Murder." But the violence is never gratuitous nor pornographically lingered over.

It's more like the inevitable pus that flows when a boil is lanced—the end result is going to be clean and painless, but getting there is pretty vile and it stinks.

The characterisation is as irresistible and powerful as the narrative drive. Dozens of people flit through the pages, but there is never confusion as to who's who. Here we get the first of Hammett's strong, individualistic women, Dinah Brand. We're told before we meet her that she's devastatingly attractive, a hustler but irresistibly sexy. Then the Op comes face to face with her and we find she has "the face of a girl of twenty-five already showing signs of wear." Her large blue eyes are bloodshot, her lipstick not on straight on a lush mouth that already has lines at the corners, her coarse hair needs cutting and there's a ladder in her stocking. It's a triumph of Hammett's art that the reader is convinced that she is charming and sexy and funny. She is an up-front, three-dimensional woman with a mind and an agenda of her own—and Hammett has the nerve to kill her off rather than pair her off with the hero. At a stroke, he ends forever the conventional "happy" ending where, the murderer dealt with by Inspector Woodentop of the Yard, our hero and heroine can embark on a happy future untroubled by the murderous circumstances of the last couple of hundred pages.

Some critics complain that once you've read one hard-boiled novel, you've read them all. The best answer to that—apart from forcing them to read Hammett and Chandler's dozen novels back to back—is Bertolt Brecht's riposte. If someone cries "The same old thing again!" then he has not understood the crime novel. He might just as well cry "The same old thing again!" in the theatre when the curtain rises. The originality resides elsewhere. Indeed, the fact that one characteristic feature of the crime novel is the variation of more or less fixed elements is precisely what gives the whole genre its aesthetic quality. It is one of the properties of a cultivated branch of literature. Besides, the ignorant man's cry of "The same old thing again!" is based on the same fallacy as the white man's idea that all blacks look the same.

Dashiell Hammett's novels are far from reruns of the same tale. In *The Glass Key* there is no casual violence, the plotting is as cunning as any Christie, and characterisation skilful, economical and assured. *The Maltese Falcon* is as tense as any novel in the genre, its moral twists and turns fascinating, its conclusions devastating. The writing is stylised, true, but always spare, with never a word wasted. I'd argue that these books stand comparison with anything written by Dos Passos, Faulkner or Hemingway in the same decade. They illuminate a society as well as shed light on men's notions of what it is to be a man.

Critics often pan *The Thin Man* because they think it was a waste of Hammett's talent, the first sign that he was to become nothing more than a Hollywood hack. But to me, it shows another side to the man; a lighter side, a talent to amuse, in places almost a gentleness. It's no coincidence that the book came out of a time when he and Lillian Hellman were first together, happy and supportive, with few outside problems to assail them. And he did tell Hellman that Nora Charles was based on her, so we shouldn't expect her to be as double-crossing and self-seeking as some of the other foils to Hammett's detectives.

Chandler too was a writer who never repeated himself in the novels. *The Little Sister* and *The Long Goodbye* are the most tightly plotted and therefore the most satisfying. But even when the plot goes hopelessly awry, we mostly don't notice because we're too caught up in the social and human background. The classic example is the old story about the filming of *The Big Sleep*. When the film version starring Humphrey Bogart was being shot, Chandler's phone rang one afternoon. It was the film's director, demanding an answer to the crucial question of who killed the chauffeur. That was the moment when Chandler realised that not only had he failed to reveal this, but that he didn't actually know.

In spite of occasional slipshod plotting, Chandler is always a joy to me to read. He had a great feeling for the sound and value of words, and he brought a literary quality to the hard-boiled genre that most of his fellows and his followers signally lacked. He had a sound knowledge of English literature, and that underpinned his work, though never in a showy way. When Chandler speaks of Eliot and Dante, the reader feels informed. It's the opposite sensation to that given by the supposedly intellectual aristo sleuth of the cosies, who puts us poor foolish readers in our ignorant places. Chandler's literary style is probably a large part of the reason why he was the first of the American *noir* novelists to make any serious impact on the British book buying public. Even his wisecracks run smooth, and mostly still produce a smile of amusement, or at least admiration.

Chandler's debt to English literature is nowhere more evident than in the construction of his hero. Marlowe is a romantic hero in the true sense of romance. He is the knight of the Grail Quest, the man set apart by his mission, a man at one with his environment, whatever that environment is. It's no surprise that Chandler originally planned to call him Mallory. In his own words, Chandler created "a complete man and a common man and...to use a rather weathered phrase, a man of honour." It's a sharp contrast to the corrupt world he inhabits and sometimes one that is impossible for me to swallow. Marlowe's knightly valour sentimentalises him; it might be possible to imagine a very parfit knight in the world of the medieval courtly romance, but it's impossible to accept him as the only hero in a world entirely populated by the venal, the superficial, the brutal, the vicious and the corrupt.

I don't feel the same way about Hammett's heroes, and that is perhaps because the kind of honour Hammett gives his heroes is an honour rooted in reality rather than romance. Hammett himself was a man of honour, a man who made hard moral choices and stuck with them, to the point of going to jail. He volunteered to fight in the Second World War at the age of forty-eight, in spite of health wrecked by his experience in the first one. Less than a decade later, he went to jail on a point of principle. He was jailed for six months for refusing to reveal the names of the contributors to the bail bond fund of the Civil Rights Congress during the McCarthy witch-hunts. He didn't actually know the names, but that was immaterial to Hammett. According to Lillian Hellman, he said the night before he went to prison,

> I hate this damned kind of talk, but maybe I better tell you that if it were more than jail, if it were my life, I would give it for what I think democracy is and I don't let cops or judges tell me what I think democracy is.

This is no empty rhetoric, any more than Sam Spade's impassioned speech to Brigid O'Shaughnessy before he hands her over to the police.

> When a man's partner is killed he's supposed to do something about it. It doesn't make any difference what you thought about him. He's your partner and you're supposed to do something about it. Then it happens we were in the detective business. Well, when one of your organisation gets killed it's bad business to let the killer get away with it. It's bad all around—bad for that organisation, bad for every detective everywhere. Third, I'm a detective and expecting me to run criminals down and then let them go free is like asking a dog to catch a rabbit and let it go. It can be done, all right, and sometimes it is done, but it's not the natural thing.

There's a practicality to this display of honour that to my mind, Marlowe lacks. Perhaps if Chandler hadn't had such a smoothly middle-class life, it might have been different. But for Hammett, the exercise of honour and morality was an everyday thing.

As well as giving the genre a new kind of hero, Chandler and Hammett brought another fresh approach to crime fiction. For the first time, they used a sense of place as an integral element of the novel. It does more that create atmosphere—it provides a sense of authenticity that has a knock-on effect on the novel as a whole. I know that I rely very strongly on the real city of Manchester when I write my Kate Brannigan novels. The city acts as a kind of grid on which the story is overlaid. Readers who know the city will recognise places they know, and subconsciously they figure that if I'm telling them the truth about that, then I'm probably telling them the truth about everything else in the book. For readers unfamiliar with Manchester, my job when I'm describing locations is to give them a kind of universality so that they can latch on to something that will make them think, "Oh yes, that sounds just like Notting Hill Gate or Yonkers or West Hollywood without the glamour." A sense of place is a common feature right across the range of today's crime fiction, from P.D. James to James Ellroy, but it was Chandler and Hammett who first used it to any significant extent.

Reading many of the Golden Age cosy writers, you could be forgiven for assuming that to them, an ambience was something to go to hospital in. Here's Colin Watson again, this time on the subject of ambience.

> The world they inhabit is self-contained and never changing. We are shown the same flats in Half Moon Street, the same Tudor mansions half an hour's Bentley ride from town, with the same libraries and studies, the same french windows opening upon the same lawns.

Hammett and Chandler changed all that forever. Here's Hammett in *Red Harvest*.

> The city wasn't pretty. Most of its builders had gone in for gaudiness. Maybe they had been successful at first. Since then, the smelters whose brick stacks stuck up tall against a gloomy mountain to the south had yellow-smoked everything to dinginess. The result was an ugly city of forty thousand people, set in an ugly notch between two ugly mountains that had been all dirtied up by mining. Spread over this was a grimy sky that looked as if had come out of the smelters' stacks.

But it's Chandler who developed a real mastery of the sense of place. He set the template for what is a key element in current *noir* fiction. Robert B. Parker says:

> I think that partly because I am writing romance, I need to root it in very hard, gritty, real circumstantial realism...because you want to embed the character in such a web of credibility that his slightly larger than lifeness is not bothersome. Marlowe almost never got out of LA.... He never went any place. And the war came and went and he took no notice of it.... He made a little go a very long way.

Chandler's sharp eye and his evocative prose gives us California in all its glory.

> It was one of those clear, bright summer mornings we get in the early spring in California before the high fog sets in. The rains are over. The hills are still green and in the valley across the Hollywood hills you can see snow on the high mountains. The fur stores are advertising their annual sales. The call houses that specialise in sixteen year old virgins are doing a land-office business. And in Beverly Hills the jacaranda trees are beginning to bloom.

He can do decay too.

> Back from the highway at the bottom of Sepulveda Canyon were two yellow square gateposts...I turned in and followed a gravelled road round the shoulder of a hill, up a gentle slope, over a ridge and down the other side into a shadowy valley. It was hot in the valley, ten or fifteen degrees hotter than on the highway.... Off to my left there was an empty swimming pool, and nothing looks emptier than an empty swimming pool. Around three sides of it there was what remained of a lawn dotted with redwood lounging chairs with badly faded pads on them. The pads had been of many colours, blue, green, yellow, orange, rust-red. Their edge bindings had come loose in spots, the buttons had popped and the pads were bloated where this had happened. On the fourth side there was the high wire fence of a tennis court. The diving board over the empty pool looked knee-sprung and tired. Its matting covering hung in shreds and its metal fittings were flaked with rust.... The place seemed to be as dead as Pharaoh.

I've outlined some of the innovations of two writers characterised thus by Somerset Maugham: "To my mind, the two best novelists of the hard boiled school are Dashiell Hammett and Raymond

Chandler who have created characters that we can believe in. They are only a little more heightened, a little more vivid, than people we have all come across."

But what is their legacy? What can we point to today and say, "That comes from Dashiell Hammett, that from Raymond Chandler?" The short answer is, most of the images of detectives that permeate the most popular media of TV and the movies. I'm not denying the worldwide popularity of Miss Marple and Inspector Morse, but even they haven't got anything like the penetration of the thousands of series and movies featuring hard-boiled private eyes and the cops who have expropriated their style and their sense of honour. Clint Eastwood's Dirty Harry is a direct-line descendant of Bogart's portrayal of Sam Spade and Philip Marlowe.

Those early movies have branded us with a visual image of a private eye that we will never shake off. Down at heel, tough, self-contained and short of cash. His office is dingy and small, the furniture basic and battered. Fifty years on, rock band Dire Straits tops the charts with *Private Investigations*, a song that could come straight from a post-modernist version of *The Maltese Falcon*. For us now, the private eye will always wear a trench coat and a trilby. It's an image that lingers and pervades consciousness. It's what we expect a private eye to be. He'll always be Bogey, even though he was a man at odds with the physical descriptions in the books—Marlowe is tall; Sam Spade like a "blond Satan," described to sound more like Alan Rickman than Humphrey Bogart.

These films have created their own mythology. They've been spoofed dozens of times, sometimes even in full-length feature films like the 1979s pastiche *The Black Bird*. Of all the new movies out last week, what did the critics review? The release of a new print of *The Big Sleep*. But it's impossible to escape the books. These are not film versions that stray so far from the original that the book is lost forever. The script of *The Maltese Falcon* consists almost entirely of speech taken directly and without modification from the written novel. There are very few novels that have so vital, vernacular and concise command of language for that to be possible.

But the movies do lose something in translation, and that's the elusive something that Chandler and Hammett brought to their chosen form that takes it closer to literature than pulp fiction. What the books lose in translation is the discursive passages, those elements that take us to the heart of the philosophies of these heroes and their creators. For example, the film of *The Maltese Falcon* loses the long parable that Spade relates to Brigid when they are first growing close. It's about a man, a middle-aged, middle-class businessman with a good job and a wife and family who mysteriously disappears one day between lunch and going back to the office in the afternoon.

It turns out that the man had had a near-miss accident when a beam fell from a construction site and narrowly missed him. It forced him to look at his life, and how easily he could be parted from it by mere chance. So he decided to walk away from the rut he was in and wander the country. But when Spade found him five years later, he was living with a new wife, new job and new family. As Spade says, "He adjusted himself to beams falling, and then no more of them fell, and he adjusted himself to them not falling." It's a crucial point; how in spite of everything we have learned about the unpredictability and irrationality of our world, we continually try to behave rationally, sensibly and responsibly. The story is morally ambiguous, the extraordinary is told calmly and without flash and flourish. It's an unexpected set piece. It's not what we expect in a racy detective story. Yet the ideas that it lays out permeate the novels. But it's lost in the films, and so it's easy to see how cinema has failed these novels and spawned hundreds of superficial imitators that don't even come close, perhaps because they haven't got that solid philosophical underpinning of the originals.

If we're looking for the true legacy of Hammett and Chandler, we must therefore concentrate on the written word, as they did when they were producing their finest work. American crime fiction has never been divorced from the mainstream to the extent it has in Britain. You only have to look at the review pages of the "serious" journals to see that. Part of the reason for that is that the early British crime writers simply weren't in the same league as serious literary writers. The work of Agatha Christie or John Dickson Carr bears no resemblance to that of Graham Greene or Elizabeth Bowen, and no reasonable person could accuse the former of having influenced the latter in any way. But the distinction between Hammett and Hemingway, although real, is mainly a question of register and range, and critics far more eminent that I have suggested that Hammett did influence Hemingway. This relationship remains true today with the work of the dirty realists like Richard Ford and Brett Easton Ellis often bordering closely on work by writers like James Lee Burke, James Ellroy or James Crumley. Or indeed anybody else called James.

Chandler and Hammett have spawned hundreds of imitators, at both extremes of their stylistic spectra. There are novels written in lush literary language liberally loaded with simile and metaphor till they collapse beneath the weight of their own pretensions. There are the slangy and spare songs of praise to violence, inextricably larding it with sadism and exploitation. Much recent American hard-boiled fiction seems to me to be following the latter course. There is more violence used purely for stomach-churning effect, more sex inextricably woven into that violence in a strange pornographic dance. My objection to this strand of crime fiction is that I find it offensive—not simply because of its subject matter and the lingering pleasure the writers clearly take in it, but mostly because it's badly written. The masters these writers claim to follow would have binned it because it wasn't good enough.

The two male writers most highly praised and lauded as the successors of the masters are Walter Mosley and James Ellroy. I find it interesting that both choose to write historically—Mosley set his first novel, *Devil In A Blue Dress*, in 1948 LA, Ellroy set *The Blue Dahlia* in 1947 LA, both prime Chandler country. Both men deal with the sort of corruption among police, politicians and businessmen that engaged Chandler and Hammett. Mosley writes from the black perspective, yet although he addresses racism in what he writes, his characters seldom confront it in the way they confront the more financial sorts of corruption. Both writers also exhibit a disturbing level of violence against women.

My personal view is that their writing is misogynist to a degree that interferes with my enjoyment of their work, even though at times their writing is among the best being produced now. I say this not in any spirit of political correctness; I have no desire to censor anyone's work. But my personal response is that I find some of their underlying assumptions and attitudes deeply offensive, and that puts a barrier between me and the writing.

I have heard the argument that they are simply reflecting faithfully the period they've chosen to write about and its attitude towards women. It's also true that there is precedent for their contemptuous attitude to women in Chandler's work, where the female gender is almost exclusively represented by vamps, vixens and victims.

Here's Marlowe on women:

> There are blondes and blondes and it is almost a joke word nowadays. All blondes have their points except perhaps the

metallic ones who are as blonde as a Zulu under the bleach and as to disposition as soft as a sidewalk. There is the small and cute blonde who cheeps and twitters and the big statuesque blonde who straightarms you with an ice-blue glare. There is the blonde who gives you the up-from-under look and smells lovely and shimmers and hangs on your arm and is always very, very tired when you take her home. She makes that helpless gesture and has that goddamned headache and you would like to slug her except that you are glad you found out about the headache before you invested too much time and money and hope in her. Because the headache will always be there, a weapon that never wears out and is as deadly as the bravo's rapier or Lucrezia's poison vial.

And all that because she had the nerve to say no to Marlowe? Can you honestly say, knowing how much the guy smokes and drinks in the average twenty-four hour period, that she's being unreasonable?

It goes on, this splenetic but nevertheless very funny rant against blondes.

> There is the soft and willing and alcoholic blonde who doesn't care what she wears as long as it is mink or where she goes as long as it is the Starlight Roof and there is plenty of dry champagne. There is the small perky blonde who is a little pale and wants to pay her own way and is full of sunshine and common sense and knows judo from the ground up and can toss a truck driver over her shoulder without missing more than one sentence out of the editorial in the Saturday review. There is the pale, pale blonde with anaemia of some nonfatal but incurable type. She is very languid and very shadowy and she speaks softly out of nowhere and you can't lay a finger on her because in the first place you don't want to and in the second place she is reading *The Waste Land* or Dante in the original or Kafka or Kierkegaard or studying Provençal. She adores music and when the New York Philharmonic is playing Hindemith she can tell you which one of the six bass viols came in a quarter of a beat too late. I hear Toscanini can also. That makes two of them.
>
> And lastly there is the gorgeous show piece who will outlast three kingpin racketeers and then marry a couple of millionaires at a million a head and end up with a pale rose villa at Cap d'Antibes, an Alfa Romeo town car complete with pilot and co-pilot and a stable of shopworn aristocrats, all of whom she will treat with the affectionate absent-mindedness of an elderly duke saying good night to his butler.

Going back to Mosley and Ellroy and their cohorts, to me, the operative phrase is, "the period they've chosen to write about." To choose actively a period where misogyny, homophobia and casual racism were the norm and then to choose characters who largely reflect that prevailing social behaviour says more about writers like Ellroy and Mosley than they would perhaps like. For it is not the case that those were the only possible views of women available to the hard-boiled private eye novelist in the Golden Age. If vamps, vixens and victims were the rule, then Dashiell Hammett is the golden exception.

As we've seen already with Dinah Brand in *Red Harvest* and Brigid O'Shaughnessy, Hammett writes about strong, three-dimensional women who have individual weaknesses, not just the supposed generic weaknesses of their sex. Even the subsidiary characters like Effie Perrine, Sam Spade's secretary, are given a personality and a life. She's not just a cipher there to open the mail and channel the clients through to the boss.

Hammett's view of women gives an extra dimension to his novels. He writes about both genders, giving them their place in the world. That's one of the reasons why I'm convinced that his natural heirs are to be found among the women private eye writers who have emerged since the early 1980s. Sara Paretsky's V.I. Warshawski seems to me to be the natural child of Sam Spade and Philip Marlowe. Like them, she is the lone individual who pits herself against corruption. In Warshawski's case, that corruption is found in big business, in politics, in police departments and in their personal transactions between individuals. But she is no mere Marlowe in a frock. Paretsky has moved the form forwards, addressing the concerns of her era just as her predecessors did in theirs.

Warshawski has a sense of honour. She's as bloody-minded as the best or worst of them. Like the Continental Op in *Red Harvest*, when she's told to lay off an investigation because someone doesn't like the dirt she's digging, she treats it as a spur rather than a stop sign. Like Chandler, Paretsky is a fine writer, peppering her work with wry wisecracks that illuminate what she's saying. And, like Hammett, she gives both sexes their own place in the world.

And like both of them, Paretsky has a sense of place. Here's the opening of *Indemnity Only*, the first novel featuring V.I. Warshawski.

> The night air was thick and damp. As I drove south along Lake Michigan, I could smell rotting alewives like a faint

perfume on the heavy air. Little fires shone here and there from late-night barbecues in the park. On the water a host of green and red running lights showed people seeking relief from the sultry air. On shore traffic was heavy, the city moving restlessly, trying to breathe. It was July in Chicago.

Christopher Wren's epitaph is carved in the wall of St. Paul's Cathedral. It reads, *Si monumentum requiris, circumspice*. If you seek a monument, look around you. Earlier this week, Raymond Chandler's adopted city of Los Angeles finally honoured the man who put its mean streets firmly on the map of the mind. The intersection of Hollywood and Cahuenga boulevards has now officially been named Raymond Chandler Square. The idea came from a Chandler *aficionado*, 30 year old law student Jess Bravin. After the official dedication ceremony, he told waiting reporters: "I hope you guys write about this. After all, there's not a week goes by without you either quoting Chandler or trying—badly—to imitate his style." *Si monumentum requiris...*

St. Hilda's College, Oxford, August, 1995

Val McDermid
Biography

Val McDermid grew up in a Scottish mining community, then studied English at St. Hilda's College, Oxford. For sixteen years she was an investigative journalist, the last three serving as Northern Bureau Chief of a national Sunday tabloid. While now a full-time writer, she continues her long association with the press by writing perceptive, trenchant book reviews for the *Manchester Evening News*. Her first mystery, 1987's *Report for Murder*, arose from her professional experience and features journalist Lindsay Gordon. Lesbian Lindsay has since pursued four other investigations. In 1992, McDermid began her series with Manchester PI Kate Brannigan, a womansleuth in the Kinsey Millhone mode. Its third entry, *Crack Down*, was short-listed for the CWA Gold Dagger Award in 1994. Her 1995 serial killer thriller, *The Mermaids Singing*, did win this glittering prize. She has also published the fascinating *A Suitable Job for a Woman: Inside the World of Women Private Eyes*, an effort to answer the question of "just how big the gap was between the creatures of my imagination and the real-life women private eyes who take on the cases that make real differences in people's lives." Interviewees come from both sides of the Atlantic; their experiences form a fascinating background for fictional sleuths, and supply fuel for her paper read at *AZ Murder Goes...Classic*.

Bibliography

Novels:
    The Lindsay Gordon Series:
        Report for Murder, 1987.
        Common Murder, 1989.
        Final Edition, 1991.
        Union Jack, 1993.
        Booked for Murder, 1996.

    The Kate Brannigan Series:
        Dead Beat, 1992.
        Kick Back, 1993.
        Crack Down, 1994.
        Clean Break, 1995.
        Blue Genes, 1996.
        Star Struck, 1998.

    The Tony Hill Series:
        The Mermaids Singing, 1995.
        The Wire in the Blood, 1997.

Other:
    A Suitable Job for a Woman, 1995.

Edward Marston

♦

John Dickson Carr

John Dickson Carr
(1906–1977)

Biography

John Dickson Carr was born on 30 November, 1906, in Uniontown, Pennsylvania. He was educated at Hill School and Haverford College, Pennsylvania, where he published numerous early stories. In 1928 he sailed to Europe for further studies; marrying an Englishwoman, he lived in her country from 1932–48. His first novel appeared in 1930; thereafter he wrote another 70 mysteries as himself, Carr Dickson, Carter Dickson and Roger Fairbairn. His particular strength lay in the "miracle problem" or "impossible crime" with its emphasis on the "locked-room murder." A number of his detections were historical, some turning on actual crimes or time-travel. During the war he was a reviewer for the BBC and wrote numerous radio plays in addition to his novels. From 1969–1977 he was a reviewer for *Ellery Queen's Mystery Magazine.* His novels earned him two of The Mystery Writers of America's Edgar Allan Poe Awards in 1949 and in 1969; and Grand Master Award, 1962; he also served as its president, 1949. Carr married Englishwoman Clarice Cleaves in 1931; three daughters. He died on 17 February, 1977.

FOLLOW THAT CARR— AND STEP ON IT!

Before I say a single word about John Dickson Carr, lock all the doors. Secure the windows. Block any ventilation ducts. Let us get the conditions exactly right. Because the man whose work we are about to discuss is the Master of the Locked-Room Mystery, the hideous crime committed in a sealed chamber or in some other location impossible to enter or leave.

The sealed chamber may be a room, a prison cell, a tomb, a bank vault and so on. Other locations include a ship or, in *The Problem of the Wire Cage*, a tennis court—the wire cage is a protected area with four high walls. A murder victim is found lying on the court with no footprints in the sand surrounding it. How did the killer get in and out of the cage? Carr offers five different explanations, the most ingenious of which is that the murderer donned a pair of ballet shoes and made his way along the white baseline on his points before committing the crime, later making his escape by the same balletic route.

Imagine, if you will, Arnold Schwarzenegger playing the villain in a film version of this novel and having to turn himself into a ballet dancer to commit this perfect crime. What works superbly on the page would simply not work in visual terms.

My title for this talk is *Follow That Carr—and Step on It!* Because no matter how fast you drive, John Dickson Carr always stays ahead of you. Just when you think you're catching him up, you come to a traffic island with a series of roads leaving off it. One is called Supernatural Street. A second is Historical Avenue. A third is Locked-Room Lane. A fourth is the Ghost Boulevard. Other roads lead to radio plays, to short stories, to essays, to articles, to anything and everything which can be produced by the pen of an indefatigable crime writer.

The moment you believe that you've pinned him down, Carr turns into something else like a shape-changing alien. What always remains constant, however, is the cunning of his plots and the brilliance of his imagination.

Let me give you a profile of a writer. He's a foreigner who marries an Englishwoman and who learns to write her language superbly. A man who falls in love with English history and who takes it to the point of an obsession. A dramatist with a love of the medium of radio. A man who reinvents himself with pseudonyms. A versatile and prolific author, who, having mastered one type of crime story, immediately turns his attention to another.

Well, that's enough about me. Let's talk about John Dickson Carr, an author with whom I feel a deep affinity although I could never match his variety or his remarkable output.

I will not dwell too much on the life of my subject. The definitive biography is *John Dickson Carr: The Man Who Explained Miracles*. It is written by Douglas G. Greene and is a wonderful piece of scholarship. I urge you to read it as an example of how an author's life is dictated by his compulsion to write. Note the subtitle: *The Man Who Explained Miracles*.

Carr makes the crimes appear miraculous but there is always a logical explanation for them.

John Dickson Carr was born in 1906 in Uniontown, Pennsylvania. He studied at Haverford College. His father was a lawyer and an activist in Democratic politics, becoming a member of the House of Representatives. Carr's first published detective stories appeared in *The Haverfordian*, his college magazine. And even at that age, we can see flashes of a rare talent and identify the themes and material that were to attract him throughout his career.

With foolish optimism, his parents sent him to the Sorbonne in Paris for an education. What he found in the swirling Bohemian atmosphere of the Left Bank in the 1920s was confirmation of his destiny. He would be a writer. Not for him the security of the law or any other respectable LeCarré profession. In a Paris where Hemingway, F. Scott Fitzgerald and other literary figures flourished, Carr was in his element.

Before we take him any further, let us see what his relation is to some of the other classic writers being discussed at this convention. Carr did not get on at all with Raymond Chandler or with Dashiell Hammett. Indeed, he had battles with both in print. They were the chief representatives of the hard-nosed, hard-boiled, down-these-mean-streets detectives from the *Black Mask* school. Preoccupied as he was with playing fair with his readers, Carr felt that his rivals cheated.

He described Chandler and Hammett as "clueless" in the sense of disdaining clues that would make the solution of a mystery more credible. "The clueless meandering which runs riot through their works" is how he described it in a letter to a friend. Carr took issue with Chandler in particular and they locked horns. Chandler called him a "pipsqueak" in print, but stronger epithets were no doubt used of Carr in private. Hammett was less objectionable as a writer to Carr and there were aspects of Hammett's work that he praised. But the Hammett world was so far removed from his own that they could never be looked upon as kindred spirits.

Dorothy L. Sayers was one of his idols and her favorable reviews of his work were an immense help to him. She was the revered president of The Detection Club, the elite society of crime writers he was eventually invited to join. And he spent many happy evenings at club meetings, discussing his work with her.

Edmund Crispin—also to be honoured with a paper at this convention—described Carr as "One of the two or three best detective writers since Poe." When you recall that John Dickson Carr also wrote as Carter Dickson, you might wish to amend that judgement to read that he was "at least two of the best three detective writers since the great Edgar Allan." Crispin made his comment in the 1940s, a time when there were so many fine crime writers at work. You can see what a supreme compliment it was.

Carr also worshipped Arthur Conan Doyle and co-authored a biography with Doyle's eldest surviving son, Adrian. Whenever Carr worked on a non-fiction book, its impact could be seen on his subsequent novels. He learned much from Conan Doyle but he was never one to ape another writer slavishly. Carr could be influenced by others without seeming in any way derivative.

So here we have a man who is right at the heart of our classic territory, writing mainly in the 1930s, when it was said of him that one of the great joys of reading was that one could count on no less than *four* new novels a year from his tireless pen. Each one maintained the same high standard. Having a facility to write is not the same as being facile. Because Carr was so fertile, he must not be dismissed as a machine that turned out books. He was a true professional with an unending flow of ideas for stories and an eagerness to put them on paper.

The concept of fair play lies at the centre of his work. I believe that this is because of his crucial meeting with Clarice Cleaves, the charming young Englishwoman whom he encountered on a transatlantic voyage. Marriage to Clarice was not only a consummation of his love affair with England, it encouraged him to emigrate from America and it instilled in him the peculiarly English obsession with fair play.

This obsession was best seen in the sporting arena in the great English public schools of the nineteenth century. It was vital to strive hard in any sporting contest but always within the rules. "Play up! Play up! And play the game!" It was still a powerful idea in the 1930s when Carr came to England. National teams did well in a variety of sports. When they were beaten by foreigners, the most frequent complaint was that the victors had cheated—they had played dirty.

Carr had this Anglo-Saxon commitment to fair play. He felt that it was essential for an author to stick by the rules with his readers and play the game. He gave them a wide sprinkling of clues in his books and allowed the reader to discover them at exactly the same time as his detective. When Gideon Fell or Sir Henry Merrivale surprises us with deductive powers, they are working from material which has been set out honestly before us. They do not produce vital clues out of the air or know something deliberately kept from the reader.

This means that Carr had to work out his novels in advance in great detail. His carpentry is first-rate. Everything is dovetailed. The reader never gets splinters.

His professional career began when he reworked a short story which had first appeared in *The Haverfordian*. It was called *It Walks By Night*. The Gothic title was appropriate for a novel with many supernatural elements and some splendid excesses. His protagonist is Henri Bencolin, prefect of police in Paris. What sets him apart from Carr's later and more famous detectives is that Bencolin is French and comes from a wholly different culture. Again, he is a professional with the resources of a police department at his back. And, finally, he has very clear principles of detection. When other sleuths rely on intuition and guesswork, Bencolin employs a procedural method.

Carr does not make his detective a shining hero. Indeed, he is keen to throw the emphasis on the crime rather than on the man who is trying to solve it. Listen to this description of Henri Bencolin from *It Walks By Night*. This is how the readers first made his acquaintance.

> Your first impression...was one of liking and respect. You felt that you could tell him anything, however foolish it sounded, and he would be neither surprised nor inclined to laugh at you. Then you studied the face, turned partly sideways—the droop of the eyelids, at once quizzical and tolerant, under hooked eyebrows, and the dark veiled light of the eyes themselves. The nose was thin and aquiline, with deep lines running down past his mouth. A faint smile was lost in a small moustache and a

pointed black beard.... He rarely gestured when he spoke, except to shrug his shoulders, and he never raised his voice; but whenever you were in this man's company, you felt uncomfortably conspicuous.

Bencolin is not brought in with a roll of drums nor is he given the handsome features of the standard hero. He is a rather shadowy figure, quiet, reserved, and yet formidable. He investigates the murder of a young woman, an aristocrat, whose dead body is found half-naked. This was a bold touch in the 1930s when half-naked ladies were simply not found in novels, even when they were set in France. It put a sexual element in the crime which was quite daring for its day.

The novel pursues a wild and sometimes uproarious course with moments of Gothic vividness. Bencolin solves the crime in a manner familiar to readers of Agatha Christie. He gathers his suspects in a room, dissects the motives and behaviour of each one in turn, then identifies the killer. In the earlier version he had them chained to their chairs, but Carr wisely omitted this extravagance in the published novel.

Five more Bencolin novels were to follow, and a clutch of short stories, but Carr wanted to create an English detective who worked in the beloved country which the author had adopted. That is when Carr's finest character, Dr. Gideon Fell, stepped on to the page. The name was inspired by the famous epigram:

> I do not love thee, Doctor Fell.
> The reason why I cannot tell;
> But this alone I know full well,
> I do not love thee, Doctor Fell.

Gideon Fell is a glorious amateur. Physically, and in other ways, he is based very clearly on G.K. Chesterton, the creator of the immortal Father Brown. Chesterton was a massive man with an international reputation in the literary field. His agile brain and keen sense of humour made him a distinctive personality. Carr admired him enormously and there are traces of that admiration in the portrait we get of Gideon Fell in his first outing, *Hag's Nook*. But what is surprising about this book is its lyrical opening, a reminder that Carr was no mere purveyor of mechanical plots. He had the gift of language.

> The old lexicographer's study ran the length of his small house. It was a rafted room, sunk a few feet below the level

> of the door; the latticed windows at the rear were shaded by the yew tree, through which the late afternoon sun was striking now.
>   There is something spectral about the deep and drowsy beauty of the English countryside; in the lush dark grass, the evergreens, the grey church spire and the meandering white road. To an American, who remembers his own brisk concrete highways clogged with red filling stations and the fumes of traffic, it is particularly pleasant. It suggests a place where people really can walk without seeming incongruous, even in the middle of the road. Tad Rampole watched the sun through the latticed windows, and the dull red berries glistening in the yew tree, with a feeling which can haunt the traveller only in the British Isles. A feeling that the world is old and enchanted; a sense of reality in all the flashing images which are conjured up by that one word "merrie".

After this lyrical and sentimental opening, we are introduced to the great detective himself. It is not a dramatic entry but Gideon Fell quickly establishes his presence.

> Dr. Fell wheezed a little, even with the exertion of filling his pipe. He was very stout, and walked, as a rule, with two canes. Against the light from the front windows, his big mop of dark hair, streaked with a white plume, waved like a war banner. Immense and aggressive, it went blowing before him through life. His face was large and round and ruddy, and had a twitching smile somewhere above several chins. But what you noticed there was the twinkle in his eye. He wore eyeglasses on a broad black ribbon...he could be fiercely combative or slyly chuckling, and somehow he contrived to be both at the same time.

The resemblance to Chesterton is unmistakable. Carr was an admirer of his work and of his flamboyant personality. He dearly wanted to meet Chesterton, then president of The Detection Club. By the time that Carr finally joined this exclusive group, Chesterton had died and his admirer was unable to develop the friendship with him he had sought. In the person of Gideon Fell, however, G.K. Chesterton was to live on.

Fell is described as a lexicographer but he is not really compiling a dictionary. Nor does he have Chesterton's passionate interest in Roman Catholic theology. Fell's labour of love is his history of the drinking habits of the English nation, research for which is often of a liquid nature. His quaffing of English ale has given him his Falstaffian girth.

The archetypal Fell novel is *The Hollow Man*. Its American title was *The Three Coffins*. It shows Carr at his best and the Locked-Room Mystery at its most baffling. The plot concerns a certain Grimaud, who we assume is French, who meets with a group of friends each week to talk about ghosts and the supernatural. A stranger called Pierre Fley bursts in and warns Grimaud that the latter's brother will try to kill him. Fley announces that he must go because he, too, fears the brother. When the strange visitor rushes out, the only clue he leaves behind is a visiting-card: *Pierre Fley, Illusionist*.

It is a vital clue to the reader, who is being warned to take nothing on its surface appearance. Illusion is the art of disguise, of showing one thing in order to conceal another. It may involve the cunning use of light, mirrors or special devices and it is a key part of Carr's own stock-in-trade.

When Fell comes on the scene, he discovers that Grimaud has been killed in a locked room. It is a study on the top floor and a plan of that part of the building is given in the book. The study has been locked from the inside by the key in the door. There is a painting, propped up lengthwise against the bookshelves. Chairs, sofa and rug have been disarranged. The murder victim lies in the middle of the room.

Here is the ultimate locked room with no means of entry or exit for the killer. How has the crime been committed? Fell smokes a cigar as he listens to statements from those in the house, then he makes his own deductions. Pressing his hands to his temples and ruffling his mop of hair, he startles them all with his insights.

> You see, neither Grimaud nor Dumont is any more French than I am. A woman with those cheek-bones, a woman who pronounces the silent 'h' in honest never came from a Latin race. They're both Magyar. To be precise: Grimaud came originally from Hungary. His real name is Karoly, or Charles, Grimaud Horvath. He probably had a French mother. He came from the principality of Transylvania, formerly a part of the Hungarian kingdom, but annexed by Rumania since the War. In the late nineties or early nineteen-hundreds, Karoly Grimaud Horvarth and his two brothers were all sent to prison. Did I tell you he had two brothers? One we haven't seen, the other now calls himself Pierre Fley.

All the information given here is waved before the reader's eyes in advance. For instance, Hungarian translations of Shakespeare's plays are on the bookshelf. In the course of his analysis, Gideon

Fell says that the three brothers were imprisoned for some unspeakable crime. The three coffins are also mentioned. And the link with Transylvania is set up.

Earlier in the story, Carr has mentioned one of the logical explanations for the Dracula myth. When the contorted and blood-covered bodies were found in graveyards, they were said to be the victims of Count Dracula. Carr argues that they could just as well have been plague victims, who were sometimes buried before they were properly dead and who, reviving in their coffins, tried desperately to scratch and force their way out. Hence, their contorted limbs and the blood over their hands, face and body.

When the story moves towards its climax, Gideon Fell breaks off to give us *The Locked-Room Lecture*, the best and fullest description of this phenomenon. Fell does not cheat. He has other people in the room, who question him at every stage and challenge him in the way that the reader would. A crime is committed in a hermetically sealed room from which no murderer has escaped because no murderer was actually in the room. Here are Fell's possible explanations in *The Hollow Man*:

> 1. It is not murder, but a series of coincidences ending in an accident which looks like murder.
> 2. It is murder, but the victim is impelled to kill himself or crash into an accidental death.
> 3. It is murder, by a mechanical device already hidden in the room and planted undetectably in some innocent-looking piece of furniture.
> 4. It is suicide, which is intended to look like murder.
> 5. It is a murder which derives its problem from illusion and impersonation.
> 6. It is a murder which, although committed by somebody outside the room at the time, nevertheless seems to have been committed by somebody who seems to have been inside.
> 7. It is a murder in which the victim is presumed to be dead long before he actually is. The victim lies asleep (drugged but unharmed) in a locked room. Knockings on the door fail to rouse him. The murderer starts a foul-play scare; forces the door, gets in ahead and kills by stabbing or throat-cutting.

Fell juggles all the possibilities and comes up with an answer which is truly ingenious and which makes *The Hollow Man* such a classic of the genre.

Carr's other great detective is Sir Henry Merrivale, who made his first appearance in *The Plague Court Murders* (1934) and went on to feature in over twenty more novels. All of them were written under the pseudonym of Carter Dickson because publishers could not cope with the prolific output of John Dickson Carr.

Sir Henry Merrivale is very different from his predecessors. He is not a professional detective like Bencolin but he does have an important job as Chief of the Military Intelligence Department in the War Department. This would seem more to qualify him for tales of espionage than of criminal investigations, but Carr usually assigns him the latter brief. Even where Merrivale is involved in his official function, Carr avoids any discussion of the political implications of his work.

In *The Plague Court Murders*, we have our first encounter with the idiosyncratic Merrivale. Bencolin was not an especially likeable person; Fell was much more appealing and interesting. Carr is keen to establish Merrivale as another talented, outrageous and popular figure.

> I thought again of that high room over Whitehall, which I had not seen since 1922. I thought of the extremely lazy, extremely garrulous and slipshod figure who sat grinning with sleepy eyes; his hands folded over his big stomach and his feet propped up on the desk. His chief taste was for lurid reading-matter; his chief complaint that people would not treat him seriously. He was a qualified barrister and a qualified physician, and he spoke atrocious grammar. He was Sir Henry Merrivale, Baronet, and has been a fighting Socialist all his life. He was vastly conceited and had an inexhaustible fund of bawdy stories.

There is a clownish aspect to Merrivale that is constantly played on in the novels, but his brain is acute. In the end, he is always able to solve the apparently insoluble crimes. Like Gideon Fell, he has a wife and he talks very fondly about her in *Night at the Mocking Widow*. The fact that her name is Clementine—always referred to as "Clemmie"—has confirmed some people in the belief that Sir Henry Merrivale is based loosely on Winston Churchill. There are certain physical similarities, it is true, and Churchill's wife was also called Clementine but one cannot imagine Churchill holding Merrivale's eccentric political opinions or committing any of the grammatical solecisms which litter Merrivale's speeches.

Sir Henry Merrivale—or H.M. as he is usually called—has a great concern for his dignity. He is a figure of authority who expects to be accorded the proper respect. H.M. is, in every way, a fully-rounded character who gets involved in a whole range of fascinating cases but he never achieves the lift-off which Carr gives to Gideon Fell. H.M. is amusing where Fell can be hilarious; the former is discursive where the latter is incisive. And though we get more surface information about Sir Henry Merrivale, we somehow get to know Gideon Fell better.

In *Nine—and Death Makes Ten* (1940), H.M. is seen at his most characteristic. The British edition was published under the title of *Murder in the Submarine Zone*. It is one of Carr's most sombre works and is based on a transatlantic voyage which he and his wife, Clarice, made in September, 1939. Sailing from New York to London was a traumatic experience for them. German submarines had already sunk many Allied ships and there was no mercy shown to civilians on liners. When the *SS Athenia* was torpedoed on September 4th, 1939, over a hundred passengers lost their lives.

Carr sets his story in January, 1940, when the menace of German submarines had grown. The liner *Edwardic* sets sail from New York across an Atlantic Ocean infested with U-boats. Its destination is withheld for security reasons because the luxury ship has been converted into a munitions vessel. It travels without a convoy, because of the explosive nature of its cargo, the liner carries only nine passengers and its crew. When one passenger, Mrs. Zia Bey, is murdered, the killer must be aboard, since no one could possibly have joined or left the ship since it sailed.

Carr builds up the tension expertly. Carrying a secret cargo through enemy waters, the ship now has another deadly secret. Fortunately, one of the nine passengers is Sir Henry Merrivale and it is H.M. who leads the murder investigation. The topicality of the subject-matter gave this book a special *frisson* but it also provides H.M. with one of his most challenging cases. Although more subdued than in his other outings, H.M. finally unravels the mystery and really does explain a miracle to us. This is a brilliant example of the floating arsenal as a locked room in itself.

Writing about an existing wartime situation, Carr must also have had at the back of his mind the sinking of the *Lusitania* by a German submarine during the First World War. This was a case when a Cunard liner was torpedoed with the loss of 1200 lives, many of them Americans and other neutrals. The German justification for the attack on a passenger vessel was that it was carrying munitions, a contention which is still disputed.

Carr adds to the ever-present danger from outside his ship by giving us the murder inside it. He begins to wonder if espionage is involved and makes this observation about the true nature of spying.

> Espionage, son, is far from being a joke these days. It's wide and it's deep and it sinks under your feet—like that water out there. It runs much deeper than it did twenty-five years ago. Not picturesque like all the legends have made it, or always dealin' with very important issues. The proper agent's an ordinary insignificant sort of person. The clerk, the small professional man, the young girl, the middle-aged woman. Not askin' for rewards or even very brainy: but all fanatical idealists. You could shoot the lot of them without causing much of a flurry to G.H.Q. But each one of those little mites, individually, is a potential death's head.

This is an interesting aside but the novel is not a spy story. H.M. really belongs to the tradition of amateur espionage which so bedevilled our intelligence service in the first thirty years of this century. Sir Henry Merrivale is worlds away from the sophistication of a John LeCarré or Len Deighton. As a sleuth, he is far more comfortable and convincing.

When the villain has been unmasked, the novel ends with a lyrical passage which conveys exactly what Carr himself must have felt when his wartime voyage to England ended safely.

> A Sunday quiet held the ship. Commander Matthews, holding the bible clumsily, stood by the improvised rostrum and watched his passengers assemble. Again he read the Twenty-Third Psalm.... There were no hymns. There was no prayer. But, as the orchestra struck up at a signal from Commander Matthews, they sang *God Save The King*. And never had those words been sung more strongly, never was more sincerity poured from the heart, than when those strains rose to the roof and the great gray ship moved up the Channel; and, steady as a compass-needle in death and storm and peril and the darkness of great waters, the *Edwardic* came home.

Gideon Fell and Sir Henry Merrivale are the two major creative achievements of John Dickson Carr but he was not content simply to feature them in alternate novels. During the war, he turned to the writing of radio plays for the BBC. Some had a propagandist value but many were sheer entertainment, aimed at taking the listener's mind off the horrors of war. Radio was a medium of prime importance at that time, the best and quickest way to reach almost every household in the land. Not only would people crowd around their wireless sets to hear the latest news of the war itself, they would switch on in search of reassurance and diversion.

Carr's most famous radio drama series was *Appointment With Fear* in which the Man in Black starred. This part was ideally cast.

Valentine Dyall, a fine classical actor with a deep and dark voice, was the perfect Man in Black and he could send a shiver down the spines of the nation. I heard these plays as a small child and was so impressed with Valentine Dyall that I longed to work with him one day. My chance came twenty years later when I had him cast as the villain in a TV drama series which I wrote. The sepulchral voice was as rich and unsettling as ever.

Carr also wrote a series called *Cabin 13*, which was heard here in the States as well. The running character was the ship's surgeon. Whenever the vessel put into port on its travels, an incident would occur and our hero would be brought in to solve the mystery and save the day. The cabin, of course, is a sealed unit so beloved by Carr, and the nautical setting harks back to that shipboard romance he had with Clarice Cleaves and which helped to shape his whole life. His mastery of the techniques of radio drama is evident in every episode of *Cabin 13*.

In a short paper such as this, I have only been able to touch on part of John Dickson Carr's astonishing output. There is no room to discuss his historical novels or his many other experiments in fiction. His reputation rests largely on the twin pillars of Gideon Fell and Sir Henry Merrivale but there are countless other supporting stanchions.

Carr's heyday was the thirties and forties. The intellectual puzzle of the locked room mystery is no longer enough for the modern reader. Expectations from the crime novel have changed. Today's audience may find Carr's characterisation sometimes sketchy and—in the case of his female characters—rather unsatisfactory. Young women tend to be pretty ciphers rather than well-delineated human beings with a serious role to play in a novel. Romances are tossed in as backdrops and there is a vein of sentimentality that seeps in at times.

But the main body of John Dickson Carr's work still stands comparison with any of our classic authors. He has survived as well as any of them and improved with age. His ingenuity, his deviousness, his watertight plotting, his warm humour and his abiding sense of fair play still make him a most agreeable writer to read. Nobody produced better brain-teasers or left his readers with such a wonderful sense of resolution at the end of his books.

Follow That Carr—and Step On It! You will never catch up with him but you will have the most exhilarating chase.

Biography

Novels:
- *It Walks by Night* (first Henri Bencolin), 1930.
- *Castle Skull*, 1931.
- *The Lost Gallows*, 1931.
- *Poison in Jest*, 1932.
- *The Corpse in the Waxworks*, 1932.
- *Hag's Nook* (first Dr. Fell), 1933.
- *The Mad Hatter Mystery*, 1933.
- *The Blind Barber*, 1934.
- *The Eight of Swords*, 1934.
- *Devil Kinsmere* (as Fairbairn), 1934.
- *Death Watch*, 1935.
- *The Three Coffins* (*The Hollow Man* US), 1935.
- *The Arabian Nights Murder*, 1936.
- *The Burning Court*, 1937.
- *The Four False Weapons*, 1937.
- *To Wake the Dead*, 1938.
- *The Crooked Hinge*, 1938.
- *The Problem of the Green Capsule* (*The Black Spectacles* UK), 1939.
- *The Problem of the Wire Cage*, 1939.
- *The Man Who Could Not Shudder*, 1940.
- *The Case of the Constant Suicides*, 1941.
- *Death Turns the Tables* (*The Sea of the Scornful* UK), 1942.
- *The Emperor's Snuff Box*, 1943.
- *Till Death Do Us Part*, 1944.
- *He Who Whispers*, 1946.
- *The Sleeping Sphinx*, 1947.
- *The Dead Man's Knock*, 1948.
- *Below Suspicion*, 1949.
- *The Bride of Newgate*, 1950.
- *The Devil in Velvet*, 1951.
- *The Nine Wrong Answers*, 1952.
- *Captain Cut-Throat*, 1955.
- *Patrick Butler for the Defense*, 1956.
- *Fire, Burn!* 1957.
- *Scandal at High Chimneys: A Victorian Melodrama*, 1959.
- *In Spite of Thunder*, 1960.
- *The Witch of the Lowtide: An Edwardian Melodrama*, 1961.
- *The Demoniacs*, 1962.
- *The House at Satan's Elbow*, 1965.
- *Panic in Box C*, 1966.
- *Dark of the Moon*, 1967.
- *Papa La-Bas*, 1968.
- *The Ghost's High Noon*, 1969.
- *Deadly Hall*, 1971.
- *The Hungry Goblin: A Victorian Detective Novel*, 1972.
- *No Flowers by Request and Crime on the Coast* (with others), 1984.

As Carter Dickson:
  The Bowstring Murders (as Carr Dickson), 1934 (the first Sir Henry Merrivale....)
  The Plague Court Murders, 1934.
  Death in Five Boxes, 1938.
  The Judas Window, 1939.
  Nine—and Death Makes Ten (*Murder in the Submarine Zone* UK), 1940.
  The Curse of the Bronze Lamp, 1945.
  The Cavalier's Cup (the last), 1953.

Short Stories:
  The Department of Queer Complaints (as Carter Dickson), 1940.
  Dr. Fell, Detective, and Other Stories, 1947.
  The Third Butler and Other Stories, 1954.
  The Exploits of Sherlock Holmes, with Adrian Conan Doyle, 1954.
  The Men Who Explained Miracles, 1963.
  Later collections, ed. by Douglas G. Greene.

Other:
  The Murder of Sir Edmund Godfrey, 1936.
  The Life of Sir Arthur Conan Doyle, 1949.
  Plays, Radio Plays, Anthologies. For a complete bibliography, refer to Greene.

Critical Studies:
  S.T. Joshi, *John Dickson Carr: A Critical Study*, 1990.
  Douglas G. Greene, *John Dickson Carr: The Man Who Explained Miracles*, 1995.

Edward Marston

Biography

Edward Marston came from Wales to read Modern History at Oxford. He has been a university lecturer, radio, television, and theatre dramatist, and in addition to writing has worked as an actor, director, and dramatist. He is the author of two mystery series, one Elizabethan in background, the other revolving around the Domesday census of 1086 A.D., and has written crime novels with golf and sports backgrounds under his actual name, Keith Miles. He was a nominee for the Edgar Allan Poe Award for Best Novel for *The Roaring Boy*, and is a well-known host and raconteur at mystery events as well as former Chairman of the Crime Writers' Association. When not traveling or fulfilling speaking engagements, he and his wife live in rural isolation in Kent.

Bibliography

Novels:
    The Nicholas Bracewell Series:
        The Queen's Head, 1988.
        The Merry Devils, 1989.
        The Trip to Jerusalem, 1990.
        The Nine Giants, 1991.
        The Mad Courtesan, 1992.
        The Silent Woman, 1994.
        The Roaring Boy, 1995.
        The Laughing Hangman, 1996.
        The Fair Maid of Bohemia, 1997.
        The Wanton Angel, 1998.

    The Domesday Books:
        The Wolves of Savernake, 1993.
        The Ravens of Blackwater, 1994.
        The Dragons of Archenfield, 1995.
        The Lions of the North, 1996.
        The Serpents of Harbledon, 1997.
        The Stallions of Woodstock, 1997.
        The Hawks of Delamere, 1998.
        The Wildcats of Exeter, 1998.
        The Foxes of Warwick, 1999.

    The Alan Saxon Golf Mysteries (as Keith Miles):
        Bullet Hole, 1986.
        Double Eagle, 1987.
        Green Murder, 1990.
        Flagstick, 1991.

    Other:
        Stone Dead (as Martin Inigo), 1991.
        Touch Play (as Martin Inigo), 1991.
        Murder in Perspective (as Keith Miles), 1997.

Other:
    Numerous other Sports Books, Screen, Stage and Television, Plays, Children's Books, and Non-fiction (as Keith Miles).

H.R.F. Keating

◆

Dorothy L. Sayers

Dorothy L. Sayers
(1893–1957)

Biography

Dorothy Leigh Sayers was born in Oxford on 13 July, 1893. She was educated at the Godolphin School, Salisbury, 1909–11, and Somerville College, Oxford, 1912–15, B.A. (honours) in French, and M.A., 1920. She taught modern languages at Hull High School for Girls in Yorkshire, 1915–1917, was a reader for Blackwell publishers, 1917–18, assistant at Les Roches School, France, 1919–20, and then spent 1922–29 as a copywriter for Benson's advertising agency, London, where she coined several famous slogans. From 1931 she was a full-time writer and broadcaster. She was a member of the Modern Language Association (president, 1939–45); and a founding member of the Detection Club (president, 1949–57). An active theologian, she acted as Vicar's Warden, St. Thomas', Regent Street, 1952–54; and St. Paul's, 1954–57. The University of Durham awarded her the D. Litt., 1950. Married Oswald A. Fleming in 1926 (died 1950); one illegitimate son. She died on 17 December, 1957.

Dorothy L. Sayers

At the *AZ Murder Goes...Classic* conference I was slated to speak after the performance by my wife, Sheila Mitchell, of Catherine Kenney's play *Dorothy L—A Dramatic Portrait of Dorothy L. Sayers*. I had been asked to talk about Dorothy L. Sayers and the Detection Club, of which I am one of her successors in the President's chair. I had prepared a moderately long talk leading from anecdotes about Dorothy Sayers and the Club into a consideration of the detective story and whether the genre to which she contributed so much is still valid. However, in the event it seemed it would be trying the patience of our audience too much to speak at length after the 90-minute, demanding play. So here I set down the latter part of what I would have said under the title....

Is the Detective Story Dead?
It is often said nowadays that the Detective Story, such as Dorothy L. Sayers and Agatha Christie wrote in the 1930s, is outmoded. It has been overtaken and even outclassed, they say, by "the crime novel," the suspense novel, and the thriller. It is true that the majority of mystery or crime fiction written today can best be described, to use an old term, as Sensation Fiction. However, to my mind all these books, which are highly attractive to the contemporary reader and not a few of which are very well-written, may nevertheless be described as the primeval slime out of which the Detective Story painfully rose up.

Slime is a harsh word to use. But it is surely hardly an unjust way of describing books that rely almost exclusively on rousing excitement or on horror, on books that feature lengthily, and lovingly, described gruesome corpses, whether seen in the forensic laboratory or with head, or worse, slashed off by the innocent roadside. These are the books all too similar to those that the Detective Story sloughed off when it came into existence, books that G.K. Chesterton, the first President of the Detection Club, castigated in the 1930s for their "incessant and reckless propagation of wicked Chinamen." The sole difference, it often seems to me, is that now the Chinamen have been replaced by serial killers, every bit as recklessly propagated.

I am not, be it noted, knocking any fiction that has in it what the late Stanley Ellin once called "a streak of wickedness." I am not advocating a universal return to "the cosy" in its most hygienic and mellow form, though such books are still written and still attract their public, not all of them in Britain. Any such condemnation would come ill from the author of, for instance, *The Rich Detective*, a novel with its full share of the underside of life, criminality, drugs, prostitution, but which yet can trace its descent from the detective story of old with its start-to-finish tug of murders and the mystery of how they were committed.

But what exactly is the Detective Story that I have described as rising from the primeval slime of Sensation Fiction? Its earliest origins are hard precisely to locate. Edgar Allan Poe, of course, laid down the basic conditions the form demands. First and foremost there was the Great Detective, that figure set up as an example of what a human being can do possessed of enough powers. Then there was the Watson (as he later came to be called), the narrator's admiring friend who could be used simultaneously to keep from the reader the startling solution to the mystery and to draw attention to the Great Detective's astonishing powers. And, at the opposite pole, Poe drew the first outlines of the unseeing police detective, the man working strictly according to the confining rules of simple reason. Together with such lesser discoveries as the Least Likely Person and the murderer who leaves false clues, there laid down for subsequent writers were the basic necessaries.

But they were laid down only in three short stories, and as such it was long and long before the ideas they postulated were taken up. Nor with Poe's magnificent successor, Conan Doyle, was the form of the Detective Story immediately established. Both *A Study in Scarlet* and *The Sign of the Four* are splendid tales, but neither of them is a classic Detective Story. Muddy traces of the primeval slime of Sensation Fiction still cling.

The Detective Story in its right and proper form did not appear, I believe, until in 1920 Agatha Christie's first book, *The Mysterious Affair at Styles*, came out, having languished in some five or six publishers' drawers before it eventually saw the light of day. In America it had to wait another six years before publication. All Mrs. Christie, indeed, thought she was doing with it was responding to a challenge from her sister to "write one of those detective stories," by which she meant only a story with a detective in it who is likely to learn much more than the reader ever gets to know before the final surprise solution.

But unwittingly (which is perhaps the best way to make a discovery) Agatha Christie had taken the one vital step out of the primeval slime.... She had written a book that contained no emotional entanglements with any of its characters. They are lively figures, of course, but as you read you never passionately want any one of them not to have committed the murder. Here, in fact, was a purely intellectual novel, not that this implied it was not wonderfully easy to read. Here, at last, was the *Pure Puzzle*.

And, thanks in no small measure to the creation of that unlikely but lively figure Hercule Poirot, the book was seen as an example to copy. Luck, as is often the case, also contributed to Mrs. Christie's success. The book came out at a time when many women, thanks to such new or newish devices as the vacuum-cleaner, had more leisure than ever before (and no radio, much less any television, to while away the time with). So, slowly at first but then with increasing rapidity, the puzzle detective story caught on until, in the year 1928, a group of writers of this sort of book felt it necessary to band together, however informally, as the Detection Club. Its sole serious object, Dorothy L. Sayers wrote at about this time, was to "keep the detective story up to the highest standards that its nature permits, and to free it from the bad legacy of sensationalism, clap-trap and jargon."

But these words had scarcely come from her pen when, as is the way with human beings, a contradictory idea came to take possession, simultaneous possession, of her mind. It was the idea she embodied in the two books she published in 1930, *The Documents in the Case* and *Strong Poison*, the latter the story in which, in flaunted opposition to her own condemnation of "heroes who insist on fooling" with members of the opposite sex, Lord Peter fell in love with Harriet Vane. However, although Dorothy Sayers disobeyed, or at least disregarded, the rule about the necessary purity of the puzzle in both these books (in *The Documents* she introduced a serious philosophical theme), she did not plunge the form back into the primeval slime.... Instead, she contrived with much skill to run as it were side by side the Novel, that is the fiction which aims emotionally to entangle the reader, and the Detective Story, the pure intellectual puzzle.

This is her great legacy to all subsequent mystery writers. She showed us how you could use the wonderfully ongoing form of the Detective Story, the puzzle demanding an answer, in the very same pages as you could do all or most of the things the Novel can do. It is an inheritance which may be said to have culminated in the novels of P.D. James, though it has dozens of other distinguished practitioners on both sides of the Atlantic. So it is particularly appropriate perhaps to recall in conclusion P.D. James's definition of the rules of the Detective Story, noting only that these are not rules outwardly imposed by the Detection Club or any other body but are simply the necessary factors required in writing in this particular form.

P.D. James then has listed them as these:

> ...a mysterious death at the heart of the book (This is what gives to what might be a trivial game its importance in the reader's mind.); a closed circle of suspects (This contributes to the game element that is still necessary by insisting on "fair play" between reader and writer.); each suspect to have a credible motive, the practical opportunity to commit the crime and reasonable access to the means with which (perhaps only eventually revealed) it is committed (A condition which the writer of the modern detective story is able to fulfill often only by limiting the number of suspects far more rigidly than to the number of suspects indicated in the American title of Michael Innes' first book, *Seven Suspects*.); finally, the central character is to be the Detective who is to solve the mystery by deduction from facts that have been shown to the reader.

Using these seemingly trivial tools, crime writers today can do almost anything that their colleagues in the world of the mainstream novel can do, but with the added advantage of keeping their readers reading, wanting to know the answer to that simple but compelling question, "Who done it?" So no, although the Detective Story may be, as it were, lurking in the shadows it is by no means dead, nor is it ever likely to be.

Bibliography

Novels:
  (Lord Peter Wimsey all titles):
    Whose Body?, 1923.
    Clouds of Witness, 1926.
    Unnatural Death (*The Dawson Pedigree* US), 1927.
    The Unpleasantness at the Bellona Club, 1928.
    The Five Red Herrings (*Suspicious Characters* US), 1931.
    The Floating Admiral, with others, 1931.
    Murder Must Advertise, 1933.
    Ask a Policeman, with others, 1933.
    The Nine Tailors, 1934.
    Six Against the Yard, with others (*Six Against Scotland Yard* US), 1936.
    Double Death: A Murder Story, with others, 1939.
    The Scoop, and *Behind the Screen*, with others, 1983.
    Crime on the Coast, and *No Flowers by Request*, with others, 1984.

  The Peter Wimsey/Harriet Vane Novels:
    Strong Poison, 1930.
    Have His Carcase, 1932.
    Gaudy Night, 1935.
    Busman's Honeymoon, 1937.
    Thrones, Dominations, completed by Jill Walsh, 1998.

  Other:
    The Documents in the Case, with Robert Eustace, 1930.

Short Stories Collections:
  Lord Peter Views the Body, 1928.
  Hangman's Holiday, 1933.
  In the Teeth of the Evidence and Other Stories, 1939.
  A Treasury of Sayers Stories, 1958.
  Lord Peter: A Collection of All the Lord Peter Wimsey Stories, ed. by J. Sandoe, 1972.
  Striding Folly, 1972.

Other:
  Plays, Poetry, Essays, Theology, Translations, and Addresses.

Critical Studies:
  Janet Hitchman, *Such a Strange Lady*, 1975.
  Barbara Reynolds, ed., *Letters of Dorothy L. Sayers*, 1996.
  Catherine Kenney, *The Remarkable Case of Dorothy L. Sayers: vol 1*, 1996; *vol. 2*, 1998.
  Barbara Reynolds, *Dorothy L. Sayers: Her Life and Soul*, 1993.
  Alzina Stone Dale, *Dorothy L. Sayers, The Centenary Celebration*, 1993.

H. R. F. Keating
Biography

There isn't enough room to detail the highly successful career of author, critic, and editor H.R.F. Keating, past chairman of the Crime Writers Association and the Society of Authors, and current president of the Detection Club, the prestigious association earlier led by Chesterton, Sayers, Christie, and Symons. Educated at the Merchant Taylor's School and at Trinity College, Dublin, he was for some years a journalist. His first Ins. Ghote mystery, *The Perfect Murder*, won the 1964 Gold Dagger from the CWA and an Edgar Allen Poe Award in 1965 from the MWA. For fifteen years, Keating was the chief crime fiction reviewer for *The Times*. He initiated a new series with *The Rich Detective* in 1993. September, 1996, witnessed a new Ins. Ghote in *Asking Questions*. In the 1980s he published three mysteries under the pseudonym Evelyn Hervey, and he has a long list of short stories, bibliography, biography, criticism, reviews, and other writings to his credit. Keating lives in London with his wife, the actress Sheila Mitchell. On May 1, 1996, Keating was presented with the Diamond Dagger Award at the House of Lords.

Bibliography

Novels:
  The Ins. Ganesh Ghote Series:
  The Perfect Murder, 1964.
  Inspector Ghote's Good Crusade, 1965.
  Inspector Ghote Caught in Meshes, 1968.
  Inspector Ghote Hunts the Peacock, 1968.
  Inspector Ghote Plays a Joker, 1969.
  Inspector Ghote Breaks an Egg, 1970.
  Inspector Ghote Goes by Train, 1971.
  Inspector Ghote Trusts the Heart, 1972.
  Bats Fly Up for Inspector Ghote, 1974.
  A Remarkable Case of Burglary, 1975.
  Filmi, Filmi, Inspector Ghote, 1976.
  Inspector Ghote Draws a Line, 1979,
  The Murder of the Maharajah, 1980.
  Go West, Inspector Ghote, 1981.
  The Sheriff of Bombay, 1984.
  Under a Monsoon Cloud, 1986.
  The Body in the Billiard Room, 1987.
  Dead on Time, 1989.
  Inspector Ghote, His Life and Crimes, 1989.
  The Iciest Sin, 1990.
  Cheating Death, 1994.
  Doing Wrong, 1994.
  Asking Questions, 1996.

  The Harriet Unwin Series (as Evelyn Hervey):
  The Governess, 1984
  The Man of Gold, 1985.
  Into the Valley of Death, 1986.

  The Detective Series:
  The Rich Detective, 1993.
  The Good Detective, 1994.
  The Bad Detective, 1995.
  The Soft Detective, 1997.

  Other:
  Death and the Visiting Fireman, 1959.
  Zen There Was Murder, 1960.
  A Rush on the Ultimate, 1961.
  The Dog It Was That Died, 1962.
  Death of a Fat God, 1963.
  Is Skin Deep, Is Fatal, 1965.
  Mrs. Craggs: Crimes Cleaned Up, 1986 (short stories).
  In Kensington Gardens, 1997 (short stories).

Plus 4 Novels, numerous uncollected Short Stories, several Radio Plays, over half a dozen Anthologies, Bibliography, Biography, criticism, and among the Non-fiction:

Murder Must Appetize, 1975.
Sherlock Holmes, The Man and His World, 1979.
Crime and Mystery: The 100 Best Books, 1987.
The Bedside Companion to Crime, 1990.

Miriam Grace Monfredo

♦

Daphne du Maurier

Daphne du Maurier
(1907-1989)

Biography

> I awoke to despondency on January 1st, 1930. What if my novel turned out to be no good? I have a sudden conviction that my book is not only dull but badly written, that it might as well be in the waste paper basket.

This lament reflects what almost surely has been believed at one time or another by every author since the birth of the written word. But the voice here belongs to British author Daphne du Maurier (referring to her first novel, *The Loving Spirit),* whose work for several decades in the mid-twentieth century appeared with regularity on bestseller lists in Europe and North America. Du Maurier was born into a family that possessed a rich historic and artistic legacy, and was one of three daughters of former actress Muriel Beaumont and her husband, successful actor-manager Gerald du Maurier. Du Maurier's parents seemed to have suffered no financial constraints and she, by her own admission, had few parental restraints. She said in her autobiography (*Myself When Young*) that she was frequently criticized for shunning publicity, for being a recluse, but that she was by nature shy and felt awkward with those outside her circle of family and friends. Du Maurier had written three novels by the time she met and married Major Frederick Arthur Montague Browning ("Tommy"), by whom she had two daughters and a son. She lived a significant portion of her life in the county of Cornwall, which became the setting for several of her books.

Du Maurier's published work consists of six collections of short fiction, two plays, eleven works of non-fiction, and fifteen novels, and she was described in her obituaries as one who helped to shape popular culture and the modern imagination. Her fiction is often labeled romantic literature, but, as we shall see, it is not that easy to pigeonhole her work.

Last Night I Dreamt I Went to Manderley Again

I would be inclined to wager that most novel readers in the English-speaking world, at least those over a certain age, will recognize that sentence as the opening line of Daphne du Maurier's *Rebecca*. In terms of recognition and endurance, it ranks right up there with "Call me Ishmael" and "It was the best of times, it was the worst of times." Why is it so memorable? Not because of its interesting cadence—many skilled writers can manage that or better than that. It is probably because *Rebecca*'s opening line does precisely what a novel's opening line is supposed to do: capture in a very few words either its viewpoint character or its motif. "Last night I dreamt I went to Manderly again" succeeds in doing both.

And of course the instant recognition factor was helped by the fact that *Rebecca* became wildly popular and remained so for years. In fact, during a few decades in the middle of the century, it seemed as if everyone who had read anything at all had read *Rebecca*. First published in 1938, it wasn't by any means du Maurier's first novel, and it wasn't necessarily her best one (du Maurier herself said, toward the end of her life, that she could never figure out why the book *was* so popular), but it was her first bestseller. And, whether it deserves to be or not, *Rebecca* remains du Maurier's most well-known work.

Her short fiction, however, comprises some of her best work. (Although collections of these are out of print in the United States and can usually be unearthed only by digging through the shelves of used and rare bookstores.) For sheer imaginativeness, originality, and skillful construction many of her short stories are superior to some of her novels. *The Birds* became the best known because of the unfortunate, Hitchcock film of the same name; and in fact, the movie bears little resemblance (surprise, surprise) to du Maurier's chilling masterpiece. Some of her other stories also stand with the best suspense short fiction of all time. One particularly powerful short, *The Blue Lenses*, shows du Maurier to be a direct literary descendant of Edgar Allan Poe and a much superior predecessor to Stephen King. *The Little Photographer*, moody and atmospheric and disturbing, is one of my own favorites.

Don't Look Now, also made into a film, is a sinister, frightening piece, and vividly demonstrates du Maurier's macabre streak. When this little gem was published, it was too far ahead of its time to receive the recognition it should have, undoubtedly because, in du Maurier's own assessment, "no one seemed to understand it." But the movie became somewhat of a cult classic and she gained a new generation of readers. *The Breakthrough*, a memorable and well-constructed story, is a science fiction short requested by Kingsley Amis, and about which du Maurier said, "...although I don't know a thing about science fiction, I thought I would have a go—it's rather a challenge..."

Du Maurier clearly enjoyed a challenge, and she took risks. In *The Rebecca Notebook*, she wrote that for years she continued to receive letters from all over the world, asking why she never gave *Rebecca*'s viewpoint character a name. The answer, she said, was a simple one. "I *could not* think of one, and it became a challenge in technique..." And she gave herself an added challenge in *Rebecca*, as there have been very few successful novels in which, before even the opening line, the main character is dead.

In addition to novels and short stories, du Maurier wrote two plays, and a travel book about her beloved Cornwall. She also did a number of biographies: one about Branwell Bronte (she said the Bronte family had always fascinated her) and two that dealt with the Bacons, Francis and Anthony. These more scholarly biographies, done rather late in her career, were not particularly well-received. But an early one that she had written about her father, *Gerald*, brought some of her first critical recognition.

She drew on her ancestors for several others books that are not among my du Maurier favorites. I want to say a few words about them, but you should be warned, since my own concentration is historical mysteries, that I may be somewhat less than trustworthy here. In du Maurier's words:

> Writers are said to draw upon their own experiences. Some, perhaps; not all. Men and women who have never lived make finer captives on the printed page, or if they have lived, and are historical, then the very knowledge that they belong to a past we have not known ourselves induces fancy.

Well, yes. But I find du Maurier's crossbreeds of fact and fancy to be less enjoyable than her other work because they lack a sure and steady hand. Or a firm rein. Or, for want of a more graceful way to phrase it, I'm not sure what direction she meant to take. She *said* that at first she intended to recreate her family by the use of fiction, but then, after poring over diaries and letters, she apparently decided that "the real thing" might be better. (In fact, her bibliographers list these books as non-fiction, which seems to me a bad idea and somewhat akin to insisting that a mule is really, mostly, a horse.) So while at times du Maurier appears to be on firm ground in relaying her family history, at other times she plainly becomes bored with these plodding ghosts and veers suddenly into the unlikely, the implausible, if not the downright impossible. For a reader, the resulting jolts can make for a bumpy ride. For an author, there is a lesson to be learned here: Writing about members of one's own family is risky business, even if they *are* all dead.

I think we should call these du Maurier hybrids *ancestral fiction*, applaud her attempt to create life after death, and recognize her as an important progenitor of the current crop of historicals. *The Du Mauriers*, set in the 1800s, is primarily concerned with her grandfather, George du Maurier, who was an illustrator (for *Punch*) and a novelist. *Mary Anne* was based on her great-great grandmother, Mary Anne Clarke, whose affair with the Duke of York was supposed to have caused quite a stir in Regency England. After du Maurier sent the finished manuscript to her editor he requested a number of changes; she complained about the length of time these changes would take, saying that she didn't even like the novel. "The whole thing is lacking in human interest and reads like a newspaper." It had, she said, one saving grace in that "it is definitely not romantic—I'm done with romance forever." (The term *romantic* had by then begun its fall from favor, taking on a pejorative cast and driving du Maurier to abandon what she had often done well.) And, sure enough, a somewhat later book, *The Glass Blowers*, is a slow-paced, relentlessly *unromantic* account of du Maurier's provincial ancestors during the French Revolution.

I will touch here on only a few of du Maurier's novels; those that, for one reason or another, I have especially liked. I have already spoken of *Rebecca*. As it happens, the first du Maurier I read was *The King's General*. (I was thirteen or fourteen when I found an old, dog-eared copy on my parents' prohibited, you're-not-old-enough-for-it bookshelves, which of course made it irresistible. I didn't know at the time that there was such a thing as story laced with history—a secondary school subject I particularly disliked—and would never have risked filching it if I *had* known.) Du Maurier had initially wanted to base this book on the history of the Rashleigh family, the original owners of her

Cornwall house. Menabilly had been built in Tudor times, rebuilt in the seventeenth-century, then burned in the nineteenth [intimations of Manderley?], leaving little of its interior intact. Du Maurier, years before she rented a restored Menabilly from Rashleigh descendants, had become besotted with the house and the remoteness of its setting. *The King's General* required, according to her, months of research, but since the Rashleigh family was not *her* family, she apparently felt less responsible to the spirits haunting an ancestral plot; she created a novel in which were mingled fictitious and historically real characters, and set them against the backdrop of the seventeenth-century English Civil War. *The King's General* also has one of du Maurier's most interesting female viewpoint characters: the crippled woman, Honor, caught in a love affair which mirrors the tragedy of the war. I recently reread the novel, and while not as intrigued with it as that first furtive time round, I still found it a solid example of du Maurier's formidable strength as a storyteller.

Jamaica Inn, du Maurier's first commercial success, is a well-constructed mystery, suspenseful and sinister and violent, and set on the Cornish coast of the nineteenth-century. The inn itself (like the Manderley to follow) takes a central role in the plot, and this was the first novel in which du Maurier demonstrated her remarkable skill in creating the malevolent, brooding atmosphere that distinguishes much of her best work. Since du Maurier, there have been only a few authors (for example, P.D. James) who have used setting to such powerful advantage.

Du Maurier called *My Cousin Rachel* "the most *emotionally-felt* book I had ever written. After it, I felt dead." The simplest explanation for this would seem to be that the title character is a significant departure from du Maurier's earlier women, such as Mary Yellan in *Jamaica Inn* and the nameless narrator of *Rebecca,* both of whom are controlled not only by markedly unpleasant men, but by the circumstances in which du Maurier places them. In stark contrast, the character of Rachel Ashley is without question the novel's controlling force, and she is the strongest female character (other than Rebecca) created by du Maurier. She is also one of the last. With the sole exception of Mad in *Rule Britannia,* du Maurier's subsequent novels featured male protagonists.

Referring to *The Scapegoat*, du Maurier wrote to a friend that, " I hoped you would see the psychological politics, and the religious significance, but I still think this will be seen only by a few, and that most people will read it as a semi-thriller." Perhaps, but it would be hard to overlook the meaning of two brothers who resemble Cain and Abel, and who are given repeated opportunity to indulge in avarice—avarice of Biblical proportions—as it rears its head at every twist and turn of this novel, and is exactly what makes it unforgettable.

The House on the Strand and *The Flight of the Falcon* are two of my du Maurier favorites that did not meet with great commercial success. But, as I said earlier, she should be given high marks for exploring new techniques, and I am an admirer of her daring and versatility even when her efforts were not entirely successful. However, and this is pure conjecture on my part, it may have been du Maurier's very versatility that in the long run contributed to the wane of her popularity. For example, her editors asked for a sequel to *Rebecca* and she refused them, which may have been for her a wise choice, although it would have spared us the eventual sequel that *was* written. She never did a series; there was in her work no continuing character, something today's reading audience appears to crave. Du Maurier's books are very different, one from another, and readers are not given what might be called "the comfort of sameness" that seems to have become more and more a requirement. Some of us authors may envy du Maurier's free spirit.

Eventually she paid for that freedom. As her work became more imaginative, more difficult to categorize, her popularity declined. In retrospect, it seems ironic that du Maurier's *Flight of the Falcon* came about because of her passing interest in the Jungian theory of subconsciously determined destiny. After submitting *Falcon* to her editor, Victor Gollancz, she wrote: "Victor is pleased with the book...I know it had some 'Deeper' Thought layers, but I'm sure Victor has not spotted them, and just thinks it's a suspense story..." This may have been overly critical on du Maurier's part. Since the swift-moving, allegorical *Falcon* followed directly on the heels of the plodding *Glass Blowers,* I think it's just as likely that Victor was simply overjoyed that his best-selling suspense novelist had come to her senses. And he was reportedly horrified when, after a $100,000 "request" from *Good Housekeeping* magazine, (surely a most curious venue for this unorthodox novel) du Maurier changed *Falcon's* original ending. She was, it seems, constantly anxious about money although she had plenty of it. A year later, she worried that she was not selling well any more: "My *Falcon*, which everyone said was a Best-seller, only sold about twenty thousand copies in England...in the old days, I sold about eighty to a hundred thousand."

In her later years, she offered some thoughts on her declining popularity. Of *The House on the Strand*, one of her last novels and one of her best, she said that as far as films went, "Not a nibble for *Strand,* despite the fact that it is heading all the bestseller lists [in England]. Ten years ago, some film person would have snapped it up, just because it sold so well. Kits [her son] says everything is sex or violence or spies, and it has to be perverted sex at that...incest, etc. Honestly, what is left!"

And those apocalyptic words were penned, believe it or not, in September of 1969.

I am probably obliged to say here that there are a number of du Maurier biographies, and I have dutifully even read a few. I don't recommend any of them. But then, I dislike biographies of authors on general principle, as anything we need to know about a writer can be found in that writer's work.

However, since du Maurier, in her own words, wanted privacy and solitude above all else, it was inevitable that there would be such titles as, *The Private World of Daphne du Maurier* (Martyn Shallcross,1992), and *Daphne du Maurier: The Secret Life of the Renowned Storyteller* (Margaret Forster, 1993). That *private* and *secret* business should immediately tip us off—we are going to be fed some juicy tidbits here. And indeed, we are treated to such things as, "the letter sent her [du Maurier] into immediate and wild fantasies." We are informed that du Maurier was "phobic;" that "her mind [was] fragmented if not seriously disordered;" that she became depressed every winter; and that she had "a paranoid view of publishers." (This last, if true of du Maurier, strikes me as being incontrovertible proof of her saneness.) It is also strongly hinted that du Maurier was schizophrenic. So have we learned something new here? Some singular pathological "secret" about Daphne du Maurier? Well, no—as on almost any given day, almost any given writer is delusional, manic or depressed or both, and in the grip of multiple personalities. Especially in winter.

One book about du Maurier can be recommended: *Letters from Menabilly; Portrait of a Friendship.* This consists of over three decades of correspondence that took place between du Maurier and the book's editor, writer Oriel Malet. Without the speculative pronouncements of a biographer, we see for ourselves the du Maurier humor, and a sense of fun not prominently displayed in her novels. And we see, again in du Maurier's own words, an author excited about her work in progress, but as uncertain as any other writer of its acceptance when finished. The tone of her correspondence seems refreshingly free of arrogance; instead, there is recognition of her strengths as well as acknowledgment of her frailties. As a writer what she most wanted, she said, was to tell a good story.

I think du Maurier is one of our most underrated mystery and suspense novelists, and I am even more certain that her unique short fiction has never received the attention it merits. She gave us imaginative, suspenseful, and sometimes magical stories with brilliantly conceived, evocative settings. She clearly guided many of us to the path of historical fiction. And while hers may not always have been deathless prose, in her best work du Maurier exhibited a strong narrative drive that has rarely been surpassed.

In short, she told a good story.

Bibliography

Novels:
    The Loving Spirit, 1931.
    I'll Never Be Young Again, 1932.
    The Progress of Julius, 1933.
    Jamaica Inn, 1936.
    Rebecca, 1938.
    Frenchman's Creek, 1941.
    Hungry Hill, 1943.
    The King's General, 1946.
    The Parasites, 1949.
    My Cousin Rachel, 1951.
    The Scapegoat, 1957.
    Castle Dor [with Sir Arthur Quiller-Couch], 1962.
    The Flight of the Falcon, 1965.
    The House on the Strand, 1969.
    Rule Britannia, 1972.

Short stories (they are listed here as they were first published in London, with the later titles below.):
    The Apple Tree (also as *The Birds and Other Stories*), 1952.
    Come Wind, Come Weather, 1940.
    Early Stories, 1959 (written between 1927 and 1930).
    The Breaking: Eight Stories (also as *The Blue Lenses*), 1959.
    Not After Midnight and Other Stories (also as *Don't Look Now*), 1971.
    The Rendezvous and Other Stories, 1981.
    The Classic Macabre, 1987.

Plays:
    Rebecca, 1940.
    The Years Between, 1945.
    September Tide, 1949.

Non-fiction:
    Gerald: A Portrait, 1934.
    The du Mauriers, 1937.
    The Young George du Maurier: A Selection of His Letters, 1951.
    Mary Anne, 1954.
    The Infernal World of Branwell Brontë, 1960.
    The Glass-Blowers, 1963.
    Vanishing Cornwall, 1967.
    Golden Lads, 1975.
    The Winding Stairs, 1976.
    Growing Pains: The Shaping of a Writer (also as *Myself When Young: The Shaping of a Writer*), 1977.
    The Rebecca Notebooks, 1981.

Other:
    Critical Studies, media adapations, and many more short stories.

Miriam Grace Monfredo
Biography

Miriam Grace Monfredo lives in Rochester in western New York state, the scene of her Glynis Tryon/Seneca Falls Historical Mystery Series. Historian and former librarian Monfredo began writing fiction in 1989. Her first mystery, the critically acclaimed *Seneca Falls Inheritance*, is set against the backdrop of the first Women's Rights Convention held in 1848. Since then she has written four more mystery novels that focus on the history of American women and the evolution of women's rights. In demand as a speaker on the history of nineteenth-century women, Monfredo lectured in seventeen states on the release of her 1998 title, *The Stalking Horse*. Her short fiction has appeared in magazines and anthologies, including two Best of the Year collections. She is also the co-editor of two historical mystery anthologies.

Bibliography

Novels:
    The Glynis Tryon/ Seneca Falls Historical Mysteries:
        Seneca Falls Inheritance, 1992.
        North Star Conspiracy, 1993.
        Blackwater Spirits, 1995.
        Through A Gold Eagle, 1996.
        The Stalking Horse, 1998.

Anthologies:
    Crime Through Time, 1997.
    Crime Through Time II, 1998.

Short Stories:
    The Vigil Table, EQMM, Feb., 1989.
    Gather Not Thy Rose, EQMM, July, 1992.
    Once Upon A Crime, 1994.
    The Apprentice, EQMM, Nov. 1993.
    The Year's Best Mystery and Suspense Stories, 1994.
    The Year's Best Fantasy and Horror, 1994.
    Suffer A Witch, Crime Through Time, 1997.
    A Mule Named Sal, Crime Through Time II, 1998.
    Buffalo Gals Won't You Come Out Tonight, Malice 8, 1999.

Peter Lewis

◆

Eric Ambler

Eric Ambler (1909–)

Biography

Eric Ambler was born 28 June, 1909, in London and educated at Colfe's Grammar School and the University of London, 1925–28. He studied engineering and then went into advertising where he was both a copywriter and director of an advertising agency. In the early 1930s he tried his hand at writing plays, but dissatisfied, turned to what was for him the greater and more alluring literary challenge, the thriller. Between 1936–40 he published six novels in quick succession, "redeeming the form by raising it from the 'pulp' level...and transforming it into a vehicle for serious political ideas" [Peter Lewis]. During World War II he served in the Royal Artillery; from 1944–46 he was assistant director of the army's filmmaking unit which prepared him for a successful career, primarily as a scriptwriter, in British film between 1946–58. Hollywood proved less welcoming; after ten years there he returned to Europe in the late 1960s. In 1951 he began writing novels once again. Ambler has been recognized by the Crime Writers Association with its Gold Dagger Award, 1959, 1962, 1967, and 1972, and its Diamond Dagger, 1986; by the Mystery Writers of America with the Edgar Allan Poe Award, 1964, and Grand Master Award, 1975; and has received other awards, an Honorary D. Litt. City University, 1993; and the O.B.E., 1981. Divorced from his first wife, Ambler married the writer Joan Harrison in 1958.

Eric Ambler

Phrases such as "subverting the genre," "rewriting the genre", "playing the genre back on itself", and "deconstructing the genre" are commonplace in current criticism of post-modernist literature, in which parody, pastiche, self-reflexivity, and technical playfulness (or "the ludic") are often conspicuous features. Such tendencies have been evident in recent mystery writing as well as literary fiction. James Crumley, for example, has explained how he deliberately set out radically to rework, unravel, and re-ravel the conventions of hard-boiled private-eye fiction as developed by Dashiell Hammett, Raymond Chandler, and Ross Macdonald. Many contemporary women writers, including Sara Paretsky and Mary Wings in the US, Val McDermid and Lisa Cody in the UK, and Marele Day in Australia, have similarly reworked, unraveled, and re-raveled the conventions with feminist intentions.

Far from being a modern obsession, such reworking and subversion of genres and conventions has a long literary history. Chaucer, Shakespeare, Cervantes, and Pope are but four of the major figures who exemplify the tendency. During the 1930s—many years before the jargon of Deconstruction became fashionable—Eric Ambler devoted himself to precisely this type of literary activity. He consciously planned to transform the thriller utterly, just as in the 1960s John LeCarré spearheaded a new form of Cold War spy fiction by turning Ian Fleming's James Bond inside out. With six novels written in quick succession during the second half of the 1930s, Ambler succeeded admirably, and for many critics the fifth of these, *A Coffin for Dimitrios (The Mask of Dimitrios* in England), remains his masterpiece, even though he went on to write a further twelve novels after the war between 1951 and 1981.

The years between the two world wars may have been a Golden Age for the mystery, but certainly not for the lowly thriller. Detective stories gained a degree of intellectual respectability in this period because of their brain-teasing puzzles. The issue of whodunit or howdunit appealed to problem-solving philosophers and scholars like Bertrand Russell. The thriller, on the other hand, was thought of as irredeemably sub-literary. As Donald McCormick and other scholars have shown, a huge number of spy adventures and other thrillers were published between 1918 and 1939, but the literary quality was lamentably poor. In his autobiography *Here Lies*, Ambler writes that at the time "the only kind of popular novel about which I had strong feelings was the postwar thriller (which) had nowhere to go but up." For the thriller, it was an Age of Lead, not Gold.

With few exceptions, such as John Buchan's and Somerset Maugham's superior contributions to the genre, the early twentieth-century thriller is so formulaic, so crudely written, and so full of clichés that Ambler defines its typical hero (Sapper's Bulldog Drummond) as someone characterized by "abysmal stupidity combined with superhuman resourcefulness and unbreakable knuckle bones." Sapper's fiction is full of daredevil melodrama, muscular jingoism, and power-crazed criminals intent on dominating the world. Politically, such novels are anti-Semitic, xenophobic, crudely patriotic, and markedly fascist in tendency. For Ambler in the 1930s, sharing the left-wing views of most young artists and intellectuals, they were not only incredible and unrealistic, but politically objectionable as well.

As a writer, Ambler initially aspired to be a serious dramatist in the wake of Ibsen and the German Expressionists, but he was dissatisfied with his efforts and in the mid–1930s changed direction abruptly. While reading the popular fiction of the time, he felt that he could do very much better than the thriller writers he encountered, and set himself the task of raising the genre from its status as the lowest of all literary forms to one that could compete with the very best crime fiction. He was not alone in this endeavour. His contemporary Graham Greene, whose career ran more or less parallel to Ambler's, was also interested in exploiting the potential of popular literature, especially thriller conventions, for serious purposes.

Ambler launched his thriller-writing career with *The Dark Frontier* (1936, though not published in the US until more than fifty years later), a strange amalgam of science fiction and political fantasy, mainly set in an imaginary Balkan country called Ixania. Partly conceived as a parody and burlesque of E. Phillips Oppenheim and comparable writers of popular thrillers, *The Dark Frontier* turns upside down the stereotypical ingredients and political values of their work. Yet the novel is more than a comic send-up of the routine thriller with its absurd plots. Ambler's treatment of serious issues, especially nuclear weapons (which did not even exist at the time except in the minds of theorists), indicates that he is doing more than poking fun at the genre. In subverting it, Ambler also suggests how an alternative type of thriller could be written, just as LeCarré's later response to Ian Fleming inaugurated a startlingly different brand of espionage novel about the Cold War.

In the other five novels of his first phase—eleven years elapsed between *Journey into Fear* in 1940 and *Judgement on Deltchev* in 1951—Ambler developed his alternative thriller without parody, burlesque, pastiche, and the other comic devices of *The Dark Frontier*. These five novels, containing no elements of fantasy or science fiction, are decidedly realistic in their settings. The political realities and conflicts of the 1930s predominate, with Europe lurching toward a second great war only a generation after the first. The polarities of Right and Left become more and more sharply defined: Capitalism vs. Socialism; Democracy vs. Totalitarianism; Marxism vs. Fascism; Stalin's Soviet Union vs. Hitler's Germany and Mussolini's Italy.

Background to Danger (1937, *Uncommon Danger* in the UK, though not Ambler's preferred title) is an exciting adventure story of intrigue, pursuit, and escape, and as such employs several standard plot devices and conforms in some respects to thriller expectations. Even so, Ambler's originality was obvious to critics at the time. For one thing the setting is highly realistic, the action emerging from the authentic political turbulence of Central Europe at the time. Furthermore, Ambler's central character, Kenton, is an antihero rather than a conventional hero, a man who becomes entangled in a complex web of political double-dealing simply by being in the wrong place at the wrong time, not because he is a spy or secret agent. It is Kenton's ordinariness that Ambler emphasizes, not the impossibly heroic qualities of the usual ultra-patriotic protagonist. Like so many of Ambler's main characters, Kenton is an average man rather than a superman belonging to the world of romance.

Equally crucial to Ambler's reworking of the genre is his undercutting and even reversal of the ideological basis of the interwar thriller. Ambler's satire of big business and monopoly capitalism in *Background to Danger*, as well as his very sympathetic portrayal of two Soviet agents, the brother-and-sister team of Andreas and Tamara Zaleshoff, establish this novel more clearly than *The Dark Frontier* as a left-wing thriller, which in the 1930s was virtually a contradiction in terms. Britain is attacked for its insular blindness to what was really happening in an increasingly fascist Europe, while Socialism is broadly endorsed.

In his fourth novel, *Cause for Alarm* (1938), Ambler repeats the basic pattern of *Background to Danger*, even using Andreas Zaleshoff as a significant character for a second time—something uncharacteristic of Ambler who generally avoids sequels and series characters. But just months before *Cause for Alarm* he published the third of these six novels, *Epitaph for a Spy* (also 1938). Despite its title, *Epitaph for a Spy* is a decidedly original variant of the detective story: not a whodunit, but a who-is-the-spy puzzle. It seems to have been this change of formula that led to Alfred Knopf's decision not to publish it in the US at the time; American publication was delayed until 1952. Knopf wanted another *Background to Danger*, with a fast-moving narrative involving travel, border-crossings, and international intrigue, and got it in *Cause for Alarm*.

Epitaph for a Spy is no less political than these two novels, but the closed setting of a hotel on the *Côte d'Azur* in the South of France inevitably brings Golden Age mysteries to mind. Agatha Christie might well have used such a setting though certainly not in the way Ambler does. There are twelve suspects in the hotel, including the first-person narrator, Vadassy, who functions as an amateur detective, though an incompetent one. As Ambler's ironic comparison between Vadassy and S.S. Van Dine's fictional detective Philo Vance makes clear, Vadassy has nothing in common with the line of super-sleuths running from Poe's Dupin and Conan Doyle's Sherlock Holmes to Agatha Christie's Hercule Poirot and other Golden Age detectives. In *Epitaph for a Spy*, Ambler creates an unexpected fusion of the spy novel and the classical detective story, sporting with the Golden Age mystery formula in such a way as to produce a highly political novel of considerable topicality. For example, Ambler incorporates an analysis of what went wrong in Germany between the Treaty of Versailles in 1919 and Hitler's accession to power in 1933, and also of the Nazi regime itself. This is a novel full of portents of war with European civilization heading into the abyss. About twenty-five years after *Epitaph for a Spy*, John LeCarré similarly fused spy fiction and the detective story in his first novel, *Call for the Dead*, and further developed this synthesis in the first novel of his *Quest for Karla* trilogy, *Tinker, Tailor, Soldier, Spy*.

As noted above, for his fourth novel, *Cause for Alarm*, Ambler returns to the more mobile, adventure-based plotting of *Uncommon*

Danger, with the sympathetic Andreas Zaleshoff again a formidable presence, but there are important differences. For one thing, the setting is now Mussolini's Italy, not Central Europe. More significantly, in both its narrative strategy and its political aspirations *Cause for Alarm* is considerably more sophisticated than the earlier novel. The cuts that Alfred Knopf insisted on for the US publication in 1939 are revealing. Knopf wanted a racy thriller with a topical background, and deleted parts of the text, including the penultimate chapter in its entirety to speed up the action According to Ambler's British editor at his London publishers, Hodder and Stoughton, Knopf was guilty of mutilating the novel, since the chapter in question was the best in the novel—a disturbing account of a brilliant Italian scientist driven mad by his treatment under Mussolini's Fascist regime. Ambler was clearly continuing his radical enterprise of redeeming the thriller by making it a vehicle for searching political analysis, just as Graham Greene was expanding the possibilities of the thriller for religious as well as political purposes at the same time in *Brighton Rock* and *The Power and the Glory*.

As in *Uncommon Danger*, the action revolves around one of Ambler's typical antiheroes, Marlow, who is trapped between the mighty opposites of Fascism and Communism, and under the pressure of circumstances is forced to choose and make a stand. Like Kenton in the earlier novel, Marlow chooses the Left, and in committing himself to Zaleshoff's plan of action, he risks his life in an attempt to undermine the increasingly powerful and warlike Berlin-Rome Axis forged by Hitler and Mussolini.

Reviewers in England lavished praise on *Cause for Alarm*, and by 1938, with four novels out in less than three years, Ambler was being described as "the best living writer of thrillers." Yet in 1939, with his fifth novel, *A Coffin for Dimitrios*, he surpassed himself, and his achievement was at once acknowledged by critics. As in the case of *Uncommon Danger*, Ambler's British publishers did not like his title, considering "Coffin" likely to turn off potential readers. Hodder and Stoughton insisted on a change and the book appeared in the UK as *The Mask of Dimitrios*. Knopf considered this change to be foolish and adhered to Ambler's original title for the US edition, but he did make a number of cuts, which while not mutilating the novel, do not enhance it either.

For many people, this is Ambler's masterpiece, and it has long been accepted as a milestone in the history of the thriller—if indeed "thriller" is the *mot juste* for a novel that is much more consciously literary than its predecessors. Ambler makes considerable demands on his readers by requiring them to piece together the story of Dimitrios between the early 1920s to the late 1930s from the various narrative fragments he presents: an assemblage of police archives, written statements, index cards, hearsay evidence, and interviews. There is a multiplicity of voices and perspectives rather than a fixed viewpoint. Here, indeed, the thriller writer takes the Modernist road. This is reinforced by Ambler's choice of a successful detective novelist in the English Golden Age mold, Charles Latimer, to be the pursuer of Dimitrios, the apparently dead but intriguing figure whose life story is the object of Latimer's quest. The novel, then, is partly a novel about a novelist and novel-writing. It contains a critique of the classic English murder mystery of the interwar years for being so escapist at a time of intense international danger and political atrocities. *A Coffin for Dimitrios* implicitly and explicitly endorses the thriller form as a much more adequate vehicle for exploring social, political, and economic realities than Golden Age detective fiction. In other words, the novel itself stakes a major claim for the intellectual respectability of the thriller, thus combating the prevailing view of the form during the interwar years as a sub-literary pulp.

Throughout the novel there is a complex interplay between the reality of everyday life, the "reality" of English detective fiction, and the different "reality" of Ambler's alternative fiction. Indeed Ambler satirizes English detective fiction as symptomatic of the naivety and blindness of the English intelligentsia and establishment in the face of the growing fascist threat. Near the end of the novel there is some particularly caustic irony in the passage about Latimer concerning himself with "more important things," namely the plot of his next detective story set in "an English country village...with cricket matches on the village green, garden parties at the vicarage, the clink of teacups and the sweet smell of grass on a July evening...the sort of thing people like to hear about...the sort of thing that he himself would like to hear about." This predates by some years Raymond Chandler's much-quoted remarks about the facetious artificiality of English Golden Age fiction in *The Simple Art of Murder*.

By abandoning the usual fast-moving, linear, and chronological basis of the thriller in favour of a complex narrative moving back and forth between past and present, Ambler is able to cover virtually the entire interwar period and to offer an interpretation of the political upheavals of those years. It was strangely appropriate that British publication coincided with the outbreak of World War II in September, 1939, since the novel is a highly ambitious attempt to analyze the new brutality and counter-civilization unleashed by an amalgam of monopolistic capitalism and fascist politics. Dimitrios himself symbolizes this new force in Europe leading inevitably to war, and in some respects his career parallels that of Hitler.

The war was to bring Ambler's career as a novelist to a standstill for many years, but before it did so, he wrote the sixth and last of this early cluster of novels very quickly during the Phony War (September, 1939–May, 1940), before the Battle of Britain and the military rout of France. *Journey into Fear* (1940) is much more orthodox in its narrative methods than *A Coffin for Dimitrios*, but it breaks new ground in other ways, being the most psychological of these thrillers. Ambler here undertakes a study in depth of one of his typical antiheroes, an English scientist called Graham who initially is presented as unimaginative, blinkered, and highly conventional. Because of his rare expertise he is able to make a significant contribution to the war effort, and as a result he is targeted by a Nazi assassination team when sent abroad. Like Kenton in *Background to Danger* and Marlow in *Cause for Alarm*, Graham is another English innocent away from home who finds himself caught up in a nasty world of political intrigue.

Mainly set on board a ship in the Mediterranean, *Journey into Fear* is a closed-world narrative like *Epitaph for a Spy* with its hotel setting. As it becomes clear that Graham's would-be assassin is also on board, the tension gradually increases in intensity. This is not a Golden Age whodunit, but a thriller variant. Which of the people travelling with Graham is his intended killer? And how can Graham escape the death planned for him? Ambler develops the thriller potential of this situation brilliantly, but as usual in these early novels he ensures that the political dimension is in the foreground. Finding himself in the equivalent of a death cell, Graham is forced to reassess his entire philosophical and political position, and experiences a form of enlightenment. Waking up to reality, he finds within himself not only the strength to resist the seemingly inevitable but also the determination to fight back. As such he becomes a symbolic manifestation or personification of the English need to take on the fascist, especially Nazi, threat. Here, in a novel written in wartime, the Amblerian antihero becomes positively heroic, an emblem of resistance to barbaric primitivism. Whatever the odds against success, he is going to battle it out rather than submit fatalistically, and, if possible, win. The onset of war resulted in a significant shift in the Amblerian antihero. In previous novels this central character undergoes a change of heart and mind because of the influence and support of others as well as the circumstance in which he finds himself. In *Journey into Fear* the antihero, alone and under intense pressure, finds inner resources to transform himself into a patriotic as well as moral hero.

When Ambler eventually returned to novel-writing after the war, his fiction understandably took a different direction while building on his extraordinary achievement between 1936 and 1940. With those six early novels he triumphantly succeeded in his aim to demonstrate that the thriller, which at the time seemed to be just about the lowest of all literary forms, could be a suitable vehicle for serious literary treatment of urgent social and political themes.

Bibliography

Novels:
    The Dark Frontier, 1936.
    Uncommon Danger (*Background to Danger* US), 1937.
    Epitaph for a Spy, 1938.
    Cause for Alarm, 1938.
    The Mask of Dimitrios (*A Coffin for Dimitrios* US), 1939.
    Journey into Fear, 1940.
    Judgment on Deltchev, 1951.
    The Schirmer Inheritance, 1953.
    The Night-Comers (*State of Siege* US), 1956.
    Passage of Arms, 1959.
    The Light of Day (*Topkapi* US), 1962.
    A Kind of Anger, 1964.
    Dirty Story, 1967.
    The Intercome Conspiracy, 1969.
    The Levanter, 1972.
    Doctor Frigo, 1974.
    Send No More Roses (*The Siege of the Villa Lipp* US), 1978.
    The Card of Time, 1981.

Other:
    The Ability to Kill and Other Pieces, 1963.
    Editor, *To Catch a Spy: An Anthology of Favorite Spy Stories,* 1964.
    Here Lies: An Autobiography, 1985.
    Waiting for Orders (short stories), 1991.
    The Story So Far: Memories and Other Fictions, 1994.
    Plus 5 novels as Eliot Reed with Charles Rodda; numerous Screenplays.

Critical Studies:
    Peter Lewis, *Eric Ambler,* 1990.
    Peter Wolfe, *Alarms and Epitaphs: The Art of Eric Ambler,* 1993.

Photo Credit: Fillinghams

Peter Lewis

Biography

Peter Lewis hails from Northumberland, England. A busy academic, he is a Reader in English at the University of Durham specializing in 18th Century literature. He has written critical studies of John LeCarré and Eric Ambler, and he has published some crime short stories. His John LeCarré won the 1986 Edgar Allan Poe Award for Best Critical/Biographical work.

Bibliography

Novels:
  Books related to mystery and crime:
    John LeCarré, 1985.
    Eric Ambler, 1990.

Essays:
  John LeCarré, in *Reference Guide to English Literature*, 2nd. ed, 1991.
  Eric Ambler, in *Twentieth Century Crime and Mystery Writers*, 3rd. ed., 1991.
  Eric Ambler and 'Eliot Reed', in *Durham University Journal*, vol. 87, no. 2, 1996.
  Eric Ambler, in *Mystery Writers*, ed. Robin Winks, 1998.

Robin Smiley

◆

Collecting Erle Stanley Gardner

Erle Stanley Gardner
(1889–1970)
Biography

E.S. Gardner, who also wrote as A.A. Fair, Carleton Kendrake, and Charles J. Kenny among others, was born in Malden, Massachusetts, on 17 July, 1889. He was educated at Palo Alto High School, California and Valparaiso University, Indiana, 1909. After some years of study in law offices, he was admitted to the California Bar, 1911, and practiced law in Oxnard 1911–18. Thereafter he worked as a salesman and in various aspects of the law, but his primary output was magazine stories, 1923–32, after which he was a full-time writer. His most famous body of work is the 82 volume Perry Mason series. He maintained an interest in case review, polygraphs, and reporting on criminal trials. The Mystery Writers of America presented him with the Edgar Allan Poe Award, 1952, and the Grand Master award, 1961. He was made an honorary alumnus of Kansas City University, 1955; D.L. McGeorge College of Law, Sacramento. Married to Natalie Talbert in 1912, separated 1935, she died, 1968; one daughter. Married Agnes Jean Bethell, 1968. He died on 11 March, 1970.

Collecting Erle Stanley Gardner

To date there have been more than 300,000,000 copies of Erle Stanley Gardner books printed in all languages and formats. In the mid-1960s, at the peak of Gardner's popularity, more than 26,000 copies of his books were purchased on an average day. It is not unreasonable to say that during his lifetime Gardner was *the* mystery writer in his readers' minds. Perry Mason, Gardner's most popular series character (although not his only one, by any means), was—and arguably still is—*the* smart lawyer in popular culture. How many real-life attorneys have had to tell potential witnesses that most legal proceedings are not like Perry Mason trial scenes?

Erle Stanley Gardner was a giant of a man, not in terms of physical stature, but in accomplishment. He was a product of his era, the sort of man our paler age no longer seems to produce. Gardner was, among other things, a legendary trial lawyer, a "one man writing factory," an outdoorsman, an explorer, an archaeologist, a businessman and a fighter for lost causes.

Gardner was born in 1889 in Massachusetts. His parents moved the family west in 1899, settling finally in Oroville, California. Erle was always very bright, but much too rebellious to be a good student. He was suspended from high school several times for pranks directed at the school's foppish principal.

Gardner finally graduated, but his parents, with one son already at Stanford, decided they could not afford to support two college students at the same time. Erle read for the law in a legal office while working there as a typist and clerk. He "didn't want to waste time" in college anyway. He did, however, enroll and spend a few weeks as a student at Valparaiso University in Indiana. His rebellious nature got him in trouble again. He dropped out of Valparaiso after being promoted as a contestant in an illegal boxing exhibition and ducking an indictment. After that episode he spent most of his time travelling around California, reading the law in various offices. He eventually passed the bar in 1911, at the age of 21.

An old boxing crony had moved to Oxnard, California, prompting Gardner to set up his law practice in what was then—and to some extent, is now—a rough adjunct to the county seat of Ventura, a graceful old town on the coast between Los Angeles and

Santa Barbara. Gardner fit in perfectly in Oxnard and made a reputation for himself right away by defending members of the local Chinese community who were being prosecuted by the district attorney for gambling. Gardner was brash and bold in his legal stratagems—and got his clients off by resorting to legal trickery. He knew they were guilty, but then so were the prosecutor and all the members of the local in-crowd, who liked nothing better than a Friday night poker game.

Gardner made enemies, but also a powerful reputation, and in a short time was invited into the legal practice of a fine corporate lawyer in Ventura. Gardner hated it there; he loved the rough and tumble of the courtroom. Looking for a way out of the office routine, he left the firm and worked as a travelling salesman until the post-World War I recession forced the business into bankruptcy. Gardner was left flat broke and wondering where to turn next, when an unnamed Chinese man made a $200 deposit into his bank account. Gardner was never broke again.

But he *was* back in an office, although he continued searching for a way to make a living without being confined to one spot. In 1921 he took up writing. By his own admission, he was not a gifted writer. In fact, he claimed that he had no aptitude at all. In time he came to be—even in his own estimation—a good plotter, but never a great stylist. Gardner forced himself to be a writer by writing all the time, submitting his stories, digesting any criticism they received, and then writing some more.

He sold nothing right away; the stories were "awful." But by the end of the year his story *Nellie's Naughty Nightie* made it into a pulp magazine called *Breezy Stories*. It was his first published work. He reportedly gave the acceptance check to his mother, who refused to cash it because of the story's *risqué* title. (Her practical side eventually won out.)

On a typical day, Gardener would go to court in the morning, spend all day working there, return to his office to do some research after hours, and then go home at night and write. Often he would finish a story at one in the morning and start another before falling asleep in his chair after two. He would awaken at five, shower, shave and do some more writing before leaving for the office. Setting a goal for himself of 100,000 words a month, a standard he maintained for the rest of his life, he wrote anything for publication in the pulps. He included Westerns in his repertoire, although he soon dropped them because his deeply Western sensibility made them too authentic for Eastern publishers.

Gardner wrote under a number of pen names: Charles M. Green, Kyle Corning, Grant Holiday, and several others he abandoned after he became an established novelist. He created several series characters, among them Lester Leith and Speed Dash, the human fly, who was also a detective.

Pulps paid only two or three cents per word in the mid-1920s, but Gardner knew he wasn't yet a sufficiently polished craftsman to publish in the higher paying "slicks." He was making more than $10,000 a year from his law practice—enough to support his new wife and growing family in good style—and he wanted the writing to be more than just an income supplement. He continued to work at learning and refining his craft.

Eventually, with the aid of some criticism (Gardner always listened carefully to criticism about his writing, since he felt it could never be worse than any he received daily during his courtroom battles), his writing improved and some of his stories were published. Along with Carroll John Daly and Dashiell Hammett, Gardner became one of the backbones of *Black Mask* magazine. By the early 1930s, Gardner had excellent agency representation and two book-length manuscripts strong enough to be considered for serialization by *Collier's* and *The Saturday Evening Post*.

Both magazines rejected the manuscripts, but then they fell into the hands of the young president of William Morrow and Company, Thayer Hobson. Hobson loved the stories and wanted to publish them as books. He suggested that Gardner rewrite them as the first two entries of a courtroom series. Gardner agreed to do so, and in the rewriting process created Perry Mason. In March, 1933, Morrow published *The Case of the Velvet Claws*; *The Case of the Sulky Girl* appeared in September. Eighty more Perry Mason books would follow.

Early in his writing career Gardner typed his own copy, using the two-finger method, pounding so hard that by the end of a writing session his fingers would bleed. Later he dictated his manuscripts to his secretaries—at any time he had between three and six of them—and would edit and polish their transcriptions. There is a story, possibly apocryphal, that sometime in the early 1950s Gardner dictated half a novel into his Dictaphone before leaving a verbal note to the unfortunate secretary who had been transcribing the book: "Sorry, but I think I've written this one before."

Gardner's output was so vast that from a collecting standpoint it makes sense to discuss his books in groups rather than as individual titles. The Perry Mason series was the first Gardner series to make it into print. It is his most popular—and, needless to say, the most publicized—the most numerous, and the most widely collected of Erle Stanley Gardner's works. Each Perry Mason title begins with the same four words: *The Case of the...* (Unfortunately, some titles that are not Perry Masons also begin with that phrase, causing some identification problems.)

The first two Masons, *The Case of the Velvet Claws* and *The Case of the Sulky Girl*, are the only Gardner books that have cracked the thousand dollar barrier. Both had two Morrow printings. *Velvet Claws* may have had a first printing of about 2,000 copies, and a second printing of perhaps another thousand. The exact numbers are not known. The book is scarce, particularly in collector's condition. Its predominantly black dust wrapper is especially prone to wear. The printings for *Sulky Girl* were reportedly a bit larger, but even fewer copies of this title are seen. According to Morrow publicity, each book in the series added to its popularity and each of the first printings of the 1930s titles was larger than that of its predecessor.

The books' central characters were in place from the beginning. Perry Mason was a handsome and slick defense lawyer, entirely committed to his clients' interest and willing to use any device necessary to win in court. However, his maneuvers were always within the law; he never suborned perjury or intimidated a witness. Della Street, his capable and dedicated secretary, was in her twenties. Her loyalty to her boss was absolute, and their relationship was absolutely platonic. Paul Drake, Mason's rangy private investigator, was a deceptively easygoing character.

Mason's antagonist in the early books was Sergeant Holcomb of the Los Angeles Homicide Squad, a big, dumb cop. Holcomb was gradually phased out of the series in favor of Lieutenant Tragg, a suave, sophisticated detective. With the advent of the television series in the late 1950s, the literary Tragg underwent a metamorphosis that brought him into line with the TV character played by Ray Collins, a laconic, ironic, witty variation on the original. In the sixth Mason book, *The Case of the Counterfeit Eye*, District Attorney Hamilton Burger—"Ham Burger"—was introduced and became a fixture in the series. Burger never changed; he was always a self-righteous, bumbling pursuer of the obvious.

Gardner's style was established from the first book. His characterizations were brief (unappreciative critics call them sketchy), his pace fast and his courtroom scenes were always punctuated by

Mason's delicious legal gymnastics. Gardner worried that in his novels there was a distinct pause between his early chapters, in which the mystery was established, and the later courtroom scenes, where it was solved. He thought he might lose his readers in the interim. He need not have worried. The courtroom scenes were the ones that gave the Perry Mason novels their distinct flavor, and his readers relished them above any others.

The first two Perry Masons are the most difficult to find and the most expensive, but the balance of the prewar titles (often called the "thick" books, these were published before 1943, when wartime production codes were instituted and a scarcity of materials forced a reduction in book size and format) are also elusive and highly prized. They range in price from a low of a hundred dollars or so for the most readily available titles to nearly a thousand dollars for the scarcest. Although all are difficult to locate, the toughest Perry Mason titles from this period are *Lucky Legs*, *Howling Dog*, *Counterfeit Eye*, and *Perjured Parrot*.

The wartime titles—the "thin" books, published from 1943 to 1945—featured wonderful period dust wrapper art, the best being *Black-Eyed Blonde*, *Golddigger's Purse*, and *Half-Wakened Wife*. The paper used for the text was brittle and fragile, but more of these books than might have been imagined have survived in decent condition. The reason for this serendipity is not known. The dust jackets of these titles, and for the titles published from 1945 (when the paper quality improved) through 1954, are in themselves enough to ensure collectability. The outstanding wrappers in this run are *Fandancer's Horse*, *Vagabond Virgin*, *Negligent Nymph*, and *Grinning Gorilla*. Abundant and inexpensive until just a few years ago, these books have begun to disappear and, not surprisingly, to appreciate in price. Any of them fine or better in jacket will command at least $50.00. At that price they are bargains.

Gardner's popularity was at its peak during the mid-1950s through the mid-1960s, due in part to the weekly *Perry Mason* television show, starring Raymond Burr and produced by Gardner's own production company, Paisano Productions. The books from this era are the most abundant and—in terms of their dust wrappers—the least inspired. Still, even these books are appreciating, although collectors should hold out for fine or better copies.

Titles published at the end of Gardner's career (roughly from 1966 on), from *Worried Waitress* to the last, posthumously published Perry Mason, *Postponed Murder*, are still relatively inexpensive, but surprisingly hard to find. In all, locating just the Perry Mason titles presents a formidable challenge to collectors. But they comprise only a little over half of Gardner's output.

The second most widely known Gardner series, featuring Bertha Cool and Donald Lam, was published under a pseudonym Gardner used in his pulp days, A.A. Fair. The first twelve titles, from *The Bigger They Come* (1939) to *Bedrooms Have Windows* (1949), were simply identified as the work of A.A. Fair. In 1952, the dust wrapper of *Top of the Heap* confirmed the long-rumored fact that Fair was, in fact, Erle Stanley Gardner. This book and each of the sixteen Cool and Lam titles that followed it were identified as the work of "Erle Stanley Gardner writing as A.A. Fair."

Bertha Cool owns a private investigation agency. She is big, crude, and stingy. Bertha likes to adorn herself with a large tonnage of gold jewelry and likes physical exertion only a little better than spending money—that is, not at all. Her brightest operative (later her partner) is Donald Lam, a lawyer whose frank trickiness has run him afoul of the powers that be in the bar association, causing him to change his profession to private eye. Lam is tiny, weighing maybe 120 pounds. Bertha carries nearly that much weight around in the form of her gold jewelry. Donald is bright, fearless, and treads always on the edge of the law in the service of his clients. He also likes his female clients a little too much, and not always platonically. Bertha finds his womanizing dangerous, if endearing. It has been argued that Donald Lam is the Gardner character who comes closest to the author's own personality and experience. The Bertha Cool/Donald Lam books rank with the best Masons; some readers like them better.

The first twelve A.A. Fair titles tend to be scarcer and even a little more expensive than contemporary Perry Mason titles. The first Fair, *The Bigger They Come,* is priced at better than $300, when it can be found at all. Some of the titles are seldom encountered. *Owls Don't Blink* (1942) is a true rarity in dust wrapper; *Cats Prowl at Night* (1943) is much tougher to find than wartime Perry Mason titles.

The Fair books published after the author's true identity was revealed are more readily available, and command prices comparable to later Masons. Surprisingly, one title infrequently seen is the last Gardner book published during the author's lifetime, *All Grass Isn't Green* (1970).

Gardner's other major series, the nine Doug Selby *D.A.* books, were published between 1938 and 1949. Selby reveals another side of Gardner's early experience, that of a young lawyer practicing in a small county seat. These are good courtroom dramas, but prosecutor Selby never rivalled defense attorney Mason in popularity, and Gardner gave him up in later years.

Most of the books in the *D.A.* series were published during the "thick" book era and tend to be more available than the corresponding Perry Mason books. The first series entry, *The D.A. Calls It Murder* (1937), is by far the scarcest. The third one, *The D.A. Draws A Circle* (1939), may be the most common of all the pre-war Gardner books.

Two other detectives made more than one appearance in Gardner books. Terry Clane, a District Attorney who specializes in cases dealing with Orientals, is the hero of two books, *Murder Up My Sleeve* (1938) and *The Case of the Backward Mule* (1946). Interestingly, the first title is much more commonly seen than the second. Gramps Wiggins, an independent, ageless curmudgeon, also appeared in two books, *The Case of the Turning Tide* (1941) and *The Case of the Smoking Chimney* (1943).

Two Clues (1947) may qualify rural sheriff Bill Eldon as a series hero. The book is comprised of two novellas featuring Eldon as a detective. Rob Trenton made only one appearance, in Gardner's *The Case of the Musical Cow*.

Early in his career as a novelist, Gardner published under pseudonyms from his pulp days two books that did not develop into series: *The Case of the Forgotten Murder* (1935) by Carleton Kendrake, and *This is Murder* (1937) by Charles G. Kenny. Each is immensely difficult to find in jacket. To collectors trying to find them, good luck!

The nonfiction books Gardner published later in his career are collected by both Western Americana enthusiasts and Gardner completists. In some ways, these books about Gardner's life as an outdoorsman were the author's favorites. He gave many presentation copies to friends. Gardner was fiercely loyal to his friends; he could be an unforgiving enemy to anyone who crossed him. Many of his "nature" titles bear long inscriptions in his hand. In their way they have become mystery books on their own: it takes a detective to decipher Gardner's handwriting. There were 13 of these "outdoors" books, from *The Land of Shorter Shadows*, written in 1948, to *The Host with the Big Hat*, published in 1970. These appear quite frequently on the market. Inscribed copies can bring upwards of $100.

Gardner wrote two nonfiction books on the law that are becoming increasingly difficult to find. *The Court of Last Resort* (1952) is about his own experiences in fighting for wrongfully convicted criminals. He also penned a book on the legal ramifications of the unrest of the Sixties, *Cops on Campus and Crime in the Streets* (1970).

Erle Stanley Gardner published 142 books during his lifetime. The tally of his work is increased to 147 titles when the Morrow books published after his death are added to the list, and to 155 with the addition of recent books of short story compilations. And yet, this is not all his body of work. Most of his early writing has yet to be published in book form. He wrote many nonfiction articles, pamphlets, and magazine pieces on numerous subjects. Gardner was a giant in each of his fields of interest. He was a phenomenon in the publishing industry. Not bad for a writer with no natural ability.

Gardner was a fortunate man in many ways. Not the least of these was that his official biographer was no less than the great critic, newspaperwoman, and mystery novelist Dorothy B. Hughes. She championed Gardner novels from the start and her *Erle Stanley Gardner: The Case of the Real Perry Mason* (Morrow, 1978) is required reading for Gardner collectors or anyone interested in the life of a unique literary personality.

Bibliography

Selected Novels
  (Perry Mason in all titles):
    The Case of the Velvet Claws, 1933.
    The Case of the Sulky Girl, 1933.
    The Case of the Howling Dog, 1934.
    The Case of the Curious Bride, 1934.
    The Case of the Perjured Parrot, 1939.
    The Case of the Lazy Lover, 1947.
    The Case of the Hesitant Hostess, 1953.
    The Case of the Lucky Loser, 1957.
    The Case of the Footloose Doll, 1958.
    The Case of the Troubled Trustee, 1965.
    The Case of the Careless Cupid, 1968.
    The Case of the Fenced-In Woman, 1972.
    The Case of the Postponed Murder, 1973
      (posthumous).

Other:
  8 Doug Selby D.A. novels, 30 Bertha Lam/Donald Cool novels as A.A. Fair, other detective novel series with Terry Clane, Sheriff Bill Eldon, and Gramps Wiggins, 10 collections of various detective tales, 3 collections of other short stories, at least 75 articles in the *Court of Last Resort Series*, True Crime, Travel. For a complete bibliography, compiled by Ruth Moore, refer to Hughes.

Critical Studies:
  Alva Johnston, *The Case of Erle Stanely Gardner*, 1947.
  Dorothy B. Hughes, *Erle Stanley Gardner: The Case of the Real Perry Mason*, 1978.
  J. Kenneth Van Dover, *Murder in the Millions: Erle Stanley Gardner, Mickey Spillane, Ian Fleming*, 1984.

Robin Smiley
Biography

Robin Smiley, publisher of *Firsts: The Book Collector's Magazine*, has degrees in history, psychology, and film and has been a teacher, writer, actor, and a vocational photographer. He and wife Kathryn, editor of *Firsts: The Book Collector's Magazine*, relocated their business and residence from California to Tucson in 1994. He has participated in several programs on book collecting for The Poisoned Pen and is glad to share his passion for opera with any fan.

Steven Saylor

◆

Stuart Palmer

Stuart Palmer
(1905–1968)

Biography

(Charles) Stuart Palmer was born in Baraboo, Wisconsin, on 21 June, 1905. He was educated at the Chicago Art Institute, 1922–24, and the University of Wisconsin, 1924–26, the University of California at Los Angeles, 1961. He published his first novel in 1931 and began his screenwriting career in 1932. During World War II he served as liaison chief for official U.S. Army filmmaking, 1943–48. Five times married; one daughter and one son. He served as president of the Mystery Writers of America, 1954–55. He died on 4 February, 1968.

Stuart Palmer

It is a curious thing, how quickly and completely a writer of considerable renown can vanish from the scene. A case in point: the mystery writer Stuart Palmer.

Palmer was once routinely mentioned as one of the best authors in the genre, and his intrepid heroine of fourteen novels and dozens of short stories, a spinster school teacher named Hildegarde Withers, was once ranked among the immortal sleuths of fiction.

John Dickson Carr, in his introduction to the 1952 anthology *Maiden Murders*, wrote: "Here are the old craftsmen, the serpents, the great masters of the game: Mr. Ellery Queen, Mr. Stuart Palmer, M. Georges Simenon." That old serpent Ellery Queen himself, Fred Dannay, spoke of Palmer in the same breath with Dashiell Hammett and Raymond Chandler. And the dean of mystery critics, Anthony Boucher, in *The Case of the Seven of Calvary* (1937), cited Palmer as a top exponent of the puzzle story along with Erle Stanley Gardner and John Dickson Carr. In 1954 his fellow authors elected him president of the Mystery Writers of America.

As for Miss Hildegarde Withers, Boucher named her "one of the first and still one of the best spinster sleuths" (*Four and Twenty Bloodhounds*, 1950), and as recently as 1987, in their introduction to *Uncollected Crimes*, Bill Pronzini and Martin Greenberg could confidently pronounce: "Ask any knowledgeable mystery reader to name the quintessential little old lady sleuth, and the response will invariably be either Agatha Christie's Miss Jane Marple or Stuart Palmer's Hildegarde Withers."

And yet, at a recent gathering of well-read, dyed-in-the-wool mystery fans where I delivered a talk about Palmer, when I asked for a show of hands from those who knew his work, or at least had heard of him, hardly a hand went up.

Who was Stuart Palmer? We know that he was born in Baraboo, Wisconsin in 1905, was educated at the Chicago Art Institute and the University of Wisconsin, and variously worked (by his own account) as a "supercargo, iceman, publicity writer, newspaper reporter, advertising copywriter, apple-picker, literary ghost, poet, editor, special interviewer, Hollywood script-writer, etc." Physically, he was a big man, standing a bit over six foot, two inches tall. In private life, he was definitely a ladies' man; Palmer's first marriage was at age 23 in 1928, his fifth and last at age 61, two years before his death in 1968.

Palmer's first novel, not a mystery but set among criminals, was a curiosity called *Ace of Jades* (1931). The book's heroine is a wisecracking gangster's moll and the tone is meant to be charming, but for this reader the humor is too dated and the storytelling too flimsy to come off. Frankly, I couldn't get through it.

But apparently the legendary publisher Powell Brentano did, and saw in Palmer the makings of a mystery writer. This is how (in a letter to Fred Dannay, probably written around 1949) Palmer recounted the genesis of his second novel, *The Penguin Pool Murder* (1931), and the creation of the sleuth who would be with him for decades to come:

> The origins of Miss Withers are nebulous. When I started *The Penguin Pool Murder* (to be laid in the New York Aquarium as suggested by Powell Brentano, then head of Brentano's Publishers) I worked without an outline, and without much plan. But I decided to ring in a spinster schoolma'am as a minor character, for comedy relief. Believe it or not, I found her taking over. She had more meat on her bones than the cardboard characters who were supposed to carry the story. Finally almost in spite of myself and certainly in spite of Mr. Brentano, I threw the story into her lap. She was based to some extent on Fern Hackett, an English teacher in Baraboo High School who made my life miserable for two years. Once I came to get her permission to transfer to another class and she said okay, only she'd be lonesome and bored without our arguments; that I was the only student in the class whom she thought enough of to bother with. I think she started me as a writer. Fern was a horse-faced old girl, preposterously old-fashioned, fine old New England family run to seed, hipped on Thoreau and Emerson.

Thus was born Miss Hildegarde Withers, who makes her first appearance in *The Penguin Pool Murder* escorting some of her elementary school students on a field trip to the New York Aquarium. When a dead body appears in the penguin tank, Hildegarde's career as an amateur sleuth is off and running, with frequent assistance from Oscar Piper, a gruff police detective as stubborn as she is. (When they first meet and Piper asks who she is, Hildegarde archly replies, "I'm a school teacher, and I might have done wonders with you if I'd caught you early enough!") At the end of *The Penguin Pool Murder*, in a peculiar burst of passion, the two run off to get married, but in the sequel, *Murder on Wheels*

(1933), we discover that they came to their senses before they went through with it; Palmer no doubt realized that domesticity would kill their chemistry. In the novels that follow, Hildegarde and Oscar develop an engaging, endearing cat-and-dog relationship.

The Penguin Pool Murder was made into a film in 1932, starring two redoubtable character actors, Edna May Oliver as Hildegarde and James Gleason as Oscar. Oliver's portrayal was so vivid that it influenced Palmer's own conception of Hildegarde. From the same letter to Dannay:

> Then of course when Edna May Oliver played in the first picture (she did three) I fell in love with her, she was so much Miss Withers. I slanted the character even more in her direction, so that the line between life and art became very vague. In her last years Edna played the part of Miss Withers, wore the funny hats and carried the same umbrella she used in the pictures. I wish she'd run up against a murder, but she didn't. Nowadays I find myself limited in writing about Miss Withers to the scenes that Edna could and would play, and when I write a line of dialogue I hear her crisp Bostonian voice delivering them and milking them dry for every bit of comedy and punch.

More novels about Hildegarde, and more movie versions, followed. Palmer himself moved to Hollywood and collaborated on scripts for classic sleuths like Bulldog Drummond, the Falcon, and the Lone Wolf. Off the lot, he played polo with Spencer Tracy and Darryl Zanuck. During World War Two he served as liaison chief for official U.S. Army film making. But he always went back to Miss Withers, working on new novels and short stories right up to his death. And he never forgot his initial success with *The Penguin Pool Murder*; drawings of penguins, on his letterhead and beside his signature, became his lifelong personal trademark, and in a 1950 humor piece for *Ellery Queen's Mystery Magazine* called *Some of My Best Friends*, he supplied thumbnail sketches of famous fictional detectives from Dupin to Charlie Chan, all in the guise of penguins.

Sometimes Palmer managed to inform the world of Hildegarde Withers with his insider's view of the movie business. In *The Puzzle of the Happy Hooligan* (1941), Miss Withers goes to Hollywood to serve as technical advisor on a movie biography of Lizzie Borden. In *Cold Poison* (1954), she becomes involved in a murder at an animation studio. The studio's trademark cartoon character? Peter Penguin! In 1957, after Palmer appeared on Groucho

Marx's television show, *You Bet Your Life*, Groucho then appeared (along with Miss Withers) in a Palmer short story also titled (though with a more literal meaning) *You Bet Your Life*.

This kind of playful nudging and cross-referencing runs throughout the Withers series, which takes the New York spinster sleuth as far afield as Catalina Island (*The Puzzle of the Pepper Tree*, 1933), foggy England (*The Puzzle of the Silver Persian*, 1934), and Mexico City (*The Puzzle of the Blue Bandarilla*, 1937).

While Palmer had a long-running career in Hollywood, Miss Withers, alas, did not. After making three features as Withers, Edna May Oliver left RKO just as the studio decided to commit itself to the series. The actresses who followed as Hildegarde, Helen Broderick and ZaSu Pitts, were dolefully miscast, and the scripts deteriorated; after three more features, the series ground to a halt. Agnes Moorehead, who might have made a marvelous Hildegarde, was approached to play the role in television series in the 1950s, but the project never materialized. In 1972 a TV pilot called *A Very Missing Person* starred Eve Arden as the spinster sleuth.

One of Palmer's most important relationships, both professionally and personally, was with his friend and sometimes-collaborator Craig Rice, another once-celebrated, now largely forgotten mystery writer (so forgotten, in fact, that it may be necessary to remind readers that Craig Rice was female, despite her first name). Rice's sleuth was the hard-living, hard-drinking John J. Malone, whose vices were shared by his creator. When Rice fell into a personal and creative slump in the 1950s, Palmer came up with the idea to do a series of stories teaming Hildegarde and Malone, on which the two authors would ostensibly collaborate. In fact, Palmer ended up doing most of the writing, though he and Rice shared equal credit.

In a series of letters to Dannay, who bought the stories for *Ellery Queen's Mystery Magazine*, Palmer's comments about the ongoing "collaboration" provide sad glimpses of Rice's deterioration and of Palmer's patience, loyalty, and perennial good humor in dealing with her:

* * *

> I have almost finished the Malone-Withers yarn. Having done most of it alone (Craig took my outline and did the first eight pages very rough) I have thrown most of it to Malone out of gallantry or something. I tried to see Craig when in Los Angeles Monday, and talked to her mother. She is some better, but under a psychiatrist's care in some nursing home.

* * *

Here is *Rift in the Loot*, the Withers-Malone story I told you about. Craig was so anxious to get into the act that I let her make some suggestions on the ending, but couldn't use more than a slight percentage. She is no better, I am sorry to say.

* * *

What of Craig? She seems to have dropped out of sight. Last I heard she was engaged to a millionaire from Lichtenstein and needed a quick fifty which I didn't have.

* * *

Spent three hours with Craig, and wrote you a long letter about it last night which I have torn up. I am much distressed, as the situation is very much worse than you or I or anyone imagined.

* * *

Glad you feel the same way about Craig as I do. When she is herself she is a charming, brilliant, talented woman. I don't intend to be a fair-weathered friend I should have included an outline of the story, but did not since it would have been 99 per cent Palmer and I wanted Craig, for her own sake, to have a hand in it.

* * *

Wrote Craig and asked her if she felt up to reading it [*Cherchez La Frame*] and adding dialogue or anything, but haven't heard from her and imagine she is off to Chihuahua with or without Mr. Bishop, who has a police record as long as your arm—and my arm too. Maybe someday the old girl will get back in the groove again but it won't be in the immediate future, I'm afraid.

Finally, this curious passage, from a letter to a mutual friend:

Craig Rice is necessarily on the wagon, and will spend the rest of her life in a wheelchair, and has finished a novel. She expects to break out of the hospital soon; her children are going to find her an apartment. I have not been down to see her in spite of many invites; the prospect of trying to cheer up an old lady with white hair and no teeth is not inviting. She lives for her New York lawsuit, with high hopes of getting it made—I don't know if [this] was the accident where she fell down an elevator shaft into the basement of St. Nicholas' Arena and then was bitten on the situpon by the watchman's dog, or not. Something along those lines. She wants to borrow money so that her daughter Iris can fly back to testify; what Iris could know about it all is beyond me, and so is the quick fifty.

Craig Rice died in 1957. A collection of the Palmer-Rice short story "collaborations" was published in 1963 as *People vs. Withers and Malone*. Early on, two of the stories were bought by MGM and made into the film *Mrs. O'Malley and Mr. Malone* (1950), with James Whitmore cast as Malone. Hildegarde was unceremoniously dropped, however, and replaced by the very different title character, played by, of all people, Marjorie Main. Much to his chagrin, Palmer saw his beloved Hildegarde Withers transformed by Hollywood into Ma Kettle!

Like his friend Craig Rice, Palmer's creative powers declined in his later years, though not so precipitously. He continued to write new Withers short stories, some of them as good as ever. His attempt to break away from Hildegarde and create a new sleuth, newspaperman-turned-PI Howard Rook, resulted in one fairly good novel, *Unhappy Hooligan* (1956), which drew on Palmer's lifelong fascination with the circus (his native Baraboo was famous as the birthplace of Ringling Brothers Circus). Twelve years passed before the appearance of the disappointing sequel, *Rook Takes Knight* (1968).

Just as Palmer had stepped in to ghostwrite for his ailing friend Craig Rice, so Palmer's final, posthumous work was actually completed by another writer, though with less satisfactory results. Using Stuart's outline and unfinished manuscript, Fletcher Flora received co-author credit for *Hildegarde Withers Makes the Scene* (1969), which jarringly places Hildegarde among California hippies. Regrettably, Flora infused the novel with a mean-spirited edge very unlike Stuart Palmer.

It also resulted in one very bad novel, *Rook Takes Knight* (1968), very little of which may have actually been written by Palmer himself. Just as Palmer had stepped in to ghostwrite for his ailing friend Craig Rice, so Palmer's final, posthumous work was actually finished by another writer, though with less satisfactory results. Fletcher Flora is credited as coauthor of *Hildegarde Withers Makes the Scene* (1969), which jarringly places Hildegarde among California hippies and has a mean-spirited edge very unlike Stuart

Palmer. I suspect Flora may also have been chiefly responsible for the clunky *Rook Takes Knight*, which is equally uncharacteristic of Palmer. Ironically, Stuart Palmer's final credited works are the worst of his career—and may not have been written by him at all.

Today, most of Palmer's books are long out of print. Bantam brought back a few titles in paperback in the 1980s with handsome Art Deco-inspired covers, and more recently International Polygonics has reprinted a few (with cover art best left unmentioned). Otherwise, the man once ranked with Simenon and Queen is largely forgotten, his work unavailable to readers, his sleuth best remembered, when remembered at all, by her screen incarnation. (The Hildegarde Withers films show up regularly on cable television's American Movie Classics.)

Palmer's critical stature is equally murky. The only thing approaching a serious critique that I have been able to find is a brief essay written in 1985 by H.R.F. Keating as an introduction to Palmer's *Cold Poison* (reprinted under its British title *Exit Laughing* in a series called, appropriately, *The Disappearing Detectives*). Keating cannot seem to muster much enthusiasm:

> Odd to reflect that of the dozen fictional detectives I have attempted in this series to prevent disappearing entirely from reader's view Stuart Palmer's Hildegarde Withers, Hildy, is by and large the one least deserving of it.
>
> She was picked out in 1983 as one of some 90 "People of Crime" in an encyclopedia I edited called *Whodunit*. Yet really in many ways she does not deserve quite this preeminence. Hildegarde Withers is, frankly, no more than a cartoon figure.
>
> Conceived originally as a schoolmarm sleuth from a tough New York school, she was equipped with a rag-bag clutch of possibly useful characteristics: her apricot poodle Tallyrand, a series of outrageous hats, a love for fish-tanks and their denizens. But she was never allowed more depth than a penny piece.

And yet, I would argue that the early novels in the Withers series have an immense if arguably quaint charm, which comes largely from their setting, Manhattan in the early years of the Great Depression, with a flavor as unique and delectable in its own cozy way as the British country manors and small villages of Christie or Sayers or Ngaio Marsh. Unconscious details of American social history, together with Palmer's sense of humor, make these books a treasure. And from the outset Palmer understood the sheer enjoyment to be derived from dependable, likable (if often irascible) characters who share an offbeat but endearing relationship and exhibit predictable traits and habits. You know you're hooked on these novels when, at the first mention that Hildy and Oscar are setting out for their traditional spaghetti dinner, you feel like you're sinking into an easy chair.

I would also argue that some of Palmer's later, more mature novels display the power of a master craftsman, and that their expert plotting and pacing make them models of the puzzle school of writing. Two, especially, have had a powerful impact on my own work.

The highly atmospheric *Miss Withers Regrets* (1947) is set in an upscale Long Island suburb after the war. For this reader, at least, Palmer pulls off a dangerous but enviable trick: toward the end of the book, you think you see the solution coming, and it's perfectly logical, and you feel satisfied, more or less, but just a tiny bit let down, since you managed to figure it out, after all—and then, *voilà!* Palmer springs the real solution on you. This diversionary tactic—the subtle emotional trick of intentionally (though temporarily) disappointing the reader—is very daring, I think. I have done my best to emulate it myself.

In *Nipped In The Bud* (1951), the murder is discovered in the first few pages. You see all the details with your eyes wide open—and yet, there's a nagging sense (which become stronger and stronger as the novel progresses) that something, some detail or other, must have been left out of these opening pages—but what? I remember going back to reread the beginning several times as I was approaching the end, and, right up to the last, not being able to put my finger on it. To be made aware of a puzzle, even to the point of being able to see exactly where the missing piece is located in the book, and yet still being unable to figure out the shape of that piece—for me, that was a glorious and rarefied experience.

If I can ever give such an experience to a reader of one of my novels, I will feel quite privileged to have entered the esteemed company of Stuart Palmer, whose influence perseveres, no matter that his work may have fallen, for the moment, into an undeserved obscurity.

Bibliography

Novels:
  Miss Hildegarde Withers Series:
    The Penguin Pool Murder (first Withers), 1931.
    Murder on Wheels, 1932.
    Murder on the Blackboard, 1932.
    The Puzzle of the Pepper Tree, 1933.
    The Puzzle of the Silver Persian, 1934.
    The Puzzle of the Red Stallion (*Puzzle of the Briar Pipe* UK), 1936.
    The Puzzle of the Blue Banderilla, 1937.
    The Puzzle of the Happy Hooligan, 1941.
    Miss Withers Regrets, 1947.
    Four Lost Ladies, 1949.
    The Green Ace (*At One Fell Swoop* UK), 1950.
    Nipped In The Bud (*Trap for a Redhead* UK), 1951.
    Cold Poison (*Exit Laughing* UK), 1954.
    Hildegarde Withers Makes the Scene, with Fletcher Flora, 1969.

  The Howard Rook Series:
    Unhappy Hooligan (*Death in Grease Paint* UK), 1956.
    Rook Takes Knight, 1968.

  Other:
    Ace of Jades, 1931.
    Omit Flowers (*No Flowers by Request* UK), 1937.
    Before It's Too Late (as Jay Stewart), 1950.

Short Stories:
  The Riddles of Hildegarde Withers, ed. by Ellery Queen, 1947.
  The Monkey Murder and Other Hildegarde Withers Stories, ed. by Ellery Queen, 1950.
  People vs. Withers and Malone, with Craig Rice, 1963.
  The Adventure of the Marked Man and One Other (reprint of two Sherlock Holmes pastiches, plus an homage to Doyle, *The IOU of Hildegarde Withers*), 1973.
  Once Upon a Train and Other Stories, with Craig Rice, ed. by H. Straubing, 1981.

Other:
  Numerous Screenplays, Articles.

Steven Saylor

Biography

Steven Saylor grew up in Texas where he earned a B.A. (honors) in history from the University of Texas, Austin, in 1978. 1980 found him in San Francisco where he worked as a magazine and newspaper editor and a freelance writer before publishing *Roman Blood* in 1992. He now lives in Berkeley with his longtime partner, Rick Solomon. He has published five novels set in Ancient Rome featuring Gordianus the Finder. A volume of collected Gordianus short stories, *The House of the Vestals*, appeared in 1997; *Rubicon* follows in 1999. Saylor, a winner of the 1993 Robert L. Fish Memorial short story award, the 1993 Lambda Award for his novel *Catilina's Riddle*, and the 1995 Critics' Choice award for his novel *The Venus Throw*, is currently working on a Texas-based historical mystery due out in 2000.

Bibliography

Novels:
    The Gordianus the Finder Series:
        Roman Blood, 1991.
        Arms of Nemesis, 1992.
        Catilina's Riddle, 1993.
        The Venus Throw, 1995.
        A Murder on the Appian Way, 1996.
        Rubicon, 1999.

    Other:
        Honor the Dead, 2000.

Short Stories:
    The House of the Vestals, 1997.

Susan Moody

♦

The Oxford Detectives

The Oxford Detectives

Biographies

Nicholas Blake
(Cecil Day Lewis, 1904–1972)

The Poet Laureate was born in Ballintubbert, Ireland on 27 April, 1904 and brought to England in 1905. He was educated at Wilkie's Preparatory School, London, 1912–17; Sherborne School, Dorset, 1917–23; Wadham College, Oxford, 1923–27, B.A., M.A. His long academic career embraced posts at a wide number of schools, colleges, and universities; he was Professor of Poetry at Oxford University, 1951–56, and Norton Professor of Poetry, Harvard University, 1964–65. He was a reader at John Lehmann, Ltd, publishers; and a reader, later director from 1954 at Chatto and Windus. In addition to his own poetry, he served as editor of many collections and anthologies of other poets, and issued many translations. Under his pseudonym, he published 20 detective novels, most with amateur sleuth Nigel Strangeways. His honours and awards are too numerous to list. Married to Mary King from 1928–51; two sons; remarried to Jill Balcon, 1951; one son, the actor Daniel Day Lewis, one daughter. He died on 22 May, 1972.

Edmund Crispin
(Robert Bruce Montgomery, 1921–1978)

Edmund Crispin was born on 2 October, 1921, in Chesham Bois, Buckinghamshire, and educated at the Merchant Taylor's School, London, and St. John's College, Oxford, B.A. 1943. He was first a schoolmaster at Shrewsbury School, 1943–45; then, being a gifted musician, he derived his income from composing choral and orchestral works, songs, and film music, and from his writing. Crispin was married; no children. He died on 15 September, 1978.

Michael Innes
(J.I.M. Stewart, 1906–1994)

Michael Innes was born in Edinburgh on 30 September, 1906. He was educated at the Edinburgh Academy and at Oriel College, Oxford, where he was a distinguished scholar (B.A., honours, 1928). A Lecturer in English, University of Leeds, 1930–35, he became the Jury Professor of English, University of Adelaide, Australia, 1935–45; Lecturer, Queen's University, Belfast, 1946–48; Fellow of Christ Church, Oxford, 1969–73. In 1961 he served a term as Walker-Ames Professor, University of Washington, Seattle. Honours include: D.Litt., University of New Brunswick, 1962; University of Leicester, 1979; University of St. Andrews, 1980. His literary output was enormous; in addition to the Appleby detections infused with a donnish sensibility, he wrote other crime novels and 20 novels as J.I.M. Stewart, dozens of short stories, and many works of scholarship. Married to Margaret Hardwick (1932–79); three sons, two daughters. He died on 12 November, 1994.

The Oxford Detectives

My subject is Oxford detectives, but I'm going to concentrate for the most part on just one.

In England, magazines and newspapers often have little fillers at the end of the page, small items in which they ask the rich and/or famous to write about such trivial subjects as:

The worst day of my life.
What's on my night-table for bedside reading.
Who I would most like to spend an evening with.

Were I ever rich and famous enough to be asked the latter question, my answer would undoubtedly be with Robert Montgomery, the man whose alias is Edmund Crispin—wine lover, sophisticate, cultured, witty, *bon viveur*, knowledgeable. And above all, charming.

In *vino veritas*—possibly. In Crispin's case, it was *in scribendo veritas*, most definitely. A writer may make every effort he can to be un-autobiographical, but nonetheless, every word he writes says something about the sort of man he is. Only a charming man could have produced such a charming protagonist as Professor Gervase Fen.

I first came across Crispin's work as an impressionable schoolgirl in Oxford, and was immediately overwhelmed by the deliciously dissolute picture of the author on the back cover of his books. At the time, I also thought the author blurb which he'd obviously written himself was absolutely hilarious...I was younger then! Unlike most authors, Crispin wrote, he had never been a lumberjack, bartender, advertising agent, ship's cat, lecturer in metallurgy, gigolo, and Member of Parliament. What he had been was a schoolmaster and it was to this period of his life that he attributed his knowledge of human nature in general and of criminal human nature in particular.

Already, before a book has even been opened, we have a flavour of the man.

Kingsley Amis, one of our foremost novelists and father of the perhaps more famous Martin, and Philip Larkin, probably our leading poet, were both up at Oxford with Montgomery, during the war. Amis describes the first time they saw him as a real undergraduate. Amis writes:

This man along with an indefinable and daunting air of maturity, had a sweep of wavy auburn hair, a silk dressing-gown in some non-primary shade and a walk that looked eccentric and mincing, though I found out later that it was the result of severe congenital deformity in both feet.

When more fully attired, he inclined to a fancy-waistcoated, suede-shoed style, along with cigarette holders and rings. They made me uneasy, especially the last two items, which at about this time were apparently compulsory for villains in British films.

Even Philip Larkin, himself no ascetic in matters of dress, disapproved.

"I say. I don't much care for those rings of Bruce's," he said.
"They're flashy."
"Yes, and foreign."
"Yes, and common."

Can't you just imagine the pair of them, jealous as hell of this undergraduate sophisticate?

A brief biography. Robert Bruce Montgomery—his real name—was born into a family where there were already three daughters. The youngest of these was five years older than he was, and by the time he was seven or eight, all his sisters were away at school. Because of his feet, he had to undergo annual operations until he was fourteen, which obviously limited his activities, and made him somewhat solitary. Music and books—playing and writing—were the obvious things to occupy himself with: amazingly, he was largely self-taught.

Montgomery was one of those unfortunate people who peak early. By the time he went up to Oxford, he was already something of a polymath. Although he entered St. John's College in 1940 as Organ Scholar, he also read modern languages. He became the college choirmaster and also conductor of the Oxford University Musicians' Club. He spent much of his time hanging out with actors at the Oxford Playhouse. And, crucially, he was already a frequenter of hotel bars, while his gauche fellow undergraduates were still hoisting pints in the local pubs. I hope this important transatlantic distinction translates.... To add to his cosmopolitan image, he was also rumoured to have written a book called *Romanticism and the World Crisis*, he possessed a grand piano, and was known as something of a painter.

In 1944, while still an undergraduate, he published his first crime novel, *The Case of the Gilded Fly*—or as his friends called it: *The*

Gelded Fly. He wrote this in two weeks, during the Easter vacation, using a silver penholder, and published it under the pseudonym of Edmund Crispin. Predictably enough, Amis and Larkin, who planned to be successful novelists themselves, tore it to critical shreds.

After leaving Oxford, Montgomery taught for a time at Shrewsbury, a famous private school for boys. The crime novels came out yearly until 1952. In 1953, he published a collection of short stories. For a while, he occupied himself with giving concerts and recitals. Because of his music, he frequented the world of film studios, and was occasionally seen escorting busty blonde starlets about the West End. These were circles which seemed unimaginably glittering to his duller contemporaries.

But by 1960, he had retired to Devon to do nothing more demanding than write a bit more music for the cinema, fill in the *Times* crossword, anthologise sci-fi stories, and write reviews of crime and science fiction.

After that, there was a twenty-five year gap until in 1977, the year before he died, he produced *The Glimpses of the Moon*, the ninth novel which, as Kingsley Amis rather bitchily puts it, "we had all been rightly dreading." His publishers announced on the cover: "Worth Waiting For!" Sadly, it wasn't.

So...what happened? We get a glimpse of the reason in a letter from Philip Larkin, who describes Montgomery's time as a schoolmaster at Shrewsbury as "beer-drinking interrupted by brief bursts of teaching."

What happened to him, Amis says, was very simple and dreadful. Crispin had two genuine and precocious talents—music and authorship—which both dried up quickly and completely when he was about thirty. By this time, he was rich and to some considerable extent famous, both as Edmund Crispin, the crime writer, and also as Bruce Montgomery, composer of film music. Yet at that time, he reportedly said to Amis: "I can see no point in anything more and don't get any fun out of anything I do."

So, like Hammett before him, he simply allowed alcohol to destroy his cultural output. Amis remarks: "It took Dylan Thomas 20 years to drink himself to death. It took Edmund Crispin 27."

The question has to be asked: does Edmund Crispin count?

Of course! He counts, first of all, over and above any other consideration, because of the wit and humour of his books, the grace of his style, and the personal charm of his protagonist, Gervase Fen, Professor of English Literature and Language in the University of Oxford, who is surely among the most delightful sleuths in the entire genre.

He is totally unalarming, endearingly boyish, his dark hair ineffectually slicked down with water, though a few mutinous spikes always stick up on the crown of his head. He had blue eyes—obviously some Irish ancestry in there somewhere—but wait until the villains start trying to get the better of him, and see just how quickly those blue eyes grow icy cold.

It is not his looks which entrance the reader, however, but his behaviour. This is clearly a man who has never grown up, an academic Peter Pan. I've always loved Fen's exuberance, his extrovert character, his unconventional behaviour, his fitful enthusiasms. He is always larger than life, whether singing lustily and raucously to the hedgegrows as he walks down a country lane; driving dangerously through Oxford in his little red sports car; improvising a speech to be delivered to the rural voters in a bid to enter Parliament; or simply grumbling, which he does frequently and with gusto.

He likes to be the centre of attention. He makes frightful puns—"Oxford is the City of Screaming Choirs" or "The home of lost corpses"— are among the worst. Left alone with sticks of greasepaint, like a child, he cannot refrain from experimentally daubing them all over his face. At the drop of a hat, he will start boring on about the crime novel he is about to write. When he feels unwell, he lets everyone know about it.

Yet his intellectual ability is never in doubt. This is, after all, a renowned literary critic, author of several learned works as well as a Professor of English Language and Literature.

Not that this particularly impresses people. In *The Moving Toyshop*, a friend he hasn't seen for some time says,

> "You weren't a professor when I saw you last. The University had more sense."
> To which Fen answers firmly, "I was made a professor because of my tremendous scholarly abilities and my acute and powerful mind."
> His friend says, "Oh? You wrote to me at the time that it was only a matter of pulling a few moth-eaten strings."
> "Did I?" Fen says uneasily. "Well, never mind all that now...."

Here's what Michael Innes has to say about dons and detective stories:

> The senior members of Oxford and Cambridge colleges are undoubtedly among the most moral and levelheaded of men. They do nothing aberrant; they do nothing rashly or in haste. Their conventional associations are with learning, unworldliness, absence of mind and endearing and always innocent foible. They are, as Ben Jonson would have said, persons such as comedy would choose; it is much easier to give them a shove into the humorous than a twist into the melodramatic; they prove peculiarly resistive to the slightly rummy psychology that most detective-stories require. And this is a pity if only because their habitat...offers such a capital frame for the quiddities and wilie-beguilies of the craft.

Much of this applies to Gervase Fen. There is no denying that some of Crispin's plots are weak, that sometimes he lapses from wit into facetiousness, that the form occasionally overwhelms the content.

But, as he wrote himself:

> I have no great liking for the so-called 'realistic' type of crime story. I believe that crime stories in general, and detective stories in particular, should be essentially imaginative and artificial, in order to make their best effect.

Yet, despite that artificiality, or perhaps because of it, the setting he chooses—the City of Oxford itself, small villages in the west of England, a film studio, a cathedral close, a boys' public school—are fully realised, fully realistic. Self-contained. Graspable. Nothing sweeping or vast. And for the all-too-short length of each book, Crispin manages to transport us into the miniature world he is describing.

And unlike many other writers, particularly those with serial characters, there is no straining to insert Fen into each new setting. Each of the backgrounds in which we find Fen seem to arise absolutely logically out of his personality and his position.

For instance, it is absolutely logical that he might appear in Sandford Angelorum as the Prospective Parliamentary Candidate for the Independent party. Someone asks him: "What put it into your head? Why are you standing for Parliament?"

Even to himself, Fen's actions were sometimes unaccountable, and he could think of no convincing reply. He said sanctimoniously,

> It is my wish to serve the community.... Or at least, that is one of my motives. Besides, I felt I was getting far too restricted in my interests. Have you ever produced a definitive edition of

Langland?... You begin to wonder if you're mad. And the only remedy for that is a complete change of occupation.

Perfectly logical. Again, it is logical that he might be visiting a friend who has temporarily taken over as organist in a west country cathedral, as in *Holy Disorders*, or present at a boys' school in *Love Lies Bleeding*, as the replacement speaker on Speech Day, called in at the last minute as an old friend of the Headmaster's.

At the Leiper film studios in *Frequent Hearses*, Fen's presence again is absolutely logical. The film studio is about to make a film about Alexander Pope, and naturally Fen, as an English Professor, has been hired as an expert on Pope's life and works.

Someone writing a history of the University wrote: "Oxford Blood is spilled with curiously exuberant passion and freedom."

And that is another of Crispin's great strengths. Oxford: how good he is on Oxford—its institutions, its eccentricities, its affectations, and its beauty?

Here's the city, glimpsed from the top of Headington Hill at night, just as the Scholar Gypsy glimpsed it years before in Matthew Arnold's poem:

> Through a rift in the trees he caught his first real glimpse of Oxford—in that ineffectual moonlight an underwater city, its towers and spires standing ghostly, like the memorials of lost Atlantis, fathoms deep. A tiny pinpoint of yellow light glowed for a few seconds, flickered, and went out. On the quiet air he heard faintly a single bell beating one o'clock, the precursor of others which joined in brief phantom chime, like the bells of the sunken cathedral in Breton myth, rocked momentarily by the green deep-water currents, and then silent.

It is worth remembering that the middle class authors of the time were writing out of a deep bedrock of certainty. Not only about themselves, but also about the world in which they—and their fictional characters—operated. The donnish school—of which the most notable classic practitioners were Michael Innes, Dorothy Sayers (in *Gaudy Night*), Crispin himself, Nicholas Blake, and J.C. Masterman—was no exception. Unlike Chandler and Hammett, their books did not treat of moral ambiguity. There are few doubts in these books, no ethical dilemmas. Good is good and bad is nearly always unmitigatedly bad.

For instance, in *Operation Pax*, by Michael Innes, Appleby tells the rabbitty little conman, Routh, that sometimes the only way out of a tough spot was through the police station. "It may be a bit bleak," he says, "but it's as safe as Buckingham palace." This was a certainty all law-abiding Brits would have enjoyed both then and, in fact, until recently. It's one that a Raymond Chandler character would not have been able to share.

As I said, in these donnish crime novels, there was little moral reflection. It wasn't necessary for the writers to keep on announcing how upright and virtuous their heroes were, as Hammett and Chandler did. There were no declarations about mean streets and men who were not themselves mean. It simply wasn't necessary. The reader would have understood that as Englishmen, what else would these protagonists be but honorable? As Englishmen, how else would they behave but as gentlemen?

It should perhaps be pointed out that by the time the Oxbridge dons turned to crime writing, the genre had attained a certain amount of respectability. By the mid 1940s, no real-time don need be ashamed to be caught reading one. Or, for that matter, writing one. Or even being the protagonist in one. As solid members of the upper middle classes, such readers did not want dispatches from beyond the frontiers of their own experience. For them, these Oxford-set novels were entertainment, an intellectual puzzle, with a delicious dash of literacy thrown in to reassure them that they were not behaving frivolously.

Later, it became the fashion among critics and the newer generations of crime writers to deride and despise the middle classes and their tastes in almost everything, for no real reason that I have ever been able to see. Even as late as 1971, Crispin was given a book to review called *Snobbery With Violence*—an overview of the contemporary crime novel which sought to show how far it had matured—with the very clear indication that in so doing, it had mightily improved, and wrote resignedly: "Oh dear: the Poor old Middle Classes have been at it again."

Nor did the readers of that kind of crime fiction want any sex or violence. Violence is very seldom described within their pages, though a great deal of disgust and abhorrence is expressed at the possibility of it. Particularly if people with German connections were involved. A high moral tone was taken, partly because of the social climate. Many of those donnish crime novels were written either as England geared itself up for war, suffered through a war, or came out at the end of a war which—with a little help from our friends—we had indubitably won.

As for sex, it was a popular fallacy of the times that the middle classes did not have sex very much, and the academic classes not at all.

At least, I assume it was a fallacy since my own father, who was an English don at Oxford managed to produce five children!

Fen is unusual for those fictional times in not having a fairly high-powered wife or companion: Ngaio Marsh's Roderick Alleyn is married to famous painter Agatha Troy whose paintings hang in the house; discerning millionaire Margery Allingham's Albert Campion married an aircraft designer—surely a ground breaking job for a woman in those days; the wife of Michael Innes' Inspector Appleby is the strongly independent sculptor, Judith. Nicholas Blake sleuth, Nigel Strangeways' wife Georgia is not only an explorer, but one of the three most renowned explorers in the world!

Fen's wife, Dolly, by contrast, is described as a plain, spectacled sensible little woman incongruously called Dolly, sitting at one corner of the fireplace in Fen's set of rooms in college. She seems to be content to look after the children occasionally uttering a calming "Now Gervase" at her husband's wilder flights of fancy. This, to me, strikes a strange note: perhaps in Crispin's time at St. John's, in the early 1940s, don's wives were in the habit of sitting in their husbands' college rooms, but I grew up in that Oxford milieu, and from my own experience, I know that wives and children were kept firmly sequestered in North Oxford—although as I grew into adolescence, I did find myself frequently calling upon my father in college in the hope of being introduced to undergraduates! I can't imagine that Dolly Fen had the same motivation.

But perhaps W.G. Moore, Montgomery's tutor, was unusual in this regard.

However...most of the information we have about Dolly Fen is contained in *The Gilded Fly*. Very little is heard thereafter and it makes me wonder whether Crispin originally intended her to take a larger part in subsequent novels—given the knitting, which is a classic crime fiction cliché, perhaps he intended her to play a Miss Marple-ish accompaniment to Fen's solo performances.

As I said earlier, although Crispin's books might at first glance appear to be classic golden age crime fiction, linear descendents of that genteel Thirties world he admired so much, the world of decent young men in flannels and plucky tennis playing girls, he cannot help including a certain amount of subtle subversion.

The classic ingredients are always there, but they often come with a dose of realism attached.

Here's a village in Devon:

> Cotten Abbas is sixty or seventy miles from London and obscurely conveys the impression of having strayed there out of a film set. As with most show-villages, you are apt to feel when confronted with it, that some impalpable process of embalming or refrigeration is at work, some prophylactic against change and decay which, while altogether creditable in itself has yet resulted in a certain degree of stagnation.

I find that description most perspicacious given the times in which Crispin was writing. In England today, there is a constant battle between those who wish to embalm what they perceive as the pleasant past and those who insist that we must engage in the march of progress, however detrimental it may be. Most classic writers would have described such a village in terms of its embattled state against that march; it is part of Crispin's subtle subversion that he so often take the unexpected view. (Though in his last book, *The Glimpses of the Moon*, he spends much of his time inveighing against the South West Electricity Board and the pylons which are making the countryside both hideous and dangerous—indeed, one of the central characters in the book is a highly excitable pylon known to the locals as "The Pisser.")

Crispin's work includes most of the standard characters we expect from classic cosy crime writing: the Doctor, the Squire, the Rector, the Chief Constable, the absentminded Professor, the conceited Actor. In his hands, all these are present and all are recognisably English, recognisably Classic, recognisably recognisable. Nonetheless, he makes of them something quite other than central casting, rent-a-crowd, stock characters, imbuing them with a strong individualism so that many of his wonderfully realised characters are almost Dickensian in their ferocious eccentricity.

Crispin loves the eccentric. Take, for example, the Rector in *Buried for Pleasure* who for eighteen years has been plagued by a teacup-throwing poltergeist but rather than bring unwelcome publicity upon his rectory, has succeeded in domesticating it, training it not to rap and throw things after midnight. As the Rector explains earnestly to Fen:

> The thing clearly enjoyed its preposterous goings-on; they did no one any serious harm; and since I might conceivably worsen

its condition by scaring it off, I felt it my duty as a Christian priest to let it alone. And I've never regretted doing so.

Or Sir Richard Freeman, the Chief Constable of Oxford, who although a policeman, would much rather be an academic writer—unlike Fen, who would rather be a policeman—and has already published three books of literary criticism.

This is the same Sir Richard who, in one of those wonderful running gags which Crispin loves, keeps interrupting Fen's detecting with querulous phone calls about the subtext of Shakespeare's play, *Measure for Measure*.

And there is the raffish Captain Watkyn, the parliamentary agent in *Buried For Pleasure*, in which we find Fen standing for Parliament as the Independent candidate. Captain Watkyn is marvellously enthusiastic, and is about to have posters stuck up all over the constituency with Fen's photograph on them and the caption: "Vote for Fen and A Brave New World." Fen demurs at this: "I scarcely think—"

But as Watkyn points out: "...you won't get into Parliament by saying: 'Vote for Fen and a Slightly Better World If You're Lucky'."

Or the two bewildered heavies hired from London to practise a spot of GBH on some inconvenient witnesses, who find themselves, without quite knowing how, being thrown into the river at one of Oxford's most well-known swimming holes, Parsons Pleasure, where elderly dons used to come to bathe in the nude.

A science don, who was standing slapping his belly on the bank, regarded them helpfully. Seeing that they could not swim, he said: "Now is the time to learn. Bring your body up to a horizontal position and relax the muscles; the surface tension will support you."

Incidentally, I remember my father telling me about the renowned Head of College who, along with a number of his colleagues was disporting himself on the river bank, stark naked, when a punt containing young ladies came by. The other dons immediately clapped towels over their private parts, but this man, Professor Joad, covered his head, explaining afterward, in reproving tones: "I, gentlemen, am known by my face!"

And it would be hard to find anything zanier than Dr. Garbin, the clergyman in *Holy Disorders*, who find himself quite by chance with a raven as a pet. As he explains to Fen:

> "A foreign sailor with a tragic history sold him to me some two years ago. He is supposed to speak, I think, but I have

never heard him do so. He is not," Garbin paused, "a companionable creature I admit. Sometimes I find his presence actually depressing. I have given him every chance to escape but he displays only apathy."

Garbin stretched out a hand to stroke the bird's feathers. It pecked at him.

I wish I had time to read you Crispin's account of Fen's visit to this man. Not only does Dr. Garbin have a pet raven, but his wife is called Lenore, and Fen takes enormous pleasure in saying things like: "I say, is that a pallid bust of Pallas, perched above your chamber door?" Or, looking at the man's bookshelves: "Here is many a quaint and curious volume of forgotten lore..." while Dr. Garbin, obviously wondering where this nutter has escaped from, is saying: "Mmm yes, I suppose that's one way of putting it."

This Edgar Allan Poe-type bird is by no means the only curious pet in Crispin's books. Crispin might well have been a fully paid-up member had there been such an association as the RSPCA—that's the Royal Society for the Propagation of Cruelty to Animals.

For instance, there is the naked parrot in the *Case of the Gilded Fly*, which has pecked out all of its feathers except for a ruff round its head, which it can't reach.

In the *Long Divorce*, there is a cat called Lavender whose IQ is non existent, so that it goes about with the hypnotic air of the feeble-witted, and seems to lack the usual cat attributes, so that it seems incapable of moving about without sending ornaments, clocks, vases, etc. crashing to the floor.

Then there is the Non-Doing pig in *Buried For Pleasure*. This graceless but faithful animal is a small, greyish, unalluring pig which never seems to grow however much it eats, though its owner says he's very affectionate and extremely faithful. At the end of the book, as the Fish Inn comes crashing to the ground, Fen sees that a jagged lump of stone has done for the non-doing pig. Not that he cares much. In his opinion, its fidelity had never adequately compensated for its basic lack of charm.

Perhaps the most memorable of Crispin's creatures occurs in *Love Lies Bleeding*. Mr. Merrythought, a clear descendant of the Hound of the Baskerville, is a grim, demented bloodhound who is given to homicidal fits every three months or so, and is consequently treated with extreme care.

At the end of the book, Fen finds himself following Mr. Merrythought through some dark and rainy woods though he has no confidence at all in the dog's tracking skills. However, it is the onset of one of Mr. Merrythought's trimensual fits which saves Fen from certain death as the dog launches himself at the would-be murderer and so gets the bullet intended for Fen.

Although Crispin was a devotee of John Dickson Carr, he always acknowledged as his master that other great Oxford crime-writing don, Michael Innes, creator of Sir John Appleby. So much so that he not only borrowed half of his protagonist's name from Innes, but also half of his pseudonym, and even one of Innes's characters, the seedy little criminal called Routh, who appears in the *Glimpses of the Moon*. Innes is unmistakably the prime example and progenitor of the donnish school of crime writing.

Yet, although Innes is better at plotting than Crispin, he handles farce much less authoritatively, and with a heavier hand. Nor are his characters as memorable though his prose is richer, and has a more purposeful intent. Although he relies on many of the same effects as Crispin—for instance, his use of literary puns, apposite quotations, excellent scene setting, robust and sometimes facetious humour—his deeper learning comes through.

There are no large insights in these books, no dark underbellies, and precious little social comment. But why should there have been? As I said, at the time they were written, detective fiction was still regarded as light entertainment for the middle classes.

When I was Chairman of the British Crime Writers' Association, I tried to get Michael Innes awarded our prestigious Diamond Dagger award, but my suggestion was voted down on the completely unfair grounds that a) he had done nothing for the crime novel, with which I violently disagreed, and b) was in any case—that dreaded word—elitist.

When I challenged people on this, asking what exactly they meant, this boiled down to the fact that his characters, like Crispin's, including or especially, the policemen, were literate, had read the great classics of English literature, and didn't mind punning on them or quoting from them when the need arose—and often when it didn't.

But in those days, dons really did and, in fact, often still do, talk like that. In one of the most hilarious scenes in *Operation Pax*, Innes gives us some wonderful Oxonian nonsense. He shows us the Senior Common room dining at High Table when one the Fellows happens to mention some careless remark of his twelve-year-old son's about seeing a man running away from some other men. Immediately the rest of them take this up, speculating in the most earnest of tones on what the son might otherwise have seen, supposing he had not in fact seen what he said he saw, offering hypothesis and conjecture to explain the truth or otherwise of the son's claims, postulating theories which gradually get wilder and wilder. At the end of the scene, you realize that Innes has been taking off the kind of patronizing discussions of textual criticism with which he must have been altogether too familiar.

But that's what Oxford is like. And dons don't change much. Nor do undergraduates, of whom there are some notable types in both Innes and Crispin. As Crispin says, in the *Case of the Gilded Fly*: in Oxford, the faces change but the types persist.

I can vouch for that, not only as the daughter of a don, but as a mother of a very recent graduate of the University.

Beside elitism, other charges have been levelled at these donnish books. Critics claim that the farceur style and the elaborate set pieces overshadow the plot, which is often true, and Julian Symons calls Innes "a writer who turns the detective story into an over-civilized joke."

They claim that the plots themselves place far too much reliance on chance and coincidence. *The Gilded Fly* is a case in point, where the murderer fires through three open windows at a girl who fortuitously happened to be kneeling in the line of fire beside a chest of drawers.

Or the frankly unbelievable timing of alibis in *Love Lies Bleeding*.

Or the clumsy denouement in *Holy Disorders*—so inept, in fact, that I like this book the least of the Crispin oeuvre.

Critics also complain that writers like Crispin show a deplorable tendency toward facetiousness where the puns quiver and rock like scenery in a village hall, and herald their punch lines well in advance, and that the introduction of literary references is self-conscious and maladroit.

However, another donnish writer seems to have been more successful at getting the balance right. Nicholas Blake, the pseudonym of Cecil Day Lewis (1904–72)—and yes, father of Daniel, the actor—although not strictly an Oxford fiction writer, is nonetheless a prime example of the donnish school of writing, and both the author and the protagonist are products of Oxford University.

Blake's detective is Nigel Strangeways, of whom Julian Symons wrote: "Nigel Strangeways was a real innovation, a genuine literary detective rather than one of those given quotations to spout."

Strangeways was originally based on W.H. Auden, both in appearance and in some of his habits, whom C. Day Lewis knew when Auden was at Oxford, both of them being aspiring poets and litterateurs, and both later occupying the post of Professor of Poetry in the University.

Nicholas Blake appears at first to be writing out of the same certainties as Innes or Crispin, larding his prose with literary references which range from the classics to more recent poets—as you would expect from a man who would later become Poet Laureate. Literary puns abound.

And yet, there is a slightly political, even a faintly radical note to his work—a faint stirring among the rhododendrons, a hint of mutiny in the servants' hall—which is missing in Crispin and Innes. He expresses left wing views. He quotes from T.S. Eliot, who at the time these books were written was considered the most iconoclastic of poets. My own father used to say dismissively that Eliot was a fine comic poet, referring to *Old Possum's Book of Practical Cats*.

I have to say that, as a setting for murder, I have never understood what is wrong with the drawing room and the cosy village. Auden wrote years ago that the "most satisfying detective stories are those set in idyllic and preferably rural conditions so that the body appears as shockingly out of place as when a dog makes a mess on a drawing room carpet."

This debate is still going on today, and in England we are currently witnessing a widening gulf between the so called realists and what they sneeringly refer to as the cosies. Writers of the self-styled realistic school of crime fiction claim that the cosy writers write about an idealized nonexistent world which has nothing to do with contemporary England, and that the only *real* crime writing deals with urban societies and urban problems.

The idea that the British countryside is invalid as a setting for a contemporary crime novel is nonsense. There is as much passion seething, as much incentive to murder, in the gardens of a stone-built Cotswold village, as there is in some high-rise block in London's East End, or the slums of Nottingham....

But despite the progress that these *realists* like to think the crime novel has made, the donnish, literary, witty crime novel continues not only to be read, but to be written. In 1963, a crime novelist began writing the sort of fiction that Blake, Innes and Crispin had almost ceased to produce, citing as her reason that she could not find the sort of books she wanted, in which conversation abounded, and what violence there was came as a shock, rather than being commonplace. Mysteries with a cast of characters who had some acquaintance with literature and fiction in which women figure as more than appendages or sex objects. She wrote:

> My sort of detective fiction, she wrote, will always be accused of snobbery. This is inevitable. I loathe violence and do not consider sex a spectator sport. I like humour but fear unkindness and the cruelty of power.
>
> One day, my heroine sprang from my brain to counter these things I loathe, to talk all the time, occasionally with wit, and to offer to those who like it the company of people I consider civilized, and a plot, feeble perhaps, but reflecting a moral universe.

These words were written by Amanda Cross, herself a professor of literature, and provide a fitting overview of Crispin and the other donnish crime writers. And how very pleasing it is that they should have been written by an American!

Susan Moody

Biography

Susan Moody now lives in Oxford, where she grew up as the daughter of a don, and is familiar with both the fictional and actual population of the university. At one time she lived in Oak Ridge, Tennessee, and her eldest son now lives in California, so she has a long acquaintance with the States. She began her writing career with two historical novels (both published in the U.S.) but turned to crime in 1984, creating an unusual sleuth: a tall black girl called Penny Wanawake. After following *Penny Black* with six more crime novels, Moody moved into writing suspense and other fiction. The 1991 story of the couple in the Gold Blend (Taster's Choice) ads resulted in the runaway bestseller, *Love over Gold*. The author returned to the mystery field in 1993 by publishing her first Cassie Swann novel starring a self-reliant professional bridge player whose skill at picking up clues in cards is duplicated in solving crimes. Moody's short stories are widely published at home and abroad; the most recent, *The Guilty Party*, was a runner up in the Crime Writer's Association short story award. In 1995, she published *Misselthwaite*, sequel to the much loved children's book *The Secret Garden.* A former Chairman of the Crime Writers Association and a current member of the Detection Club, the versatile author is an experienced instructor of writers' workshops.

Bibliography

Novels:
    The Penny Wanawake series:
        Penny Black, 1984. (Reprinted 1997 by Poisoned Pen Press.)
        Penny Dreadful, 1984.
        Penny Post, 1985.
        Penny Royal, 1986.
        Penny Wise, 1988.
        Penny Pinching, 1989.
        Penny Saving, 1990.

    The Cassie Swann Series:
        Takeout Double (*Death Takes a Hand* US), 1993.
        Grand Slam, 1994.
        King of Hearts, 1995.
        Doubled in Spades, 1996.
        Sacrifice Bid, 1997.
        Dummy Hand, 1998.

    Other :
        A Distant Shore (as Susannah James), 1981.
        Lucia's Legacy, 1984.
        Playing with Fire (*Mosaic* US), 1989.
        Hush-a-Bye, 1991.
        House of Moons, 1993.
        The Italian Garden, 1994.
        Love over Gold, (as Susannah James), 1993.
        Misselthwaite, 1995.
        Falling Angel, 1998.

Other:
    Numerous Short Stories

Margaret Lewis

◆

Ellis Peters

Ellis Peters
Edith Mary Pargeter
(1913–1995)

Biography

Ellis Peters was born in Horsehay, Shropshire, on 18 September, 1913. She was educated at the Dawley Church of England School, Coalbrookdale High School for Girls, and earned an Oxford School Certificate. From childhood she had authored numerous tales and was fixed on being a writer, but she began work as a chemist's assistant, 1933–40. During World War II she served in the Women's Royal Navy Service, 1940–45, and earned the British Empire Medal, 1944. Out of this came her timely trilogy on her wartime experiences. She published her first crime novel in 1938, and after her return to civilian life, was a full-time writer. Honours include the Mystery Writers of America Edgar Allan Poe Award, 1963; the Czechoslovak Society for International Relations Gold Medal, 1968, recognizing her numerous translations; the Crime Writers Association Silver Dagger Award, 1981, and its Diamond Dagger Award, 1994. She was a member of the International Institute of Arts and Letters (fellow, 1961). She died on 14 October, 1995.

A Tribute to Ellis Peters

"I have never wanted to live anywhere but in Shropshire," said Edith Pargeter to me as we sat a few years ago looking out over her rose-filled garden a few miles from Shrewsbury. And it was in her own house in Shropshire that she died, on 14 October, 1995, after suffering a severe stroke. In a writing career that began in 1936, her historical novels, her novels of the Second World War, her detective fiction and, of course, the chronicles of Brother Cadfael reached out to a wide and appreciative public throughout the world. Many readers from Poland to the United States mourned her death, and regretted that the fictional life of such a great favourite, Brother Cadfael, had also come to an end.

In her recent years Edith's mobility had become seriously impaired and she was no longer able to wander the narrow streets and alleyways of Shrewsbury where so many of her historical figures went about their business. Instead, her imaginary world of twelfth century Shropshire emerged from a comfortable modern house where books, photographs and music shared the shelves, and a small portable typewriter on a desk was the only clue that a writer was present. When we first met, Edith moved energetically about the house, pulling out books for me to see, discussing her wide range of friends overseas and making tea in her well-equipped kitchen. Then as her health became more fragile and after an operation which confined her to a wheelchair, Edith found, perhaps for the first time, that what she had most loved in life, her writing, was becoming impossible to achieve. Yet she remained positive in her thinking right to the very end saying, "The one thing I most want to do still is go on writing, and finding satisfactory things to write."

Shortly before she died, we corresponded about many aspects of her life and work, and I share these thoughts with you now, as we remember a much-loved writer and, for everyone who knew her, a much-loved friend.

I knew that in all of her novels the setting is a crucial factor, and because this interests me a great deal, I raised the topic again with her. Her answer confirmed the importance of this aspect of her work:

> A sense of place is always vital, for me, to setting the scene for a story. Even in my modern suspense novels the backdrop is always derived from some particular location in or near Shropshire, as the Middlehope of *Rainbow's End* is in the upper Teme Valley and the Aurae Phiala of *City of Gold and Shadows* is Uriconium. Never a facsimile, but quite identifiable to Salopians. A convincing piece of the world is essential if you want to people it with convincing characters. So place, season and weather always play a great part in my books. And accordingly, place plays the same role in my life.

From her vantage point in Shropshire, one of the quietest parts of England, Edith looked confidently out to a wider world:

> Having firm roots of your own, I think, disposes you to respect and feel interest in the roots of other people, so that the parochial and the universal are not contradictory, but mutually supportive.

Edith, who never married, had always been reticent about her private life. I asked her about the happy marriages in her novels, Hugh Beringar and Aline with their baby, George Felse and Bunty and Dominic; and found very firm views on the subject of the family:

> I am an absolute believer in the strength and importance of the family, so perhaps it was inevitable that I should stress it even in the murder mysteries. I think George must be the only happily married policeman in the genre, his wife and son assets in the main, not liabilities.

Young people feature in many of her novels and they travel freely from Italy to Czechoslovakia to India. Edith found that

> ...the growing disposition to begin travel in the teens, which I sense everywhere these days, must be good. Mutual interest and mutual understanding cannot but aid the cause of peace, as well as enriching the lives of all parties.

Two of her Inspector Felse novels with young Dominic as hero are set in India because

> I was dying to set out for other people the places and events that had entranced me after three months in that country. I could not possibly write a factual book about India after that one visit, but I could use Cape Comorin and the elephants of Periyar as backdrop to a suspense novel. Place, again, asserting itself.

Internationalism in its broadest form filled her life and many of her books. Although she herself served with distinction in the WRNS (she was awarded the British Empire Medal in 1944 "for zeal and wholehearted devotion to duty") and regarded the defeat of Hitler as being entirely necessary, her natural learnings were towards pacifism and tolerance. At the same time she did not dismiss the need for the lessons of the Second World War to be remembered:

> I think it is vital that the events of the war should be commemorated and remembered by the current generations, and accurately recorded for generations to come, or nothing will have been learned from them. I have followed the events of VE and VJ days with considerable emotion, and renewed one or two contacts from fifty years back. And felt very glad that I was able to be in it, as close as possible to combat. I would not have missed it. Nothing else then seemed worth doing.

The international summer school that she attended in Czechoslovakia in 1947 changed the direction of her life dramatically. In the years that followed, she taught herself Czech and translated sixteen books into English, maintaining her friendships in Czechoslovakia through many difficult years of political repression. A recently reprinted novel, *The Soldier at the Door*, first published in 1954, is an eloquent, deeply-felt plea against war and conscription and pleads the case for young victims of militaristic states throughout the world.

Edith never found political parties particularly helpful in leading society towards her goal of international understanding, and said:

> The only political party I have ever belonged to was the Labour Party, immediately after the war, and that only lasted about two or three years before disillusionment. I think I am incapable of staying within a political party, at least as they exist now, since all of them are so flawed, and ultimately let their idealists down. The only standard any man can guarantee is his own personal standard of behaviour, towards all other people, native or stranger, and if everyone concentrated on that, national and international affairs would have a better chance of taking care of themselves.

Discussing politics invariably led us to religion. Many people who only know Edith through her Brother Cadfael novels might be surprised to know that she placed herself at a little distance from organized religion, although as a historian she was very interested in the life of Shrewsbury Abbey: "I have always been sensitive to the appeal of the monastic life and enjoyed from the beginning the attempt to enter it imaginatively," she wrote. Invariably we had come around to Brother Cadfael, that humorous, sympathetic and sharply observant character who has become astonishingly popular to millions of readers. What marketing man or woman, when the first Cadfael novel, *A Morbid Taste for Bones*, appeared in 1977, could have predicted in their wildest imaginings that twenty novels featuring this unlikely hero would be sold in translation into twenty languages and scores of countries? But again Edith was modest about her creation: "In a way I did not choose a monk as protagonist in the first Cadfael, he was there before me, quite implicit in the story itself."

I had to ask Edith the obvious question—what are the reasons for Brother Cadfael's phenomenal appeal?—and she admitted that she had given up trying to account for his popularity.

> Certainly people have told me they find him consoling and reassuring, and look upon him as a personal friend, but I leave it to the individual reader to explain more profoundly. I'm just grateful for it, whatever the real reasons.

Cadfael always had a hearty respect for his opponents in the Crusades, and it was interesting to speculate on what his views would be on our present, multicultural society, with mosques and temples in most of Britain's major cities. Edith had some doubts about his response:

> I fancy Cadfael's reaction to the international population of his country we see now would be very mixed. The coming of the Muslims once accepted, he would certainly accept that they were entitled to their places of worship. Also, he had acquired a good deal of liking and admiration for his opponents during the Crusades, as honourable antagonists sometimes outdoing the Franks in generosity and chivalry, as well as scholarship in several fields of learning. But he had fought against the very idea of Islam, and I think the sight of mosques rising on English soil would deeply affront him, as a kind of oblique, and more dangerous, invasion of Christendom, less easy to fight and contain than the military one.

To end a conversation with Edith Pargeter left one always with a profound sense of having been privileged to share in a philosophy of life that had been carefully thought out and attuned to the modern world, even though much of her imagination had been devoted to recreating the past. The sense of contentment that surrounded Edith was a quality rarely found. I was curious as to whether, looking back over her long life, she had any regrets, and her answer was as positive as one might have expected:

> I can't think of one special aim, something that always eluded me. As a girl I wanted to do everything in the artistic line, sing, act, dance, paint, and in those years, in small, local ways, I did do a little of all of them, but writing was always at the top of the list, so I certainly can't complain of being thwarted, even if the rest had to go. I can't think of a single major regret to confess, which makes me one of the extremely lucky ones.

In the last years of Edith's life, invitations to travel abroad were regretfully declined, although she did manage to travel to Budapest to see the filming of the first series of television adaptations of her Cadfael novels for Central Television. That visit also took her to her beloved Prague, where she signed copies of a new Czech translation of one of her novels. But the world made its way to Edith's door via the postman, who delivered huge quantities of letters every day, most of which Edith managed to answer herself.

Many readers, myself included, found that her last novel, *Brother Cadfael's Penance*, explored the mind of Cadfael in a most interesting way. Edith told me that in the future she wanted to focus more on Cadfael's pathway towards old age, with more time being spent developing character and less on solving mysteries. Yet there is a valedictory quality in *Brother Cadfael's Penance* that in many ways makes it a fitting ending to the series. It is set in November, and many of Cadfael's thoughts at the opening of the novel are of the season's end:

> The colours of late autumn are the colours of the sunset: the farewell of the year and the farewell of the day. And of the life of man? Well, if it ends in a flourish of gold, that is no bad ending.

His vision of St. Winifred, with the scent of hawthorn blossoms on a May morning, brings his life back to the first mystery, *A Morbid Taste for Bones*, and provides reassurance that the peace he seeks on his return to the Abbey will be waiting there for him:

> All the more to be desired was this order and tranquility within the pale, where the battle of heaven and hell was fought without bloodshed, with the weapons of the mind and the soul.

Such tranquility and fruition was also wished to his creator at the Memorial Service to give thanks for the life and work of Edith Pargeter, held in the Abbey Church, Shrewsbury on Sunday, 18 February, 1996. Many people from all parts of the United Kingdom attended, on a cold and frosty winter's day. Speakers included the Public Orator of Birmingham University, Professor Anthony Bryer; the Reverend Barry North, Rector of Ironbridge; Deborah Owen, Edith's literary agent; Martin Brookes; and Sir Derek Jacobi, the television Cadfael, who read from *Brother Cadfael's Penance*. Edith's great love of music was recognized by the contribution made by a number of choirs, the Abbey organist and the Pontesbury Bellringers.

The window was installed in September 1997, in an Abbey overflowing with well-wishers from all over Britian.

Stained-glass window depicting Saint Benedict who was the founder of the order to which Brother Cadfael belonged.

Bibliography

Novels:
    Murder in the Dispensary (as Jolyon Carr), 1938.
    Death Comes by Post (as Jolyon Carr), 1940.
    The Victim Needs a Nurse (as John Redfern), 1940.
    Death Mask, 1959.
    The Will and the Deed (*Where There's a Will* US), 1960.
    Funeral of Figaro, 1962.
    The Horn of Roland, 1974.
    Never Pick Up Hitchhikers!, 1976.

The George Felse Novels:
    Fallen into the Pit, 1951.
    Death and the Joyful Woman, 1961.
    Flight of a Witch, 1964.
    A Nice Derangement of Epitaphs (*Who Lies Here?* US), 1965.
    The Piper on the Mountain, 1966.
    Black Is the Colour of My True Love's Heart, 1967.
    The Grass-Widow's Tale, 1968.
    The House of Green Turf, 1969.
    Mourning Raga, 1969.
    The Knocker on Death's Door, 1970.
    Death to the Landlords!, 1972.
    City of Gold and Shadows, 1973.
    Rainbow's End, 1978.

The Brother Cadfael Chronicles:
    A Morbid Taste for Bones: A Medieval Whodunnit, 1977.
    One Corpse Too Many, 1979.
    Monk's Hood, 1980.
    St. Peter's Fair, 1981.
    The Leper of St. Giles, 1981.
    The Virgin in the Ice, 1982.
    The Sanctuary Sparrow, 1983.
    The Devil's Novice, 1983.
    Dead Man's Ransom, 1984.
    The Pilgrim of Hate, 1984.
    An Excellent Mystery, 1985.
    The Raven in the Foregate, 1986.
    The Rose Rent, 1986.
    The Hermit of Eyton Forest, 1987.
    A Rare Benedictine (prequel, three short stories), 1988.
    The Confession of Brother Haluin, 1988.
    The Heretic's Apprentice, 1989.
    The Potter's Field, 1989.
    The Summer of the Danes, 1991.
    The Holy Thief, 1992.
    Brother Cadfael's Penance, 1994.

And Relatedly:
    Shropshire, with Roy Morgan, 1992.
    Strongholds and Sanctuaries: The Borderland of England and Wales, with Roy Morgan, 1993.

Other (as Pargeter, Carr, and Peter Benedict):
    Novels, History including:
    The Heaven Tree Trilogy, 1960–63.
    The Brothers of Gwyedd Quartet, 1974–77.

Short Stories, Translations from the Czech. For a complete bibliography, refer to Lewis.

Critical Studies:
    Rob Talbot and Robin Whiteman, *Cadfael Country: Shropshire and the Welsh Borders*, 1990.
    The Cadfael Companion: The World of Brother Cadfael, 1991; rev. ed., 1994.
    Margaret Lewis, *Edith Pargeter: Ellis Peters*, 1994.

Photo Credit: University of Newcastle upon Tyne

Margaret Lewis

Biography

Born in Northern Ireland and now resident of Northumberland, England, Dr. Lewis has published several short stories, some broadcast on radio. The author of a well-researched biography of Ngaio Marsh, *Ngaio Marsh: A Life*, Lewis was selected by the editors of the *Border Lines Series* to write a literary biography/bibliography of Edith Pargeter, better known to the mystery world as Ellis Peters. She and her husband Peter are active with the Flambard Press, a small publisher specializing in books of Northern England.

Bibliography

Ngaio Marsh: A Life, 1991; US, 1998.
Edith Pargeter: Ellis Peters, 1994.
Various essays on contemporary writers (Patrick White, Paul Scott, Ruth Jhabrala) and on biography as a literary genre.

Janet Laurence

◆

Publishing in the Golden Age of Crime Fiction

Publishing in the Golden Age of Crime Fiction

Bob Barnard yesterday, in his riveting analysis of Josphine Tey's detective fiction, touched on a method of historical investigation—the collecting of small details, facts and figures in the hope that eventually they will build a picture. What follows is just that, a collection of details that I will give to you in the hope that they will form a view of publishing during the period between the two World Wars.

> What is wrong with publishing is that there are...far too many books. General publishing is fast degenerating into a gambling competition for potential best sellers. This is a profoundly unsatisfactory state of affairs which may have—will have—very evil effects upon the future of English letters.[1]

This sounds all too modern, in fact it was Geoffrey Faber in 1934.

> In 1923 there were 7,992 new books published in England.... In 1933, number had risen to 9,905.... Of this total, fiction accounted for 1,950. Every week, therefore, something like 40 *new* novels competed for attention. The congestion was actually worse because publishing concentrated bringing out new books in three seasons of the year, the spring, early summer and autumn.[2]

The Publishers of Crime Fiction

I have prepared a list of the publishing companies with the main detective novels they published between 1920 and 1940. This has been prepared from *Detective Fiction Second Edition* by John Cooper & B.A. Pike, (Scolar Press, 1994). They include all the major novelists and a number of minor during this period (see their Appendix for list). Though the Golden Age of crime fiction can be said to have extended beyond 1940, the war altered the publishing picture so much, I have chosen to end my survey at this point.

It can be seen immediately that the "heavies" of the crime publishing world were Collins, particularly after the Crime Club started in 1930, Gollancz, Hodder & Stoughton and, to a lesser extent, Heinemann and Cassell.

Throughout the period, small publishing houses came and went, usually failing through lack of capital and expertise. It was too easy to start a publishing house and too difficult to make it pay.

The U.S.
Publishers from the States visited often. British books took a substantial place on their lists. David Higham, a leading agent who started his career with Curtis Brown in 1925, said that many more became best-sellers then than do now. A number of firms had actual links with houses in London.

Harold S. Latham worked for The Macmillan Company of America from 1909 to 1952 and constantly visited England. In 1965 he looked back and commented on the publishing scene in the twenties and thirties:

> One thing that I have always envied is the English publisher's composure. Most of them never seem distracted or hard pressed for time. Those with whom I was most closely associated often arrived at the office at ten, had morning coffee at eleven, went out at twelve for a three-hour luncheon, had tea at four and left at five. And yet they accomplished a prodigious amount of work. With all our hustle and bustle I doubt that we get more done than they do.[3]

Stanley Unwin, publisher of the time, said that American publishing businesses were run much more extravagantly than British, with three times the number of people, palatial offices and unnecessarily high powered salesmen.[4]

Here's Harold Latham on some of the British publishers important to the detective publishing scene:

> *Victor Gollancz*—to work with Victor on anything was exhilarating; his excitement and enthusiasm were contagious. He was running a one-man show with his Victor Gollancz Ltd.; he issued books, in other words, in which he personally believed, and he didn't care too much about what his advisers had to say. He is an excellent example of that quality to which I have referred as being so vital to real publishing, the quality of individual, personal enthusiasm.

Harold contrasted Victor's "indescribably cluttered, noisy, and confused little office, dark and dingy, at the back of one of the business sections of his establishment on Henrietta Street, Covent Garden," with the "dignified and polished elegance of Macmillan & Co.'s quarters with roominess, shiny mahogany conference tables, comfortable chairs, fires burning in several hearths, soft rugs, an atmosphere of calm and confidence."

Of Collins: The suppressed—and sometimes not so suppressed—excitement of Billy Collins' office in the firm of W.F. Collins and Sons: editors breaking in for some last-minute decision or a reader exulting over some find of the day before, about which his superior must be told immediately, or an artist with a drawing for a frontispiece; continual rushing about and bustle, the sense of crisis in the air with Billy himself contributing to it all with a comment on some discovery he himself had just made.

Of Hodder & Stoughton: The heartiness of the welcome of Ralph Hodder-Williams, and the gusto with which he tried to interest me in all sorts of publications, many quite devoid of any American appeal. How we loved to banter about them!

Harold Latham sums up:

As I run through in my mind the various publishing houses of England which I have visited, I am struck by the fact that each has an atmosphere distinctly its own. In New York one might visit a dozen firms and not be overly conscious of their different attitudes and interests...in London, on the other hand, the publishers were individualists, and a round of calls at their offices offered a great variety of experience.[5]

So what about detective fiction?
Here's Dorothy Sayers in 1921:

I was delighted with a dictum of Philip Guedalla's in *The Daily News* "The detective story is the normal recreation of noble minds." It makes me feel ever so noble.[6]

In the 1920s Collins, up until then a mainly Glasgow based printing house publishing mass market books, began to build up a trade list in London and included a number of detective novels amongst their early acquisitions by such authors as Freeman Wills Croft, G.D.H. Cole, Philip MacDonald, and others now forgotten.

In their autumn 1926 catalogue, Collins made the following claim:

We realize that the success of a Detective Novel depends upon the ingenuity and infallible accuracy of the author in the handling of his plot. We realize, too, that mere sensation based on irrelevant episodes will never make a good detective novel.

We have accordingly set a very high standard. Only the best will do. That is why we have today the finest list of Detective Novels in existence.[7]

The finest list had just added Agatha Christie to its roll call of authors.

Colin Watson in his book *Snobbery With Violence—Crime Stories and their Audience,* in a chapter entitled *The Golden Age of Detective Fiction*:

> Novels of detection flowed from the presses month after month, year after year, in an ever-increasing tide...the weekly ration of whodunnits came to be one of the staples of life for thousands of middle-class families...by 1930 it had become respectable for literary critics and essayists to write about detective fiction. By the end of the period, detective fiction was accounting for one quarter of all new novels published in the English language.... Almost as many people turned to crime-writing as to keeping poultry or starting mushroom farms. Authorship required smaller capital investment, and the public was less fastidious about the freshness of plots than of eggs.[8]

Allen Lane (he of Penguin fame), according to his biographer J.E. Morpurgo:

> ...identified and welcomed the changing mood of the leading English mystery-writers which, in the late twenties and early thirties, was moving them away from the *roman policier*, from the puerilities of contrived detection and two-dimension characterisation, and placing them close to the "legitimate" novelist colleagues.... He listed Nicholas Blake, Michael Innes and "first and foremost Marge" [Margery Allingham] with Aldous Huxley, Graham Greene and Joyce Carey as the best and most enjoyable English novelists of our time.

Already in 1934 he was admitting, though he knew it to be disloyal (Agatha Christie was a close friend), that he "regarded Dorothy Sayers as an important novelist and Agatha as no more than a skilful entertainer."[9]

Authors and Their Experiences with Publishers

The queen of crime did not find instant acceptance. Agatha Christie wrote *The Mysterious Affair at Styles* during the war, while she was working in a hospital dispensary. She sent it to Hodder & Stoughton, who returned it. Her husband, Archie, suggested she send it to Methuen's because he had a friend in the Air Force who was a director. They kept it longer than Hodders, "I should think about six months," says Agatha in her autobiography. She couldn't remember where she sent it next but after it came back, though by now she'd rather lost hope, she sent it to John Lane, The Bodley Head, because they, in a new departure, had published one or two detective stories recently. She packed it off to them, then, in the excitement of the war's ending, her husband's return and their life together, forgot all about it.

Apparently The Bodley Head lost the manuscript. At some stage it was found by an office boy and two years later they sent a letter asking her to call.

> I was shown into John Lane's office, and he rose to greet me; a small man with a white beard, looking somehow rather Elizabethan.... He had a benign, kindly manner, but shrewd blue eyes, which ought to have warned me, perhaps, that he was the kind of man who would drive a hard bargain.

John Lane said her MS showed promise but it would need changes, particularly the last scene which Agatha had written as a court scene and he thought didn't come off (she obviously managed to improve her technique as far as court room scenes went before *Witness for the Prosecution*). Agatha writes:

> Then he went on to the business aspect, pointing out what a risk a publisher took if he published a novel by a new and unknown writer, and how little money he was likely to make out of it. Finally he produced from his desk drawer an agreement which he suggested I should sign.
> This particular contract entailed my not receiving any royalties until after the first 2,000 copies had been sold—after that a small royalty would be paid. Half any serial or dramatic rights would go to the publisher. None of it meant much to me—the whole point was, *the book would be published*.
> I didn't even notice that there was a clause binding me to offer him my next five novels, at an only slightly increased rate of royalty. To me it was success, and all a wild surprise. I signed with enthusiasm.[10]

Let's look at that contract for a moment. Nothing by way of royalties until after the first 2,000 copies sold. No advance, not surprisingly on that basis since most first novels, according to David Higham, sold no more than 900 copies, mainly to libraries.[11]

Was The Bodley Head contract usual or had Agatha, as she came to believe, been taken advantage of?

David Higham states that between the wars he could get first novel terms that were almost standard: 10% of the published price on the first 2,500 copies sold, 15% on the next 2,500, 20% thereafter; but only £30 advance based on 900 copies or so selling at 7/6. After the first book he says,

> Any novelist who had even a modest sale could have an agreement ahead for three books at a time, with provision for improvements to match success.[12]

Michael Thomas of A.M. Heath & Co., my own agent, has kindly had a quick trawl through their records and says there is quite a common pattern on advances and royalties:

> In 1933 we sold M.G. Eberhart's first book in England for an advance of £50 but a royalty rate that started at 15% and rose to 20%. By coincidence 1933 also saw a first book by a British crime writer who's happily still alive although no longer writing, Angus MacVicar. He got an advance of £25 and his royalty rate also went to 20%.[13]

In her biography of Ngaio Marsh, Margaret Lewis states that for her first book, *A Man Lay Dead*, published in 1934 by Geoffrey Bles, she earned an advance of £30 and 10% royalties.[14]

Dorothy L. Sayers' first book, *Whose Body*, was sold initially to the American publishing house Boni and Liveright, who offered $250 in advance of royalties (about £50) and brought it out in May, 1923.[15]

T. Fisher Unwin (Stanley Unwin's uncle) accepted it for English publication in October of the same year, and also published her second, *Clouds of Witness*, in February 1926. I haven't found a reference to the sum she got but here's David Higham on Fisher Unwin in 1925:

> I remember Uncle Fisher as rather morose, but ready enough to offer his £25 advance on account of 10% after the first 500 copies sold, thirteen copies to count as twelve—you had to fight most publishers on that in those times.[16]

So it would seem likely that those were the terms that Dorothy L. Sayers signed. Also that John Lane did indeed treat Agatha Christie very shabbily.

However, perhaps he did Mrs. Christie one very good turn. She wanted to write her books "under a fancy name, Martin West or

Mostyn Grey. I had the idea that a woman's name would prejudice people against my work, especially in detective stories; that Martin West would be more manly and forthright."

John Lane was insistent she kept her own name, particularly the Christian name. "Agatha is an unusual name which remains in peoples' memories" he said.[17]

The Murder of Roger Ackroyd by Martin West? I don't think it has quite the same ring!

By the time Agatha Christie submitted her fourth book, *The Man in the Brown Suit,* she was getting clued up to the writing business.

> Though I had been ignorant and foolish when I first submitted a book for publication, I had learnt a few things since. I was not as stupid as I must have appeared to many people. I had found out a good deal about writing and publishing. I knew about the Authors' Society and I had read their periodical. I realised that you had to be extremely careful in making contracts with publishers, and especially with certain publishers. I had learnt of the many ways in which publishers took unfair advantage of authors. Now that I knew these things, I made my plans.[18]

Her fourth book for The Bodley Head was *The Man in the Brown Suit*. Incidentally, it was originally called *The Mystery of the Mill House*; she changed it because she felt it sounded too much like *Murder on the Links* (I can't see the similarity myself).[19] The whole question of titles is an interesting one and I wish I had the time to go into it more closely. Even the briefest look at *Detective Fiction* reveals fascinating details. Agatha's *Dumb Witness*, published in 1937, was published in America as *Poirot Loses a Client.* They wanted to cash in on the Poirot angle, you think, then you note that *Hercule Poirot's Christmas*, 1939, in America was titled *Murder for Christmas*. John Dickson Carr's *The Three Coffins,* Harper 1935, appears in the UK from Hamilton in 1935 as *The Hollow Man.* Dorothy L. Sayers' *The Five Red Herrings*, Gollancz 1931, appears in the US as *Suspicious Characters.* But back to contracts.

Before The Bodley Head brought out Agatha's *The Man in the Brown Suit*, they suggested that they scrap the old contract (for five books) and make another one, also for five books, with more favourable terms. She politely refused to discuss the matter with them. She was willing to finish her contract with them but after that she was going to another publisher. She also decided to have a literary agent.[20]

Edmond Cork, of Hughes Massie, became her agent, as he became Ngaio Marsh's and, later, Catherine Aird's. He took Agatha's sixth book to Collins. At the time they were presented with the MS, Agatha still had two more books to go with her Bodley Head contract and Collins would have to wait two years before they could publish. Nevertheless, they thought so highly of the MS they signed a three-book contract with her on 27th January, 1924.[21]

In 1926, the waiting was over and Collins published the first of their Christies: *The Murder of Roger Ackroyd*. The first edition was approximately (approximately because Collins's detailed sales records were unfortunately destroyed during the Blitz) 5,500 copies and 4,000 were rapidly sold.[22]

When Agatha Christie disappeared a few months after the publication of *The Murder of Roger Ackroyd*, there was a considerable effect on her sales. *The Big Four* in 1927, really a collection of four linked short stories, sold over 8,500. The 1928 book, *The Mystery of the Blue Train*, described by Agatha Christie herself as "easily the worst book I ever wrote," dropped to just below 7,000. In 1929, *The Seven Dials Mystery*, a sequel to an earlier book, *The Secret of Chimneys*, neither typical Christie, rose again to over 8,000.[23]

1930 saw the launch of Collins Crime Club; according to Elizabeth Walter, the renowned postwar Collins Crime Club editor, it was the brainchild of Sir Godfrey and his nephew, young William Collins, who felt the vogue for the detective story and the enormous popularity of book clubs could profitably be linked. It was never a book club, though, merely a clever marketing idea. Each month saw a first choice and two other recommended titles and a magazine describing the books. The first title was *The Noose* by Philip MacDonald, with a first printing of approximately 5,500. A few months later came *Murder at the Vicarage*, the first of the Marple books. The publicity bonanza was over; the first printing was only 5,500. It was not until *Three Act Tragedy* in 1935 that she managed to sell 10,000 within the first year of publication and 1943 before she reached 20,000 with *Five Little Pigs*. Thereafter she never looked back.[24]

It became something of a regular pattern for authors to move publishing houses after the first few novels had established them. Stanley Unwin wrote,

> ...discovering and nursing young authors is not the same as making money or securing their gratitude. It is apt to be in fact a most disheartening process, because it is so often the publisher who reaps where other publishers have sown

who makes the money and is a fine fellow in the eyes of the author.[25]

But changing publishers often benefited an author considerably. Take the case of Dorothy L. Sayers. She found it difficult at first to find a publisher. Her first novel, referred to by her as "Lord Peter", did the rounds while she was writing the second. Ward Lock considered it, as did Hutchinson's, before she had the offer from Boni and Liveright.

Various sources say that after Unwins published her first two books, Dorothy moved to Benn with a three book contract. However, at that time the Unwin business was sold to Ernest Benn and the most likely thing is that Victor Gollancz, who at that time was running Benn, produced a new contract for her as one of the Unwin authors. This is supported by Dorothy writing to Benn after Gollancz had set up publishing on his own requesting a release, saying she had signed the contract "as an expression of my confidence in Mr. Gollancz and of my appreciation of his kind and generous attitude towards my work."[26]

Victor Gollancz was impressed with what he saw of Dorothy L. Sayers, who was very business-like in her dealings. "Writing books," she said, "is not a hobby, it is a job, a trade like any other."[27] She had personal experience of publishing, having worked with Blackwells from April, 1917 to summer 1919, as an apprentice publisher.[28]

When Victor Gollancz set up on his own (in 1927), he wanted to take Dorothy L. Sayers with him. Her contract with Benn called for two more books.

She appealed to Benn to release her from the contract but wrote to Victor that it seemed unlikely he would agree and suggesting he might like to publish the Lord Peter short stories (the contract with Benn was for novels). She had written nine short stories, six of which had been published; two, she says, were considered "too gruesome" and another had been turned down by everyone she had sent it to without a specific reason. She offered to make the stories up to a dozen or whatever number Victor considered necessary. She was apologetic in making the offer as she said she understood that short stories were disliked at the libraries and "the majority of the public—moreover, I don't think they are by any means among my happiest efforts."

Sayers ended by saying she hadn't lost hope of rescuing the novels but she didn't want a "violent row" with Benn because she felt it never paid to make enemies and, anyway, she acknowledged Benn did have legal rights.

Victor Gollancz introduced Sayers to David Higham, who took her on as a client. Higham stated in his autobiography that he sorted out her contractual problems with Benn[29], but in fact Benn appeared to have his pound of flesh as he published Dorothy's next two books. Gollancz commissioned her to edit a very successful anthology of short stories of detection, mystery and horror, with an introduction by her, which was published in four parts over several years, and published the collection of the Lord Peter short stories she'd offered him.

The difference in Benn's approach and Gollancz's in publishing the Dorothy L. Sayers' books can be seen by a look at the print runs for her first editions, kindly supplied to me by Christopher Dean, Chairman of the Dorothy L. Sayers Society:

> *Whose Body*: US first Edition, 1923, Boni & Liveright: 3,503
> UK first Edition, Unwin, 1923: Unknown at 7/6
> *Clouds of Witness*: Unwin, 1926: Unknown at 7/6
> *Unnatural Death*: Benn First Edition, 1927: 1,000
> *The Unpleasantness at the Bellona Club*, Benn First Edition, 1928: 1,000
> *Lord Peter Views the Body* (short stories) Gollancz, November 1928: 5,000
> *The Documents in the Case*: Benn, July 1930: 1,000
> *Strong Poison*: Gollancz, September 1930: 5,000
> *Five Red Herrings*: Gollancz, 1931: 4,000
> *Have His Carcase*: Gollancz, 1932: 5,000
> *Murder Must Advertise*: Gollancz, 1933: 6,000
> *Nine Tailors*: Gollancz, 1934: 6,000
> *Gaudy Night*: Gollancz, 1936: 17,000
> *Busman's Honeymoon*: Gollancz, 1937: 20,000
> *Hangman's Holiday*: (short stories) Gollancz, 1937: 3,000

Another author who moved to her advantage was Ngaio Marsh. Her first seven books were published by Geoffrey Bles. Then, according to Margaret Lewis, her agent Edmond Cork felt it would be advantageous to move to Collins. They offered an advance of £250 and royalties of 15% for four detective novels, the first of which came out in 1939. Ngaio felt guilty about leaving Bles, who had given her the encouragement she needed at the start of her career, but valued the substantial improvement in her finances and bought a new Chevrolet car. She remained with Collins for the rest of her publishing career.[30]

I mentioned libraries earlier. These were important factors in the publishing world then, even as they are now, particularly because of the circulating libraries such as Harrods and Boots and the Book Clubs such as the Times Book Club. Says Elizabeth Walter:

> These made the market for crime fiction in the twenties and thirties very different from today. They provided a steady market and a publisher had a very good idea of what the libraries would take.

And publishers knew, or thought they knew, their authors. Harold Latham wrote of Christopher Bush:

> He has a considerable public, a "steady Bush public", a public that has endured through many years. He never presents any problem to his publisher who knows exactly how many copies of a title may safely be printed for the loyal Bush fans; the number is a healthy one, too.[31]

John Dickson Carr, an American who moved early in his career to England, had considerable dealings with both American and English publishers which were made more difficult by his prodigious output and constant need for more money.

Thanks to the intervention of his friend, Ed Delafield, Carr came to an unusual arrangement with his American publishers, Harpers, that resulted in a monthly guaranteed payment, shared by his English publishers, Hamilton, instead of a twice-yearly royalty. After he started up with William Morrow in the US and Heinemann in the UK as Carter Dickson, they made a similar arrangement in the mid-thirties that resulted in Carr receiving a guaranteed monthly income from the four publishers of between $500 and $600, or over £100 a month, a large sum of money for those depression days.[32]

There was constant friction with Hamish Hamilton over possible competition between the two names, but there was nothing they could do, the two names were established.[33]

About two-thirds of Carr's income under his own name came from United States sales, one-third from British. It is likely that the ratio was similar for the Carter Dickson books and demonstrates the relative importance of the two markets.[34]

Serial and Other Rights
Throughout this period serial rights played an important part in an author's income.

When Boni and Liveright made their offer to Dorothy L. Sayers for her first book, she had hopes that the story would be published as a serial first: "That is where the money is."[35]

Agatha Christie's income from her first two books, apart from a few royalties on the second, consisted of £25 for the first and £50 for the second for serial rights in *The Weekly Times*. For her fourth book, *The Man in the Brown Suit*, *The Evening News* made her an offer for the serial rights.

> They were going to call it *Anna the Adventuress*—as silly a title as I had ever heard, I thought; though I kept my mouth shut because, after all, they were willing to pay me £500.... It seemed the most unbelievable luck. I could hardly believe it.[36]

She calls the thirties her:

> ...plutocratic period. I was beginning to be serialised in America, and the money that came in from this, besides being far larger than anything I ever made from serial rights in Britain, was also at that time free of income tax. It was regarded as a capital payment. I was not getting the sums I was to receive later, but I could see them coming, and it seemed to me that all I had to do was to be industrious and rake in the money.[37]

Until 1937 John Dickson Carr negotiated his contracts for himself, not always completely effectively. Then he became a client of David Higham, who negotiated deals for him that included retaining serial rights for his novels. Higham placed *The Four False Weapons* with the monthly *Woman's Journal* for £300. *Woman's Journal* insisted that their serialization appear before publication of the British edition of the book, which meant delaying its projected publication date of November 1937. Hamish Hamilton was not pleased since he would still have to contribute to Carr's monthly guarantee. Carr promised to write a different book for autumn publication. He finished *To Wake the Dead* in October and Hamilton managed to get printed and bound copies to the bookstores a little more than a month later.[38]

Agents

Agents were as prominent in the Golden Age as they are today. In 1924, according to David Higham, the leading firms were A.P. Watt, J.B. Pinker and Curtis Brown, known as CB, which Higham joined.

A.D. Peters had only just opened shop. Audrey Heath, once of CB, was a making a good, if strident, go of it; she had the harshest voice I've ever heard. So was Hughes, Massie; Massie also ex-CB. Charles Evans would remark, when Nancy Pearn, Laurence Pollinger and I set up on our own in 1935, "CB's pupped again".

In 1925, the atmosphere between agents and publishers could in general be called chilly, with some fog, for which the agents were partly to blame. Watt, in particular, would insist that publishers should have no direct relationship with his authors. CB himself inclined to the same attitude. Michael Joseph (under whom Higham worked until Joseph left to start his own publishing house), wanted to change all this. He argued:

> There should be a warm bond between author and publisher, preferably one of personal friendship, within which anything but money or matters involving it could be discussed. The agent could always step in on the author's side if need be. But once terms and conditions are settled the publisher and the author are on the same side: the closer they are to each other the better.[39]

Victor Gollancz always preferred to deal directly with authors behind their agent's backs, and many an agent who thought he had an unanswerable case on some contractual haggle with Victor found in his next post a letter from the writer he represented telling him not to pursue the matter. His biographer says:

> As always with Victor this cut both ways. An undefended author often got a deal worse than an agent would have secured, but some occasionally got better treatment than they would have through a pushy agent. Victor was capable of great spontaneous generosity when an author laid himself (or, more commonly, herself) open to exploitation.[40]

Book Production

The early 1920s, according to S.C. Roberts of the Cambridge University Press, were marked by a "typographical renaissance which had a notable influence upon book-production."[41] It wasn't a movement that impinged much upon detective fiction.

Victor Gollancz kept production costs low through standardization, leading Higham to comment that Gollancz could have cared little for the look of what he produced, as he appeared to buy a single cheap quality of paper in bulk and to use it for works of every kind. His typography, too, seemed invariable. What he saved on production, said Higham, he put into promotion.[42]

Hardbacks were published at 7/6. Yesterday Margaret Lewis mentioned that at that time the best West End stall seat cost 15/-, twice the price. I haven't been to the London theatre recently but I understand a similar seat now costs around £40 or £50, much more than twice the price of those hardbacks we consider expensive at around £14 or £15. According to knowledgable bookman Ralph Spurrier, after about eight months a second edition would be published at 3/6 or 2/6. Later yet a third edition might follow at 2/6, 1/- or even 6d. In the late twenties Collins Shilling Novels appeared, probably eight to ten years after the first edition. Some editions could be available simultaneously.

Ralph reckons, judging from the difficulty of obtaining Crofts and Austin Freeman books today, that their original print runs were 3,000 to 4,000, the same as Len Deighton's first book, *The Ipcress File*, published in 1963, the same year as P.D. James' and John le Carré's first books.

Maps and Plans

Colin Watson points out the practice of "meticulously drawn ground plans" that appeared in many detective novels. "Eventually [they] became a joke and had to be abandoned, but some plots were so complicated and their authors so weak on description that pictorial aid was essential."[43]

Philip Scowcroft, writer of many articles on detective fiction, says it was hit or miss whether you got a map or plan or not. Sayers' *Five Red Herrings*, which was set in an actual place, Galloway, had one, whereas the fictional setting of *Have His Carcase* didn't. However there is a letter from Sayers to Gollancz at the time of publishing *Five Red Herrings* in which she asks him to: "supply a large, handsome, clear, well executed, generous and convincing map...not like the mean, miserable, petty, small, scrimshanking, feeble and unworthy map provided by Collins for Freeman Wills Croft's book."[44] This was *Sir John Macgill's Last Journey*, also, by coincidence, set in Galloway. The map Gollancz provided is printed in *Detective Fiction* and it is indeed handsome.

Length of a Detective Story
Agatha Christie said:

> Of course, there is a right length for everything. I think myself that the *right* length for a detective story is 50,000 words. I

know this is considered by publishers as too short. Possibly readers feel themselves cheated if they pay their money and only get 50,000 words—so 60,000 or 70,000 are more acceptable. If your book runs to more than that I think you will usually find that it would have been better if it had been shorter.[45]

Dorothy L. Sayers tended towards longer books but the great majority of detective books at this time do look as though 60,000 to 70,000 words is their length.

Book Jackets
Before the first world war, detective fiction was published with beautiful embossed covers. During the war publishing had to go into economy mode and took some time to pick up afterwards. Even in the early twenties, Freeman Wills Crofts' first books came out in thin boards and with cheap paper. But by the mid-twenties the scene was improving and illustrated paper dust jackets were appearing. These were a new departure and were designed to attract the middle class audience, particularly for detective novels.

Colin Watson is scathing about them:

> Jackets were of a more or less standard character, their common features being crude colour, ill designed type, and the display, often in defiance of a book's actual contents, of a sprawled corpse in expensive-looking clothes. The inclusion of a weapon of some kind (not necessarily that mentioned in the story) was another pictorial convention, curiously wrought oriental daggers and great liquorice-coloured automatics being top favourites.[46]

Agatha Christie had a row with The Bodley Head (a house known for its excellence of design) over the jacket they designed for *Murder on the Links.*

> Apart from being in ugly colours, it was badly drawn, and represented, as far as I could make out, a man in pyjamas on a golf links, dying of an epileptic fit. Since the man who had been murdered had been fully dressed and stabbed with a dagger, I objected. A book jacket may have nothing to do with the plot, but if it docs it must at least not represent a false plot. There was a good deal of bad feeling over this, but I was really furious and it was agreed that in future I should see the jacket first and approve of it.[47]

And so she did. According to Elizabeth Walter, Agatha would

never consent to any representation of Poirot, and though she once allowed his patent-leather-shod feet to appear on the jacket of *Poirot's Early Cases,* she was never happy with even this partial representation.[48]

The colour photographs, though, in the Cooper and Pike book demonstrate a standard of design that strikes a modern eye as far from unsophisticated.

Ralph Spurrier tells of the *Reader's Library,* which started in 1929, a nice little series published at 6d. All were numbered (remind you of anything?). Inside the dust jackets was a complete listing of other books in the series. It comprised classics, modern fiction and a fairly long list of crime, including S.S. Van Dine and Edgar Wallace. Some were first editions. Primarily published for Woolworths, they had what Ralph describes as "nice, lurid jackets." For a long run of film tie-ins, the cover included hand-coloured stills of the star; these included many of the classic stars of the twenties and thirties.

Few dust jackets survive from this period and an edition with its original jacket can be ten times the value of a copy in similar condition without.

Victor Gollancz, as might be expected, flouted all the trends and put his books in plain yellow jackets with either black or red printing. His intention, it's claimed, was that the books should be instantly recognizable on railway bookstalls, an important sales outlet of the time. Gollancz's yellow jackets became a publishing trademark that survived into the eighties and has been closely associated with crime fiction.

The importance of jacket design in this period is illustrated by a story told by David Higham. Newman Flower of Cassell's took an American Book of the Month choice, which in those days carried high prestige, and put a "popular" cover on it. "Reviewers who liked books got up in that style picked it up, tried to read it and put down again. Those who didn't took one look at the jacket and let the book lie. It was hardly reviewed at all."[49]

Which story brings us to...

Reviewers

Reviewers of detective novels in this period were regarded as powerful. At the start of the twenties they were anonymous. But Victor Gollancz quickly spotted that a prerequisite for selling books was good reviews, and in 1926 craftily employed Gerald Gould, fiction critic of *The Observer,* to become a reader for

Ernest Benn Ltd. When his recommendations were published, he inevitably, and honestly, praised them. The reviews were then quoted on dust jackets and in advertisements, helping to sell books and promote reviewers. The days of the unsigned review quickly disappeared.[50]

Colin Watson sums up most reviewers as having

> ...fallen in with the notion of detective stories being in a class quite separate from "legitimate" literature and therefore not subject to the ordinary rules of criticism. Editors provided a segregated hutch for mystery novels, where they could be dealt with, a whole litter of twenty or thirty at a time, by means of a sentence apiece. There was evolved for this purpose a special style of reviewmanship. It was (and is) slightly facetious in flavour, crisp and insubstantial, like lettuce. It revealed singularly little about the books and although in most cases this was a blessing for their authors, the rare novel of quality was likely to suffer the injustice of exactly similar treatment simply because it happened to treat of crime.[51]

Punch devoted generous space in its "Booking Office" columns to detective writers such as John Rhode and Agatha Christie. In 1925 it dismissed the current batch of crime stories in verse:

> Detectives incredibly stupid
> And villains unspeakably vile,
> The usual presence of Cupid,
> The usual absence of style.
> A heroine brave and resourceful,
> Dread poisons, infernal machines,
> A hero alert and of course full,
> Whenever they down him, of beans.

and so on for three further stanzas.[52] There were, though, notable exceptions.

Arnold Bennett reviewed novels for *The Evening Standard,* including detective novels. When John Dickson Carr's first book, *It Walks By Night,* was published in the UK, Bennett's column produced the most negative of all its reviews: He criticized Carr's style, "full of primeval clichés"; his characterisation, "the French characters never show a sign of French mentality"; the dialogue, "no human being ever did or could talk as this criminal talks"; and his plot, "a bog and a morass between the full statement of the enigma and the solution."[53]

Another influential reviewer was Dorothy L. Sayers, who wrote for the *Sunday Times*. In 1933 she established John Dickson Carr overnight with a review of his eighth book, *The Mad Hatter Mystery*, comparing it favourably with G.K. Chesterton and writing,

> Mr. Carr can lead us away from the small, artificial, bright-lit stage of the ordinary detective plot into the menace of outer darkness. He can create atmosphere with an adjective, and make a picture from a wet iron railing, a dusty table, a gaslamp blurred by the fog. He can alarm with an illusion or delight with a rollicking absurdity. He can invent a passage from a lost work of Edgar Allan Poe which sounds like the real thing. In short, he can write—not merely in the negative sense of observing the rules of syntax, but in the sense that every sentence gives a thrill of positive pleasure. This is the most attractive mystery I have read for a long time.[54]

Carr's acceptance by Dorothy L. Sayers, says his biographer, meant a critical recognition that was important to his career, and for the next thirty years his publishers continued to quote from Sayers' review on dust jackets and publicity material.

Positive reviews could make a novel but the mainly brief and patronising mentions of Agatha Christie's novels didn't seem to depress her sales. Celia Fremlin studied her reviews for the memorial volume published by Weidenfeld and Nicholson in 1977. "Despite the growing fame of Poirot and his creator throughout the thirties," she says, "the review space given to Agatha Christie in most papers remained niggardly, and the reviews for the most part less than ecstatic: 'Pleasantly readable', 'a clever twist', and 'a writer of remarkable virtuosity'." Critics delighted to pick holes in the plausibility of the Christie plots and to fasten on points of detail. "Who in their right sense would use hammer and nails and varnish in the middle of the night within a few feet of an open door?" asked *The Times,* reviewing *Dumb Witness* in 1937. "And do ladies wear large brooches in their dressing-gowns?"[55]

Advertising
Geoffery Faber said in 1933:

> The most obvious [way a book can gain attention] is advertising, but almost every publisher in London will, if he is honest, tell you that it is not effective in proportion to its cost.... Far more money is spent now by publishers in newspaper advertising than was spent twenty years ago.[56]

Victor Gollancz turned advertising for books into an art form. "Instead of the dignified advertisement list of twenty titles set out primly in a modest space, there was the double or triple column, with the title of one book screaming across it in letters three inches high."[57]

Competitors quickly copied Gollancz, especially Collins and Heinemann, but Victor's innovativeness and publicity instinct kept him several jumps ahead.

If advertising wasn't cost effective, why did publishers do it? Faber answered his own question: "Advertising is ground-bait for authors. Other things being equal, authors tend to take their books to publishers who will advertise them extensively."[58]

Penguins, launched in 1936, survived and prospered without advertising. "For publicity," says J.E. Morpurgo, Allen Lane's biographer, "the Penguin would depend on word-of-mouth recommendation, on book reviews and on comment in the editorial pages." *Public relations* was as yet seldom mentioned in the larger world of commerce; though many a publisher in some limited degree practised what they did not know to exist, none before Allen had dared to depend upon public relations without advertising. Even for him it was ten years before he institutionalized his instinct by appointing the first Public Relations Manager.[59]

Allen Lane was the nephew of John Lane of The Bodley Head, Agatha Christie's first publisher. Allen Lane, then working with his uncle, did not allow the break to affect his extremely friendly relations with her.

> It was after a weekend spent with her and her second husband, Max Mallowan, in Devon in 1934 that Allen was stuck for an hour on Exeter station surveying the railway bookstalls. There was little to his liking among the piles of glossy magazines, the expensive new titles, the remainders and the shabby reprints of shoddy novels. The long, bookless journey would have been unbearable had it not set him to mulling over notions that had been present, if vague, in his mind for several years.[60]

The Penguin idea was born and Allen Lane split from his uncle (as Stanley Unwin had done many years earlier from his) and set up a separate company.

Penguins would not be the first paperbacks but their unique feature was that they would offer at 6d titles available from other publishing houses. Jonathan Cape, an innovator himself, offered Lane several titles. Other publishers were less cooperative....

Initial print runs were to be 20,000 with a break-even point of somewhere between 17,000 and 18,000 copies. Advances were £25 against royalties of one pound for every thousand copies sold, or, if really pushed £50 against royalties of one farthing a copy (or about 4% of the published price [of 6d]). No author could hope to earn more than his advance...unless his book went into a second Penguin edition...those who'd got £50 advances needed to sell 48,000 before more royalties were payable.[61]

Remember that Sayers didn't reach 20,000 for a first edition until 1938, or Agatha Christie until the early 40's. Many thought Lane was incredibly optimistic.

The first ten editions from Penguin perhaps speak more graphically than anything else of the power of the detective novel in the thirties, for amongst those ten were two: an Agatha Christie, *The Mysterious Affair at Styles*, and a Dorothy L. Sayers, *The Unpleasantness at the Bellona Club*. This can be seen as compensation for Sayers for having to provide Benn with the two further titles to complete her contract with him because Gollancz refused for many years to release any titles to Penguin. The second ten Penguins contained another detective novel, Dashiell Hammett's *The Thin Man*.

Booksellers
It was the capture of Woolworth's as a market for Penguins that ensured their success and perhaps no review of publishing would be complete without a word on the bookseller.

Geoffrey Faber said, "The job of the sales department is to sell books, not directly to the public but to the trade—to the wholesale and retail booksellers, to the export booksellers, and to the circulating libraries." Larger firms had their own travellers or representatives, smaller firms used commission men, carrying the books of several firms. Faber makes no mention of wholesalers, though they existed in the States at this time. Faber was in no doubt that a publisher's success depended almost as much upon the efficiency of his travellers as upon his own editorial flair.[62]

Allen Lane went out as a representative early in his career and his intimacy with booksellers was to stand him in good stead. "Though he could never bridge the chasm which separates the two sides of the book trade, he was, more than most of his fellow publishers, socially acceptable on the other side of the gap."[63]

There is also, of course, a gap between publisher and author. Perhaps I can end by quoting Bernard Shaw writing to Stanley

Unwin in 1929: "I always tell young authors who consult me that publishing is a gamble in which the publisher, who must make one best-seller pay for several duds, must take every advantage he can obtain, and that it is up to the author to take care of himself. That I think is sound."

Stanley Unwin replied: "I do not agree with you that a publisher *must* take every advantage he can obtain, but I do agree that the author should take care of himself and join the Authors Society."[64]

In another context entirely, Stanley once said plaintively, "Alas! in publishing, those authors one loves to see call all too seldom; it is the bores who are constant in attendance."[65]

I am conscious of many, many gaps in this brief look at publishing in the golden age of crime fiction but I hope I have been able to shed some light onto an area on which there is little readily available information.

St. Hilda's College, Oxford, August, 1995

1) Faber, Geoffrey, *A Publisher Speaking,* Faber and Faber, London, 1934, p 136.
2) Faber, *ibid*, pp 127/128.
3) Latham, Harold S., *My Life in Publishing,* Sidgwick & Jackson, London, 1966, p 131.
4) Unwin, Sir Stanley, *The Truth About a Publisher,* George Allen & Unwin Ltd., 1960, pp 217/218.
5) Latham, *ibid*, pp 132/136.
6) Reynolds, Barbara, *Dorothy L. Sayers, Her Life and Soul,* Hodder & Stoughton, London, 1993, p 110.
7) Walter, Elizabeth, *The Case of the Escalating Sales,* one of a series of tributes included in: *Agatha Christie, First Lady of Crime,* ed. H.R.F. Keating, Weidenfeld & Nicholson, 1977, p 15.
8) Watson, Colin, *Snobbery with Violence—Crime Stories and their Audience,* Eyre & Spottiswoode, London, 1971, pp 95/97.
9) Morpurgo, J.E., *Allen Lane, King Penguin,* Hutchinson of London, 1979, p 90.
10) Christie, Agatha, *An Autobiography,* Collins, London, 1977, pp 259/260 & pp 276/277.
11) Higham, David, *Literary Gent,* Jonathan Cape, London, 1978, p 186.
12) Higham, *ibid*.
13) Michael Thomas of A.M. Heath & Co. Ltd. in a personal letter to the author dated 2nd August 1995.
14) Lewis, Margaret, *Ngaio Marsh,* The Hogarth Press, London, 1992, p 70.

15) Reynolds, *ibid*, p 225.
16) Higham, *ibid*, p 129.
17) Christie, *ibid*, p 283.
18) Christie, *ibid*, pp 317/318.
19) Christie, *ibid*, p 319.
20) Christie, *ibid*, p 318.
21) Walter, *ibid*, p 13.
22) Walter, *ibid*.
23) Walter, *ibid*, pp 15/18.
24) Walter, *ibid*, and in a personal conversation with the author.
25) Unwin, *ibid*, p 80.
26) Edwards, Ruth Dudley, *Victor Gollancz*, Victor Gollancz Ltd., London, 1987, p 163.
27) Reynolds, *ibid*, p 225.
28) Christopher Dean, Chairman of the Dorothy L. Sayers Society, in a telephone conversation with the author.
29) Higham, *ibid*, p 211.
30) Lewis, *ibid*, p 70.
31) Latham, *ibid*, pp 179/180.
32) Greene, Douglas G., *John Dickson Carr—The Man Who Explained Miracles*, Otto Penzler, New York, 1995, pp 84 & 134.
33) Greene, *ibid*, p 134.
34) Greene, *ibid*, p 195.
35) Reynolds, *ibid*, pp 105/106.
36) Christie, *ibid*, p 319.
37) Christie *ibid*, p 414.
38) Greene, *ibid*, p 174.
39) Higham, *ibid*, p 132.
40) Edwards, *ibid*, pp 338 & 342.
41) Roberts, S.C., *Adventures with Authors*, Cambridge at the University Press, 1966, p 67.
42) Higham, *ibid*, p 173.
43) Watson, *ibid*, pp 96/97.
44) Reynolds, *ibid*, p 232—though Dr. Reynolds omits the word "scrimshanking", which Philip Scowcroft assured me is in the original letter.
45) Christie, *ibid*, p 341.
46) Watson, *ibid*, p 98.
47) Christie, *ibid*, pp 282/283.
48) Walter, *ibid*, pp 20/21.
49) Higham, *ibid*, pp 126/127.
50) Edwards, *ibid*, p 150.
51) Watson, *ibid*, p 98.
52) Fremlin, Celia, *The Christie Everybody Knew*, one of a series of tributes pub. in *Agatha Christie, First Lady of Crime, ibid*, p 113.
53) Greene, *ibid*, pp 72/73.
54) Greene, *ibid*, pp 141/142.
55) Fremlin, *ibid*, p 116.

56) Faber, *ibid*, p 128.
57) Edwards, *ibid*, p 168.
58) Faber, *ibid*, p 130.
59) Morpurgo, *ibid*, p 100.
60) Morpurgo, *ibid*, p 80.
61) Morpurgo, *ibid*, p 89.
62) Faber, *ibid*, pp 132/133.
63) Morpurgo, *ibid*, pp 46/47.
64) Unwin, *ibid*, pp 177/178.
65) Unwin, *ibid*, p 147.

Janet Laurence

Biography

Born in Surbiton, Surrey, on 3 December, 1937, cookery expert Laurence enjoyed a childhood marked by wartime food austerity offset by the culinary skills of a Swedish mother. All four siblings became interested in food and cooking. Following her education at St. Martin's-in-the-Fields High School for Girls—a B.A. from the Open University came in 1980—Laurence went into advertising and public relations where she became an account executive. After moving to Somerset in 1978, she started Mrs. Laurence's Cookery Courses, then began writing on food and cookery for the *Daily Telegraph*, and eventually embarked upon a career in crime writing with the publication of *A Deepe Coffyn* in 1989. Laurence has also published cookery books, a guide to food and drink in Somerset, women's fiction as Julia Lisle, and a history/mystery centered upon the painter Canaletto. With husband Keith now retired, Laurence manages frequent trips to France, the US, and abroad and is an active member of the Crime Writers Association serving as it's 1998 chairman.

Bibliography

Novels:
>The Darina Lisle Series:
>>*A Deepe Coffyn*, 1989.
A Tasty Way to Die, 1990.
Hotel Morgue, 1991.
Recipe for Death, 1992.
Death and the Epicure, 1993.
Death at the Table, 1994.
Death à la Provençale, 1995.
Diet for Death, 1996.
Appetite for Death, 1998.

>Other:
>>*The Changing Years* (as Julia Lisle), 1993.
To Kill the Past, 1995.
A Perfect Match (as Julia Lisle), 1996.
Canaletto and the Case of Westminster Bridge, 1997.
Journey from Home (as Julia Lisle), 1997.

Other:
>Several short stories, numerous cookery books and non-fiction.

Appendices

A Classic Mystery Quiz

by Carolyn G. Hart

1. Who is the founding genius of the mystery?

2. What famous mystery author's memory and works are honored by Baker Street societies?

3. Name the two most famous authors of the Golden Age of the Mystery.

4. Which Agatha Christie mystery caused an uproar over whether the author had played fair with the reader?

5. What famous mystery writer, whose first book appeared in 1908, was at one time the highest paid writer in America?

6. Which famous mystery writer disappeared for more than a week in December of 1926, resulting in enormous publicity and prompting suspicion she had been done away with by her war hero husband?

7. Name two authors who wrote books in which the butler did it.

8. Who was The Thin Man?

9. Where does Miss Marple live?

10. The murder methods in *Premedicated Murder, Death's Bright Dart,* and *Paying the Piper* are highly unusual. Name the authors.

11. Name two famous mystery authors who each wrote a mystery in which no one was murdered.

12. Who are the Australian sisters who wrote mysteries which contained the word "Black" in all but one of their titles?

13. What author once broke a contract with BBC because it used her name without the middle initial?

14. Who was Phoebe Atwood Taylor's famous Cape Cod sleuth?

15. What Craig Rice mystery featured mystery writer Marian Carstairs and her three children?

16. Who created Leonidas Witherall, the erudite sleuth who looked like Shakespeare?

17. What tart-tongued Victorian archaeologist leads readers on hilarious romps through musty Pyramids and the British Museum?

18. What remarkable sleuth pursues his vocation at the Abbey Church of Saint Peter and Saint Paul in Shrewsbury?

19. Who wrote *Where Are the Children*?

20. Who has Nancy Pickard described as the most endearing pair of new sleuths since Tommy and Tuppence?

AZ MURDER GOES...CLASSIC
Final Examination

1. Eric Ambler: Like several British writers (e.g. Somerset Maugham, Graham Greene, John LeCarré), Ambler drew on his experiences of espionage work for his fiction.

T   F

2. Ambler differs from many writers of the genre in never using the same characters in different novels.

T   F

3. In giving Dimitrios a coffin rather than a mask, Ambler's American publishers were restoring his original title.

T   F

4. John Dickson Carr: John Dickson Carr published an historical novel under the name Robin Fairburn.

T   F

5. Carr worked as a spy for British espionage during the Second World War.

T   F

6. Carr wrote a biography of Arthur Conan Doyle.

T   F

7. Raymond Chandler: Though heavily influenced by Dashiell Hammett, Chandler never met him.

T   F

8. Though schooled in the classics, Chandler purposely avoided their influences when he set out to write his detective stories.

T   F

9. Raymond Chandler never had a bestseller.

T   F

10. The Oxford Detectives: *The Moving Toyshop* is Edmund Crispin's second novel.

T   F

11. Nicholas Blake is the pseudonym of C.S. Lewis.

T   F

12. Gervase Fen is the Professor of Ancient History at Oxford University.

T   F

13. Oxford provides the setting for the 9 Edmund Crispin novels.

T   F

14. A. Conan Doyle: The phrase "Elementary, My Dear Watson," is used in the Conan Doyle story *The Hound of the Baskervilles*.

T   F

15. The only time in the Conan Doyle stories that Holmes contemplates marriage is in *The Adventure of Charles Augustus Milverton*.

T   F

16. According to Watson, Sherlock Holmes would regard strong emotion much as he would grit in a sensitive instrument.

T   F

17. DuMaurier's beloved home, Menabilly, was the setting for *The House on the Strand*.

T   F

18. Although *Rebecca* was DuMaurier's first best-selling novel, her first work of fiction was *Jamaica Inn*.

T   F

19. Alfred Hitchcock made a movie of DuMaurier's novel *The Birds*.

T   F

20. Erle Stanley Gardner: Grandmaster Dorothy Hughes wrote the Erle Stanley Gardner biography?

T   F

21. At the going rate in the 1920s, Gardner would earn $50,000 if he wrote 1,000,000 words a year?

T   F

22. Donald Lamb and Bertha Cool and D.A. Douglas Selby each appeared in more than five E.S. Gardner books?

T   F

23. Dashiell Hammett: Hammett's mother's name was Samuel.

T   F

24. Sam Spade shoots three people in *The Maltese Falcon*.

T   F

25. The Continental Op's real name was Jimmy Wright.

T   F

26. Stuart Palmer: Stuart Palmer's signature was often accompanied by his trademark drawing of a penguin—an homage to his initial success with *The Penguin Pool Murder*.

T   F

27. Stuart Palmer "collaborated" on a number of stories with his ailing friend Fletcher Flora in the 1950s (Palmer actually did almost all the work); in the 1960s his own final works were completed by another friend, Craig Rice.

T   F

28. Stuart Palmer wanted to write for the movies, but could never find work in Hollywood.

T   F

29. Ellis Peters: Brother Cadfael often heard Confesson as part of his religious duties.

T   F

30. Jolyon Carr and Peter Redfern had much in common.

T   F

31. *A Morbid Taste for Bones* was planned to be the first of a series featuring Brother Cadfael.

T   F

32. Dorothy L. Sayers: Being brought up in a vicarage strengthened Dorothy L. Sayers' belief in Christianity.

T   F

33. Dorothy L. Sayers' mother was a pipe smoker.

T   F

34. The Detection Club was founded in 1895.

T   F

35. Robert Louis Stevenson: Long John Silver is short a leg thanks to a Royal Marine musket.

T   F

36. Jim Hawkins dreams of becoming a physician like Dr. Livesey.

T   F

37. Squire Trelawney accidentally tramples Blind Pew with his horse.

T   F

Classic Mystery Quiz Answers

1. Edgar Allan Poe.

2. Sir Arthur Conan Doyle.

3. Agatha Christie, Dorothy L. Sayers.

4. *The Murder of Roger Ackroyd.*

5. Mary Roberts Rinehart.

6. Agatha Christie.

7. Mary Roberts Rinehart and Georgette Heyer.

8. A murder victim in Dashiell Hammett's novel of the same name.

9. St. Mary Mead.

10. Douglas Clark, V.C. Clinton-Baddeley, Sharyn McCrumb.

11. Dorothy L. Sayers, Josephine Tey.

12. Constance and Gwenyth Little.

13. Dorothy L. Sayers.

14. Asey Mayo.

15. Home Sweet Homicide.

16. Phoebe Atwood Taylor writing as Alice Tilton.

17. Elizabeth Peters' Amelia Peabody.

18. Ellis Peters' Brother Cadfael.

19. Mary Higgins Clark.

20. Annie Laurance and Max Darling in Carolyn G. Hart's *Death on Demand* series.

Your Score Reveals:

1–4	You read Spillane.
5–8	You haven't been paying attention.
9–12	Your'e on the right track.
13–16	Youv'e got a Christie in your briefcase.
17–20	You are brilliant and charming, a perfect companion on a desert island—if you bring the books.

Az Murder Goes...Classic Final Examination Answers

1. *False.* He was never a spy.
2. *False.* Zaleshoff is in two novels.
3. *True.*
4. *True. Devil Kinsmere* (1934).
5. *False.* He was confused with Jimmy Dickson, a real spy.
6. *True. The Life of Sir Arthur Conan Doyle* (1948).
7. *False.*
8. *False.* Quest literature; Sir Thomas Malory's *Morte d'Arthur.*
9. *False. Poodle Springs.*
10. *False.* Third novel.
11. *False.* It is Professor C. Day Lewis.
12. *False.* Fen is Professor of English Language and Literature.
13. *False.* Only half are set in Oxford.
14. *False.* This phrase is never used in any Sherlock Holmes story.
15. *False.* It is in *The Valley of Fear.*
16. *True.* This is a quotation.
17. *False.* It was Kilmarth.
18. *False.* Her first novel was *The Loving Spirit.*
19. *False. The Birds* was a short story.
20. *True.*
21. *False.* $20,000—but no tax.
22. *True.*
23. *False.* It was Dashiell.
24. *False.* Four people die but Spade kills none.
25. *True.* Wright was a senior Pinkerton operative.
26. *True.*
27. *False.* Trick question that is answered true if you switch Flora and Rice.
28. *False.*
29. *False.* He was not a priest and thus not entitled to give absolution.
30. *True.* They are two of Peters' pen names.

31. *False.* Initially it was a one-off book.
32. *False.*
33. *True.*
34. *False.* It was 1928.
35. *False.* It was a naval broadside that also blinded Pew.
36. *False.*
37. *False.* A Revenue patrol was responsible for the accident.